Out of My League

SARAH SUTTON

Golden Crown Publishing, LLC

OUT OF MY LEAGUE

Copyright © 2020 Golden Crown Publishing, LLC

For information, contact:

http://www.sarah-sutton.com

Cover Design © Designed with Grace

Image © DepositPhotos – Garetsworkshop

ISBN: 9781734232257

First Edition: June 2020

10 9 8 7 6 5 4 3 2 1

To the One whose timing is always perfect.

One

"Sophia, I know it's the last day of school, but can you at least pretend you're paying attention?"

I surrendered my gaze from my journal to focus on Mrs. Gao at the front of the room, whose dark eyes were trained on me. Two hands on her hips, two dark eyebrows raised. *Totally busted.*

My head bobbed. "I am listening."

Ha, I really wasn't. Who could blame me? Like Mrs. Gao said, last day of school and all. Who paid attention on the last day of school? But even though the year was almost over, my ears weren't working for a whole other reason.

My last journalism assignment was due in four minutes. It was a pitch for the Back to School newsletter. Our school newspaper, the *Bayview High Report*, prints out a newsletter at the beginning of each school year with all sorts of inspiring or informative pieces to spur excitement amongst the grades. The student journalist whose idea gets chosen has the entire summer to work on it, so it's ready for publication when school resumes.

Since come fall I'd be a senior, I was finally allowed to pitch my mind-blowing ideas.

Except that I had none. No ideas. Nothing.

With the pressure building up and time running out, I began to sweat. Figuratively, not literally. My brain knew how important coming up with an out-of-the-park idea was.

Winning the spot of Lead Editor would make me a shoo-in for the internship at the *Bayview Blade*, the biggest newspaper press in the county. Each fall, the press picked three seniors from the district to be their interns for the school year.

No doubt they would pick the senior who wrote Bayview's fall newsletter, and that senior would be *me*.

Lots of pressure. Okay, maybe I was literally sweating, too.

Mrs. Gao caught my eye again. Right. Paying attention.

"We're facing budget cuts for the next school year. I'm not supposed to say anything, but I trust this group." She turned to smudge the eraser along the whiteboard, wiping away any traces of the black *HAVE A GREAT SUMMER.* "I've been trying to find a way to break this to you all, but it's going to be a hard pill to swallow."

My open notebook beckoned my focus with its blank lines, taunting my lack of inspiration. For weeks now, I'd been trying to come up with an epic editorial topic. Though the Back to School newsletter was only open to seniors, I'd been writing practice entries since I was a freshman. Last year, I'd written about the environmental dangers of plastic straws and submitted it to the school board. Effective that next calendar year, Bayview High switched to only offering paper straws.

Now, when my article actually mattered, the only freaking idea in my head was *"Is Chicken Soup Better for You Than Tomato?"*

"The school has decided to cut funding for some extracurricular activities, and they've decided to cancel the newspaper, effective next school year."

Mrs. Gao's words almost went in one ear and out the other, my focus so totally elsewhere. And then it registered like a slap to the face. "Wait, wait, *what?*"

Mrs. Gao let out a weary breath, setting the eraser down on the whiteboard sill. Her shoulders slouched forward as she reached a hand to brush her black hair. "Sales are down twenty percent, and if no one's reading the paper—"

"A school paper is a necessity!" I objected, voice sounding loud and desperate to my own ears. "How else are students going to know about events, games, board meetings? How else are they going to get their information?"

A boy behind me piped up, "Uh...social media?"

I fought the urge to turn around and glare.

"Apparently, Sophia, the money for new baseball field bleachers is more of a necessity than information."

Oh, *no, no, no.* Absolutely not. My newspaper funding went to *baseball?*

Waves of blood pounded in my ears, sending a shockwave of dizziness through my senses. I gripped onto my desk to keep myself upright. This could not be happening. "They can't just cut an extracurricular to put more funding into a nonessential sports team." *Could they?*

"They can if the class size is five students."

"Nonessential, Sophia?" Tess, the main sports reporter,

turned toward me. If looks could kill, hers would've struck me down. "The newspaper isn't as important as the baseball team."

Uh, I *so* disagreed.

Any retort I might've pitched back died on my lips as a different kind of panic seized me, another fact crossing my mind. "Does this mean the seniors aren't qualified for the *Blade* internship?"

Mrs. Gao's expression confirmed my worst fear before her words did, twisting into a sorrowful mask. "It's required that applicants attend a school with an active journalism program. I'm sorry, Sophia, but yes, that means you—and the two other soon-to-be seniors in our class—will not be allowed to apply."

I was going to pass out. Right there, with two minutes left in the last day of school. I was going to pass out, knock my head against the desk, fall into a coma, and have to be airlifted to the hospital.

And there wouldn't be a school newspaper to report on it.

I *needed* that internship. My entire future depended on it. Besides the fact that interning with a major press would look great on my college applications, it was my *dream* to write for the *Blade*. Writing for the school's meager newspaper had been practice. The *Bayview Blade* was the real deal. That would make me a real journalist; it would make everything I'd been working towards worth it.

And, come on, I *had* that internship. Tess and the other senior, Shelby, wouldn't have applied. Heck, they were probably only in this class because all the other last period extracurricular had been filled. That internship would've been *mine*.

As if someone dumped my hopes in a toilet and pressed the handle, my dreams slipped down the drain. Slumping back in my seat, numb, I couldn't do anything other than blink.

"If you're not going to use your journals, please pass them to the front. Maybe they'll bring this elective back down the line and the next group can refer to our potential ideas."

Our journals. The ones we'd been given at the start of the year to record our possible article ideas. I'd filled mine with newspaper clippings, doodles, and lists upon lists of inspiring quotes and phrases. I refused—*refused*—to relinquish it. Mrs. Gao would have to pry it from my concussed, comatose fingers.

"Where do we go to appeal the board's decision?" I demanded, trying to hold some thread of hope. "There's got to be another step, right?"

It couldn't just be *over*.

"This is the school board, not Congress. I'm afraid it's out of my—and your—hands."

A certain finality clung to her words, but my heart didn't just sink. No, it rapidly swan-dived from a boat wearing a coat of concrete. The air in my lungs drowned right along with it.

The dismissal bell rang out, signaling the end of my junior year of high school, the end of the *Bayview High Report*. I sat still in my seat as the horrible sound echoed in my ears, watching the other students filter from the room.

The other journalism students didn't seem as weighed down as me, bounding past Mrs. Gao without a care in the world.

"Sorry to end the year with bad news," she said to them. "Have a great summer. Make wise decisions."

In a slow daze, I packed up my pencil case. Pencils and pens I'd used for the entire semester of this class, now never to be used in here again. My journal still sat on my desk, a beacon of hope that seemed silly now. *If I got the internship*—but what did it matter? That wasn't even an option anymore.

Everything was over.

Mrs. Gao turned to me as I approached the door, her own expression unhappy. "I know you're disappointed, Sophia. Trust me, I am too."

I hugged my things closer, the loss of possibilities insurmountable. It was like mourning the death of a loved one. In a way, I guess I was—the death of my dreams. "How long have you known?"

"The school held a board meeting last night about cutting programs, but I had an inkling that our program would be on the list. I didn't want to say anything until it'd been decided." She reached out and touched the binding of my notebook. "You can keep this. I wouldn't ask you to give it up."

My chest felt hollow, like someone carved out all my ribs and organs until I was as empty as a pumpkin. What was the point of hanging onto this thing if there was no reason to use it? No newspaper to write for; no internship.

Though it practically killed me to do so, I released my death grip on the journal. "Like you said, maybe it'll help others down the line."

She watched me for a moment, but there was nothing left

for her to say. No words of encouragement. "Have a good summer, Sophia."

A good summer? I could've laughed as I made my way through the hall. My entire summer had already been mapped out. Write a killer article—because I would've, even if my ideas were slow coming—get accepted for the internship, and start working there after school next fall.

That article would've gotten the attention of my parents, who had long since turned a blind eye.

All planned out. All achievable. Until now.

And for what? Because someone wanted to buy the baseball team new bleachers? What, the ones they bought a decade ago weren't good enough anymore?

There were callouses on my fingers from all the jampacked days and late, late nights of just sitting and writing, pen magnetized to my hand. I'd been dreaming of my chance for years, and now...it was over.

"End of the year party after the baseball game tonight!" someone shouted over my shoulder, startling me from my thoughts so badly that I dropped my pencil case. It fell to the ground with a thud, and apparently hadn't been closed all the way, because pencils and erasers scattered everywhere. Annoyance welled within me as I bent down, scrambling for my supplies. "Bring your books and homework to burn!"

Burning homework? *Sacrilegious.*

I shook my head as I tucked a pastel eraser inside, stretching for a pen just out of reach.

Just before I grabbed it, another hand snatched it up. "Here's this one."

The blue ink pen was angled so the engraving was faced out. *Sophia.* "Thanks," I muttered, yanking it back.

Feet stamped around me, threatening to trample my crouched figure. Before someone had a chance to stomp me into a pancake, I quickly climbed to my feet, fumbling for my pencil case's zipper. When I lifted my eyes, I came face to face with the person who'd helped me.

It wasn't so much the fact that *baseball* was getting my funding that made me so mad. It was that the stupid sport represented stupid people like *him.*

Walsh Hunter.

Every school had that one guy who everyone loved, right? Incredibly charming, good-looking, people fawning over him like he's God's gift to humanity? At Bayview High, that guy was Walsh Hunter. Tall, sandy blond hair, sharp jawline, and gemstone blue-green eyes.

Oh, and did I mention he was captain of the money-stealing baseball team? With his purple and gold baseball jersey on, it was obvious. Everything about him was just so *perfect, perfect, perfect.*

Ugh.

Bayview was a pretty big school, but not big enough that our paths never crossed. I saw him in the halls from time to time, or when he came up to talk to my boyfriend, who hated him as much as I did. The only time Walsh ever noticed my existence, though, was during math class sophomore year, when he tried to cheat off my test.

Upstanding citizen, that guy.

"Don't mention it," Walsh responded, looking at me—really looking at me. "You coming to the party tonight?"

Was it bad that my first thought was *is he talking to me?* Probably. I didn't even know what to say.

Walsh, though, with his glittering eyes, didn't give me much of a chance. "You should come. I think you'd have a lot of fun." After recruiting his potential partygoer, Walsh patted me on the shoulder, but his eyes latched onto something behind me. "See you tonight. Hey, Zach! Wait up a sec!"

He edged around me and back into the thick of the crowded hallway, people parting for him like he was royalty.

With an annoyed glare, I swatted at the fabric on my shoulder, as if to knock off his touch. I couldn't blame him for being so tragically oblivious. When someone was placed on a pedestal, it tended to morph one's thinking.

Or so I assumed. No one placed me on any pedestals.

"Sophia!" a new voice called through the abyss of students, all who were trying to filter from the halls as fast as possible. A small hand stuck above the heads, waving around like a buoy in the middle of the ocean. "Sophia, hang on!"

There were two things that came to my mind when I thought of Edith Bradley. One—my best friend since childhood, my ride-or-die wing-woman.

And the second thing I thought of—*short*. She liked to say she was five-foot-two, but I seriously doubted it.

Edith elbowed her way out from behind a pair of students talking, heaving a loud sigh at them. "Sheesh, why is no one *moving*? Hello, let's *go*!"

Even though my spirits were low, her good mood felt infectious. "So rude," I agreed.

"Totally. I'm glad I caught you." She looped her arm through mine, peering up at me. "I need a favor."

"I don't like doing your favors," I said immediately. "They aren't fun."

She flapped her hand, waving away the thought. "Are too. Especially this one. It's totally pain-free and really only requires your presence." She opened her dark eyes wide, trying to convey every drop expression in them. "Come with me to the party tonight."

Did she mean the burn-your-homework party I'd heard about literally seconds ago? My shoulders immediately slouched, everything in me deflating. "Those parties are for people who are less evolved than us, remember?"

"Maybe I don't want to be evolved. Maybe I want to party alongside the uncivilized for once."

I gave her a bland look. "They're not as interesting as they pretend to be."

"Come on, it'll be fun! It's going to be at Walsh's. And before you say no—" Her words became rushed, cutting off any sort of denial I was about to say, "—you owe me. Don't ask me why you owe me yet. I've got to come up with something."

I stopped in front of my purple locker, picking up the lock but not twisting it. Everything in me absolutely did not want to go to a party tonight—especially not if it was at Walsh Hunter's house. Parties weren't really my thing in general; I only went to back up Edith. And besides, I was in mourning. Mourning my ruined dreams, which were broken and shriveled and dead. I planned on spending my night crying under the covers, *not* partying.

Celebrating the end of school—an end of a journalism era —seemed so wrong.

"Pretty please with a cherry on top?" Edith asked again, pressing her palms together. "I need my motivator. You can help me talk to boys."

Ah, yes. She said boys plural, but I knew there was a certain boy in particular on her mind. Edith had been crushing on the same guy since the sixth grade. Zach Balker. You'd think after all these years of crushing on him, *something* would've happened, but nope. Their relationship never strayed out of the platonic zone, not that it ever discouraged Edith.

"I'm not sure I'm up for being a motivator tonight," I told her, finally twisting the dial on my lock, popping my locker open. A bare metal box greeted me, devoid of any stickers and mirrors and textbooks from when I'd cleared it out earlier in the week. Only my tan backpack hung on the hook, and I had no journal to pack into it. Heartbreaking. "Maybe we can just do something tomorrow?"

"Have you broken the news to you-know-who yet?" she asked me, leaning her hip along the lockers.

I knew exactly what news she meant, and exactly who I was supposed to break what to. But the mere idea of doing so made everything in me tie up in knots. "Not yet."

"Sophia." The word was a scolding. "You deserve better. You know you do."

"I've never broken up with anyone before," I told her almost desperately, willing her to drop it before anyone overheard. "I'll get to it."

Really, I'd been thinking about breaking up with my

boyfriend, Scott, for a few weeks now, but wanted to hold off. Wanted to wait and see if the spark I'd felt at the beginning of our relationship would relight.

I'd also been putting it off because I had no idea how Scott would take it. I'd never broken up with someone before —I needed to have a boyfriend first to be able to break up with them. How did one break up with their first boyfriend? I had no clue.

So, of course, I just put it on the back burner, pretending things would resolve themselves. Good strategy, I think.

Before Edith had a chance to respond, no doubt saying something to encourage me further down Breakup Avenue, a shadow fell over my locker, a low voice quick on its heels. "There you are. I was starting to think you decided to stay in class all summer."

Looking over, I locked eyes with Scott, my boyfriend of nearly two months now. He leaned up against the locker beside mine. After hearing Walsh Hunter's voice right in my ear, looking at Scott was a nice contrast to the perfection of the baseball captain. Safe brown eyes, straight black hair. Scott had been trying to grow a mustache for the last month, though it resulted in nothing but a patchy line above his lip.

Normal and simple, not stuck-up and self-absorbed.

"I was talking to Mrs. Gao," I told him. "We...we were just talking about the article." *And about when we're hosting a funeral for it.*

I already missed the familiar weight of my journal, naked without it. I wanted to tell Scott about what happened, but as short-stop on the baseball team, I doubted he'd be too broken-hearted to hear where the funding had been wired.

And quite honestly, I wasn't sure he'd really listen.

"I'll talk to you later," Edith said, shooting Scott a glare from the side of her eye, already beginning to back away.

I frowned after her for a moment. "How was your last day, Scott?"

"I should've just skipped like I *planned to do*. But *my girlfriend* talked me out of it."

I fought the urge to roll my eyes at his pouty tone. "Hey, you didn't have to listen to me. You can take your own risks."

"Risks," he huffed. "What's risky about skipping the last day of school? You're just a goody-two-shoes."

"Being a goody-two-shoes is better than having to come back in the summer for detention."

Scott brushed off my words with a scoff, one that I got so often.

Don't fight with him, I told myself while gritting my teeth, shutting the locker door gently. I didn't *want* to fight with him, but the urge came so easily lately. Scott had a massive tendency to be a Negative Nelly, and I didn't even think he meant to. It was just a personality trait of his. Normal, simple, negative.

"Are you going to come over before your game tonight?" I asked him.

"Will your parents be home?"

I held in a sigh, already knowing his answer. "Probably."

"Then no thanks. You know I don't like to be around them."

Scott's dislike of my parents was no secret, but I guess I couldn't really fault him for that.

He had yet to shake the sour expression. "Why did you wear your glasses today?"

This time, I couldn't hold my sigh in. "My eyes were really dry this morning." To punctuate this fact, I slipped my finger underneath my glasses, rubbing.

"Did you use eye drops? You should've used eye drops." He didn't wait for me to answer—which was probably a good thing, because I was seriously about to snap at him. "I've got to talk to Ryan about tonight. Walsh is throwing a party, and I have to know if I'm supposed to bring chips or something."

Jeez, *again* with this stupid party. But his tone was different than Edith's. Scott's voice turned acidic when he spoke, like he tasted something bitter.

Scott held animosity for everything around him, and Walsh was no exception. In the two months since we started dating, I heard it all: how Walsh got to be captain instead of Scott, how Walsh started turning all the other boys on the baseball team against him, how Walsh was just evil incarnate. I wasn't sure I agreed with Scott to that extent, but it was a little refreshing to find someone else who did not bow down to Mr. Perfect.

Scott said, "I'll see you..."

"Later." It was the noncommittal way Scott usually finished that sentence, and today, I found that I didn't care. After a load of crap-tastic news, I just wanted to be by myself.

Scott brushed past me, not offering a kiss or hug goodbye, but that was our usual. PDA was strictly off-limits, and for me, that was totally fine.

My eyes followed his back, watching as he walked up to the gaggle of baseball players at the far end of the hall. Seven or eight of them stood around, spending their first day of summer in the halls of the school, laughing about something that couldn't possibly be that funny.

Walsh stood in the middle, and I didn't miss that everyone's eyes pointed in his direction.

I glared toward them, at the people and their stupid leader. People like them—they were all just so...so...entitled. Selfish. Stuck-up and shallow, and they ate my newspaper funding without even batting an eye. Sure, other people's dreams and passions were sucked dry, but at least the baseball team got new stuff.

It made me want to scream.

Just then, the universe, for whatever reason, had Walsh lift his eyes straight to mine as if he'd heard my angry thoughts. How did a guy like him get everything he wanted, everything handed to him, every single time? Was he in league with the devil or something?

Walsh still watched me from across the hallway, probably wondering why I was staring at him like I wanted to commit murder.

There was nothing I could do. The school freaking idolized the baseball team. Baseball in this school—in this county—was worshipped. Why else would the county division agree to extend their baseball games until the middle of July? Why else would the town dedicate an entire *park* to the Bayview Royals?

Heck, I wouldn't have been surprised if Coach Glassmore got nominated as mayor next election term.

Why could no one else see how conceited those players were? Did *everyone* turn a blind eye?

If we still had a school newspaper, I might've written an article about the unfairness of it all. Honestly, I was surprised I never had before. I'd point out the biased treatment they got from the teachers—*positive* biased treatment, of course—the unfair funding they received, all the parties, all the drinking, all the rottenness that the players tried to hide with their pretty smiles.

An article displaying all the dirty little secrets of the baseball team. I could've exposed it all. Now *that* would've been a home run for sure.

The thought sat in my mind for a moment, festering, until it finally clicked. Without wasting another second, I hurried down the hallway, praying that my breakthrough hadn't come too late.

two

*M*rs. Gao was already locking up her classroom door when I got to her, probably wanting to jumpstart her summer vacation as well. She had to have heard my tennis shoes slapping the ground, echoing through the now empty hallway as I got close.

"Sophia." Her eyes widened. "Are you all right?"

"Let me write the article," I gasped, my lungs heaving. A sharp pressure in my side sent me doubling over, leveling my forearms against my knees. I *so* needed to workout more. "The Back to School newsletter—let me write it."

Mrs. Gao blinked. "Um, there *isn't* going to be a Back to School newsletter."

"I'll write it anyway. I'll write an amazing article, we'll present it to the board, and then they'll realize how important it is to have a school newspaper." Several strands of my auburn hair caught in my face and I frantically tucked them back, peering up at her with a puppy-dog gaze. "It'll knock their socks off and they'll *have* to reinstate it. It'll work, Mrs. Gao."

Okay, sure, maybe it was a long shot. The school board finalized their decision. But if I had a chance to reverse their totally bogus ruling, I had to try. I wouldn't be able to live with myself if I let the newspaper slip from my fingers without a fight. I'd beat myself up for the rest of summer—heck, maybe even the rest of my life.

One last chance to stop my dreams from going down the drain.

"Sophia," she said gently, grasping for words. "I know you're dedicated and passionate about this. I do. But do you have any ideas that *would* knock their socks off? Something other than the horrors of non-recyclable straws, I'm afraid."

See, even *she* understood my dilemma. "I know, I know. I can find a good topic, I swear." *And I might even already have one.* It just needed a bit more fleshing out, and I didn't want to risk telling her the details, just in case she tried to talk me out of it. "It might not work, and the school board might not listen, but it's a chance, Mrs. Gao."

"You're confident, Sophia. You *have* been writing these articles for the past three years—if there's one thing you're good at, it's telling a story. I can understand why you want to try one last time. for your love of writing."

Or, you know, to prevent my life from ending. Same thing.

"If you can get me the article by the last Sunday of July, I can present it at the board meeting that Monday. If anything, we can see about publishing it on the first day of school. But I can't promise anything."

The deadline was so easy-peasy. My recyclable straw article took me less than two weeks to gather information and compose. And I already knew my topic: exposing the bias for the baseball team. If the school board hoped that no one noticed the unfairness before, too bad. When I was done, everyone would finally open their eyes to the truth of Bayview baseball. "All I need is a chance."

Mrs. Gao reached into her tote bag and withdrew my writer's notebook, corners well-loved and stickers dotting the cover. The mere sight of it made the world feel right again, like everything would end up okay. Color burst into my black and white world, making me feel alive again.

"Tap into your genius, Sophia," she told me. "You'll need it."

When I went into the 9th grade, the family dynamic in my household shifted drastically. My parents bought me a bicycle for my birthday, a coral one with a white woven basket, and told me the world was my oyster.

At the time, I didn't realize what they really meant was that the I was on my own.

That birthday was a milestone for us all. Mom and Dad started treating me less like a child and more like an adult. Like a friend. Like a roommate, living in the same house but interacting on the minimum. Me being on my own gave them more time to focus on each other. They starred in their own version of a soap opera, playing different parts and creating drama where it wasn't warranted.

I liked to call it *The Old and the Angry*. They'd have a full-on argument over who left a dirty cereal bowl in the sink, kiss in the living room, and threaten to break up with each other. All in the span of ten minutes.

It was exhausting to keep up, so I tried not to.

Not that they didn't love me. My parents weren't bad parents. They didn't neglect me. They still cleaned around the house, they gave me an allowance each week, they paid the bills on time. There were even certain days where they'd cook dinner.

And independence had its perks. Like being able to come home from Edith's house at two in the morning, or being able to sneak Scott up into my room to watch a movie with the door closed.

Okay, fine, the perks were bogus, but that was my fault. I wasn't an interesting person.

At eight o'clock, I hurried downstairs in a clatter of flip-flops, freezing on the bottom step when I saw Mom. She was perched on the edge of the sofa but wasn't really watching the TV. She just stared at the wall like she was willing it to change color. Her auburn hair, which matched mine almost identically, was still up in its bun, her workout clothes still on.

I cleared my throat, shoving my notebook into my purse. "I'm heading out."

Mom startled, turning in her seat. Her makeup had rubbed off from the day, creating rings around her eyes. "Oh, Sophia, I didn't hear you come in. Are you just getting home from school?" Mom didn't even hesitate a second before pressing a hand to her forehead. "Not school. It's after six, isn't it?"

"It's after *eight*. And I've been home."

I had the strangest urge to mention the Back to School

article to her, ask her if she had any tips or thoughts about it. Maybe because she mentioned school.

I wanted to ask, but I didn't. "I'm actually going out."

Mom nodded at me, moving to actually sit down on the couch rather than rest precariously on its arm. "Have fun."

The hardest part about my wide berth of independence was I could still remember a time when things were different. Like when Dad used to take me on boat rides down on the bay. Or when Mom and I used to go on overnight trips out of town, no boys allowed. I could remember family dinners, movie nights, happy times.

And now it was all different. Quieter. Lonelier.

"I'll be out late," I said, trying in vain to get a reaction.

Mom didn't even say anything this time; she merely gave me a thumbs up.

I clenched my jaw together as she turned up the volume of her TV show, making it too loud to talk around. Drawing in a deep breath, I shook off the heaviness weighing on my shoulders. No need to be disappointed. This was just the way things were.

I didn't glance back as I headed outside, yanking the zipper on my purse closed.

three

I had my game face on. I was tapping into my inner genius. How was a girl like me, no social life whatsoever, going to dig up information on the highly-worshipped baseball team? Well, I had a plan. I had some-what of an informant already, if I could find a way to trick insider information out of Scott.

Obviously, if he knew why I was asking him so many questions about baseball, he wouldn't tell me anything. But if I could find a way for him to confess, he would be invaluable.

I'd just need to ask him questions that weren't too obvious.

Honestly, it should be easy enough. Once he talked about himself or about baseball, it was hard to get him to stop.

And since he would not come to me, I guess I'd just have to go to him.

"Thanks for coming with me," Edith said, reaching over and patting my knee. She pulled her seat all the way up to the steering wheel, her legs stretched straight to reach the pedals.

"You know I feel a lot more confident with you around. Too bad we're not one person."

"What are friends for?" I returned with a smile, gazing out the passenger's side window.

Trees and foliage surrounded Walsh's long driveway, bright and alive, the colors of summer clinging to the leaves. The setting sun sifted through the tree limbs, orange rays filtering through the branches. It wouldn't be long until darkness won out.

Edith, bracelets jingling, twisted the steering wheel around the last bend of the driveway, letting out a whistle as the trees parted and exposed the house.

And I seriously had to redefine my idea of what a house was because this giant fortress was no house. With the mix of gray siding and a sandy-colored brick, it almost looked like something from a fairytale, set on a steep, grassy hill. It glowed like a giant jack-o-lantern, each window lit from the inside. Jeez, I didn't even want to know what the electric bill looked like.

The parties that Edith and I went to were usually thrown by Zach or a guy in Greenville, and their houses, though not tiny, were nothing compared to this. Walsh had never hosted a party before, but given how massive his property was, he totally should've.

And, okay, did Walsh live in Bayview or some other world entirely? I never even knew there was a corner of Bayview that looked like this.

I slouched in my seat, glaring at the structure. "You didn't tell me Walsh lived in a freaking castle."

"Why do you think I'd know what his house looks like?"

"You know *everything*."

She seemed satisfied with my response. "I knew he lived on the edge of the higher-end part of town, not like *this*."

Oh, *not* in the middle of the forest in a castle with bay access in the back. I could see the dark water beyond the edges of his house. It was like someone took a slice of every perfect view and gifted it to him.

Perfect, perfect, perfect.

Edith eased behind a shiny SUV, getting as close as she possibly could without kissing the bumper.

"So do we want to split up when we go in?" I asked Edith as I undid my seatbelt, shrugging on my game face. "I'll find Scott, you find a cute boy, and we'll meet up in a bit?"

She started picking at her cuticles, eyeing the house. "Someone from school said something about a volleyball net being set up in the backyard. That'd be great for me to practice."

"As if you need practice," I snorted. "You're the best one on the volleyball team."

And she was, even if she wasn't totally confident in it. I always loved telling her that she was the best *and* the shortest, which was a feat in and of itself. Edith's been on the volleyball team her entire high school career. I would know, of course. I'd been the one who'd gone to every game of hers, with homemade signs that said, to some effect, "*My Best Friend Can Bump It.*"

Pretty cringe-inducing, sure. Writing articles was my forte; I wasn't at all artistic.

But her confidence had been shaken since last season, and I held back from saying "you're going to get on the team" because I knew it would only make her more nervous. No way she'd be cut from the team her *senior year*.

"Are you going to do it?" Edith asked, glancing my way. "Finally break up with Scott?"

"That would be horrible if I did it at a party," I said, knowing that was the coward in me showing. I looked at the house looming before us, hand hesitant on the car door. "And besides, I need his help for my article."

"So, you're going to prolong your crappy relationship just to use him for information?"

Well, when she put it that way, it sounded horrible. "That's kind of messed up of me, isn't it?"

Edith lifted a shoulder, unbuckling her seatbelt. "After everything he's put you through, he deserves it."

Now that the hum of the car shut off, the music filtered, muffled, into the sedan. Butterflies worked their way into a fervor in my stomach. Even though I deemed myself a journalist, I wasn't a people-person. I didn't mind being around them, but I was totally content to stay at home with my Persian cat, Shiba.

But Shiba wasn't giving me any information for my article.

My glasses fogged a bit as I hopped out of the air-conditioned car and into the summer air, the humidity eating at me instantly. I pulled my purse tighter against my hip, drawing in a deep breath. Through the fabric, I could feel the edge of my notebook, a familiar pressure. I was an undercover journalist now, ready to soak up any baseball secrets I might hear.

I nearly ran into Edith's back as she pulled to a halt. "What are you doing?" I asked, noticing that she kept twisting her fingertips, picking at her nails. "Come on, Edith. It's going to be fun."

"I know," she said under her breath. "I just think—I think I left something in the car."

I pressed a hand against her shoulder blades, pushing her forward. "You're going in. Walk."

"I-I was just admiring the landscaping. Look, is that a horse-shaped bush?"

"Uh-huh, cool." I nudged her again to mount the porch steps. "Walk."

When we opened up the door, I realized that there was a strong possibility that I'd made a mistake. There were so. Many. People. So many bodies clustered together inside, shadows mixing along the walls. Did all these people go to Bayview? Sure, it was a big school, but hardly any of these faces seemed familiar.

And, of course, the inside of this giant house was beautiful.

Everything was white and clean and pretty, like a model home from the inside of a magazine. I couldn't help but wonder what it looked like without so many high schoolers ruining its classy vibe. A giant homemade banner hung above a marble fireplace in the living room, scrawled with black lettering: *SCREW SCHOOL*. A group of boys tried to get an empty beer can stuck in the crystal chandelier that hung above the stairs, hooting and hollering each time it knocked against the crystal and fell free.

"Ladies!" Out of nowhere, Walsh Hunter materialized with his hair hanging into his eyes, his black button-down untucked from his chinos. He looked like he planned on attending a fundraiser or something fancy rather than hosting a high school party. "Well, don't you two look lovely tonight?"

However immune I was to Walsh's charms, Edith was not. That was one of her downfalls: she allowed herself to be schmoozed by Mr. Perfect's stupid smile. "This is an amazing party, Walsh."

"I didn't have a hand in it, unfortunately," he said, raising his voice louder over the music. He glanced over to his living room, where everyone danced and talked. "Ryan decided it was time for me to host my first party and people just started showing up."

Right. Ryan decided. And I bet Walsh didn't complain.

"It's Edith, right?" he asked, those blue eyes trained on her. "You played volleyball last season. You got a concussion midway through."

I glanced at my best friend from the corner of my eye, watching for a shift in her expression. That game against the Greenville team was a touchy subject for her, the leading cause in her volleyball-induced anxiety. At the game, Edith did some sort of jumping thing—a spike?—but Eloise Xiang, a girl from the other team, blocked it, sending the flying ball back. There hadn't been any time for Edith to dodge it before it hit her square in the face.

That concussion pulled her from the rest of the season. I only knew the girl's name because Edith declared her a sworn enemy, never to be spoken of again.

Edith normally hated when the fateful game got brought up, but now she nodded, the widest smile spreading across her lips. "That was me, all right. And this is my best friend, Sophia."

Walsh's blue eyes shifted ever so slightly to me, taking in my appearance. "You're the girl from the hallway. Nice to exchange names, Sophie."

Great, now I had two nicknames. "Girl from the hallway" and "Sophie." Oddly enough, I preferred the former.

"It's *Sophia*," I corrected him with a voice that could've frozen the summer air, squaring my shoulders.

Amusement colored Walsh's features, as if he couldn't tell I was being snarky. "Fire's out in the back. There's a keg on the porch if you're looking for something to drink, Edith. Harder stuff's in the kitchen." Walsh gestured off to the side while looking at me. "There's some juice boxes in the fridge if you'd like one, Sophie. Bottom shelf."

"Juice box?" What did he think I was, ten?

"I stock them for the designated drivers. Something a little better than water."

My jaw locked together with an almost audible click. I didn't know what was worse: the fact that he offered me a juice box or that he automatically assumed I was the DD.

"Music's going to be playing 'til dawn, so dance the night away, you two," he said with one last smile, turning to disappear amongst the dancing people.

We both stared after him a moment, neither speaking.

Until Edith sighed. "He's so dreamy."

"More like a nightmare," I muttered, my annoyance meter measuring to a million. At least he was gone now so we could focus. Or, really, so *Edith* could focus. "So, do you see any boys worth talking to?"

Meaning: *do you see Zach Balker?*

Edith glanced around, standing up onto her tip-toes to get

a better view. I didn't think that extra inch would help her much, but she sucked in a sharp breath. "I think I see one over by the speakers."

I raised my chin to peer around the dancing bodies, finally spotting where a boy leaned against the far wall.

Sure enough, Zach stood there, sandy brown hair curled behind his ears, eyes focused on the red cup in his hand. He was also conveniently all alone.

"Oh, now's your chance," I told her, turning with a grin. "He's all by himself."

"Maybe we should get a juice box first."

I reached out, grabbing her hands to stop her fidgeting. "Come on. Let's talk to him and then I'll find Scott." I could wait a little longer to talk to him about baseball.

With a deep breath, Edith nodded, taking a step forward. All at once, the tension seeped from her skin, like a thin coat she shrugged off. As nervous as she'd been moments before, no one could tell now. That was her thing. She was nervous until she wasn't. Until she decided she needed to be a brave social butterfly.

See, Edith was in her element here, surrounded by dancing bodies and laughter, making a beeline for Zach.

I kept my eyes peeled, looking for Scott anywhere in this massive living room. He'd have been here by now surely, but the lights were too dim and there were too many people for me to spot him.

Edith held her arms close to her center as she approached Zach. "What's a guy like you doing over here all by himself?"

If I knew Edith well enough, I knew she wouldn't have been watching Zach's expression. She would've focused on the cup in his hand or the way the collar of his jacket was slightly folded over. When she got nervous, she tended to keep her gaze off of people's faces.

So she would've missed the way Zach's eyes curved when he saw her, the green in them brightening in an instant. "I'm just waiting for the right person to walk up to me I guess."

"Hopefully we suffice," she said with a breathy chuckle, one that couldn't have oozed any more flirt if she tried.

Zach jerked his chin ever so slightly. "Hey, Sophia. How goes it?"

See, *Zach* knew my name. We hadn't spoken that often before—just when Edith approached him at a party with me trailing behind, as always—but at least he remembered and got it right. "It goes...good, I guess."

If I could just find Scott.

Zach's gaze flicked past me in a moment, locking on something behind me. His eyes narrowed, and Edith must've glanced up at him, because she turned too. "What are you looking at?" All at once, the color drained from her face. "Sophia—"

I almost didn't want to turn around, to figure out what captured both of their attentions. A couple making out in the throng of people? Someone trying to scale the fireplace? Neither would've surprised me.

A few feet from us, people parted just enough to reveal a girl with dark, curly hair with her slender arms around the neck of a boy with a purple and gold varsity jacket. It was funny, because I only had one thought running through my mind as recognition stole over me: *she's a perfect height for him.* The top of her head rose to his eye level. He and I were the same height, and we always made awkward eye contact.

Scott and I met at junior prom of all places, where I merely attended to cover it for the newspaper. Both of us were dateless and sitting alone during a slow song. He'd broken the ice by asking if I was from a different school because there was *no way* he'd miss someone like me walking down the halls of Bayview High.

We never went on dates—Scott didn't see the need to go out in public—and only saw each other a handful of times each week outside of school. He wouldn't come over to my house often since he didn't like my parents, and he'd never invited me to meet his.

Now, staring at him with his arms around another girl, I figured out why.

For a brief, fleeting moment, I wondered if I had already broken up with him. If maybe I'd just blocked it from my memory and we were already separated. Because surely he wasn't at this party embracing another girl. Surely he wasn't *cheating* on me. Surely if he wanted to see other people, he'd have the guts to cut ties with me first.

The lead feeling in my stomach rooted me in place.

"Sophia?" Edith's voice was nervous behind me, soft. She must've stepped away from Zach, coming up just behind me. "What do you want to do?"

What did I want to do? About what? About the fact that my boyfriend's mouth was in close proximity to another girl's? His gaze was trained only on her—on her *lips*, really. His own angled up in a smirk.

My hands at my sides twitched, fingers aching to curl into

fists, but there was a certain part of me that couldn't get properly mad. Like I was separated entirely from the scene
before me.

Until Scott's eyes lifted from the girl, meeting mine.

Just leave, my brain told me, the franticness of my
thoughts almost making me dizzy. *Don't make a scene. Don't
be like your parents. Talk to him about it later.*

Edith stood directly behind me, though, a silent support
that didn't allow me to turn.

Scott's arms unraveled from how they wrapped around
the stranger. I expected him to be defensive, to deny what
was so clearly obvious and try to talk me down. But what he
did was the exact opposite. "Come on, Sophia," Scott said
with an eye roll. "Don't give me that face."

Energy buzzed in my chest, like my body longed to jump
into action, but my brain didn't know how to react. I was way
too aware of the eyes that trained on us, on the dancing
bodies that slowed to a standstill. "What face?"

"That 'you're breaking my heart' face." Scott came close
enough that he didn't have to talk so loud anymore, didn't
have to draw the attention of anyone else in the room, but he
didn't give up that power. In fact, his voice still sounded so
loud in my ears. "Are you really that surprised?"

"Am I—*what*?" His words made literally no sense. The
urge to laugh came, but nothing about this situation was
remotely funny. "Am I surprised about what? You with—
whoever that is?"

The girl peered around him, her blank gaze on me. Her
brown curls hugged over her shoulders, a bit tangled as if

someone run their fingers through it. She wasn't even remotely familiar.

"We're polar opposites, Sophia. You never come to any of my games. You always have your nose stuck in a book. And your parents—well, the apple doesn't fall far from the weird department."

I flinched, from his words and from his tone. The breath of air I tried to take in stuck in my throat, the harshness of his words making my chest ache. Yes, he was a Negative Ned more days than not, but never *cruel*. Not like this.

I didn't want to look around me, to lock eyes with anyone in this horrible room.

But just over Scott's shoulder, I saw Walsh, who looked back with an unreadable expression. A jolt of warmth splintered through me, but not the warmth of comfort—the heat of *anger*. Of course he got to witness this.

Everyone did.

"I want to have a good summer," Scott went on, lifting a shoulder in a blameless shrug. "It's better this way. You'll be busy with your article and I'll be busy...having fun. Doing what I want to do. Win-win, right?"

He kept talking, kept moving his thick jaw, but the numbness started to fade as the burn of tears built in my throat. My cheeks filled with fire, the heat from the room filtering into my body. "You're breaking up with me because I'm not *fun enough*?"

"I've tried to make it work," he sighed loudly, like *he* was the one being dumped. "I've tried to fix it. Fix us, fix *you*, but I just can't do it anymore."

Fix me. Fix *me*. Like I was broken. Like there was something wrong with *me*.

My gaze slipped past Scott once again, but this time, Walsh was gone.

For a moment, my brain sat completely empty of thought. The words burrowed their way into my skin, into my very being, making me feel wrong inside. Sick. Like his words were a slimy film covering every inch of me, getting in my eyes, sticking to my mouth. I took a deep, resetting breath. Mom did that sometimes when Dad ticked her off. She'd close her eyes, breathe in, hold it. Breathe out. Open eyes.

It didn't seem to work for me.

Something hard and heavy landed over my shoulders in an instant, jarring me enough that I sucked in a loud, sharp breath. I almost thought someone shoved me, as if Edith reached out and pushed against my shoulders. But no, it wasn't that. It was—

No. Freaking. Way.

"Scottie," Walsh Hunter said with a slight tilt to his voice, jostling his arm to bring me closer against his side. He matched Scott in volume, making sure every ear could hear him over the hum of the party music. "Is that any way to talk to a lady?"

No. Freaking. Way.

"No one needs you butting in, Walsh," Scott said, annoyance shooting across his features.

"Oh, I'm not butting in. I actually want to come clean about something—I want everyone to know the truth." Walsh moved away from me just enough so he could tip his head and peer into my eyes—that is, if I looked at him. I could barely move a muscle with the weight of his arm over me, and I *so* did not want to even *glance* his way. His voice held a dramatic edge to it, putting on a performance. "I've always had the biggest crush on Sophia."

Now I did jerk my gaze up to meet his, no doubt disgust transforming my face. "What do you think you're—"

Walsh rushed to cut me off, looking directly into my eyes. "And I don't want to keep it a secret anymore. I want everyone to know how I feel about you. How we feel about each other." He gave me a soft smile, one that a lover might get before a first kiss. A flash of fear nearly had me gagging. *If he kisses me, I swear to God—* "Now that Scott's out of the picture, it can be you and me. Nothing is standing in the way of us being together anymore. Give me a chance. You're worth it all, and I'll prove it to you. What do you say? Go out with me?"

Fear of him kissing me transformed into rage. What exactly was he saying? Was he—was he *freaking* implying we had some sort of *love affair?* That we both had secret feelings for each other and were fighting to hide them? In front of all these people?

Of *flipping* course he was. There was nothing I could do but gape at him, jaw completely unhinged.

Everyone was staring at me—at *Walsh* and me—trying to catch a glimpse of what was going down. I caught one, two, several phones pointed in our direction, no doubt recording every single second of this nightmarish moment.

Have I died and ended up in hell?

I couldn't form any sort of coherent response, and I couldn't be in the room anymore, under the stares of everyone in the entire county. If I stayed, I really would end up crying —or screaming—because the pressure built more and more as my mind raced.

So I didn't wait another second or answer Walsh's insane question. I shrugged off his arm, brushed past Edith's shocked expression and the gathered crowd of people, and ran out the back door that led into the night.

four

I stood at the cliff behind Walsh's massive house, the wind lancing across my cheeks, numb to the breeze. I gritted my teeth together, staring into the darkness ahead of me and picturing what it might've looked like in the daytime, with the sunlight cresting over the horizon.

And I guess technically this was more of a pathway that led to the beach below than a cliff, but the drop-off loomed at least ten feet, so steep that a railing had been embedded into the ground to keep anyone from falling over onto the sharp rocks below.

I'd gone outside in search of air, slipping past the bonfire that attracted laughter and happiness. My hidden spot was far enough away from the flames that the music and voices were a distant hum, static sound that could be easily ignored.

Everything felt so jumbled in my head, like a gathering of string tied into several knots. After two months together, Scott just dropped me as if he couldn't care less.

No, wait—he cared. He cared enough about himself to

need someone new. Someone *fun*. Someone that didn't need to be *fixed*.

My cheeks heated to a near painful degree, humiliation rooting itself deep. That was what I struggled with, really. I was more humiliated than heartbroken. I'd been trying to find a way to break up with him anyway, so that was accomplished, but I wished that it hadn't been like this. So public, so hurtful. So many people witnessed him dumping me—so many people heard every horrible thing he said.

And jeez, everyone saw Walsh step in and declare his undying love for me.

See, this? *This* was why I didn't go to parties.

Stupid Walsh Hunter. Stupid Scott. Stupid baseball for eating my newspaper funding. I wanted to crawl under a rock and never come out.

All of the air *whooshed* from my lungs as I realized something. Scott dumping me now meant that he wasn't usable for my article. Any information and secrets he knew, I could kiss them goodbye. Maybe I could figure out a way to work him into the article, though. Highlight his chauvinistic tendencies, perhaps?

Who was I kidding? The article was a joke now.

I reached for my purse, leaning so fully against the metal railing that it dug into my stomach. My journal with my stickers emblazoned over the cover laughed at me, at my compounding failures.

This notebook, this part of me, was the problem. Looking at it now made everything in me ache. I should've left it with Mrs. Gao, given up the shred of hope instead of clinging to my future that was DOA. The pieces of writing inside weren't good enough to save my class, save my future. Even the fact that I had it at a party was a testament to who I was. Someone who wasn't *good enough*.

And the funny thing was that if I hadn't come to the party tonight in search of secrets, I probably never would've found out about Scott cheating.

Without giving it a second thought, I pitched the stupid journal over the side of the railing, wishing it would reach the ocean and I'd hear a satisfying *splash*. But only silence made its way up to my ears.

I didn't feel any better. In fact, with the wind brushing against my now-empty palm, I felt even worse.

"Isn't that sacrilegious?"

The voice, throwing a rock at my perfectly built wall of self-misery and despair, made me jump against the railing. I whirled around with daggers in my eyes, ready to throw my glare at whoever dared to interrupt.

Walsh Hunter stood before me, the boy with epic timing. He looked at me with those blue-green eyes that shouldn't have been wasted on a guy like him.

"Go away," I growled, turning back to face the shadowy beach. I couldn't see my journal, but surely it'd landed somewhere in the sand. My pride kept me rooted where I was, even though I badly wanted to go find it. "Your face is definitely not one I want to look at right now." *Offense intended.*

"Took me a minute to find you. You picked a pretty dark corner of my backyard." Walsh came to lean over the railing beside me, looking below. His elbow grazed mine, only a fraction of skin-to-skin contact, but I tugged mine away almost immediately. "So how did I do in there?" he asked, turning to face me. "Pretty believable?"

"Are you *serious?*" I demanded, and when I looked at him, I found him *grinning.* My glare was one that could've turned him to stone. "What you did in there was so not cool. And not appreciated. You don't get to just waltz up, throw your arm over my shoulder like I'm some territory to be claimed, and say 'oh, let's bring our torrid love affair to the public. Date me.'"

Walsh laughed at my impersonation of his voice. "Do I really sound so high-pitched?"

I couldn't help myself—I reached out and smacked his shoulder, hard. It only succeeded in making him chuckle, though, and created an ache in my fingers. "I am not laughing, Walsh! You totally crossed a line!"

Walsh raised his hands level with his shoulders. "Okay, okay, so I should've asked. I just thought I was doing you a favor."

"I don't need you to do me favors," I said fiercely, pointing a finger at his chest. "I am *not* some damsel in distress. And besides, for your information, I was totally fine in there and didn't need you spreading lies. Now everyone thinks we've been together—that *I* was the one cheating on Scott with *you.*" So messed up.

Though his lips lost their amused curve, his eyes still held onto a glimmer, shining just as bright as the stars. "I think it sounded romantic. *Torrid love affair.* I like that."

My eyes squeezed shut so tightly that I saw stars, jaw aching from grinding my teeth together. Yeah, he'd saved me from Scott's cruelty, but it wasn't his right to. I meant what I said. He was no Prince Charming, and I definitely didn't need saving.

"I really came to just see if you were okay."

"Well, my boyfriend just dumped me in the house of his archenemy because I wasn't good enough, and I threw my most prized possession into the sea to be eaten by sharks." Tipping my head back, I let out a small, almost crazed laugh. "You know, I've been better."

I focused on the constellations above me, at them opposed to Walsh, a breeze rippling from the bay. Focusing on the stars was way better than focusing on everything else. I focused on, despite what just happened, that the night *was* beautiful. Not too cold, but not too warm. Just right. Such a terrible contrast to the events that unfolded.

I didn't even want to imagine what was going on inside. What Scott was doing, who he was doing it with. I just hoped everything that went down gave Edith enough to keep talking to Zach about. That embarrassing ordeal might've been worth it if her and Zach got a good conversation out of it.

I could still hear the music filtering from the house, a faint melody reaching us all the way back here.

Lost in my thoughts, I had no time to react when Walsh lifted one chino-clad leg up and over the edge of the metal railing, straddling it for a moment before his other leg followed. The toes of his shoes grazed the rusting iron, and his loose grip on the rail was the only thing keeping him from tipping over the ten-foot drop.

Five fingers released their hold and he leaned back, back.

For a moment, Walsh didn't look like he was about to

leap to his death. He looked peaceful, with the wind tearing through his hair, brushing it out of his face.

But then I realized. He was actually about to jump off the cliff.

"What are you *doing*?" I screeched, words echoing in the sky. I reached out immediately, grabbing a fistful of his shirt and the wrist that was still in reach. "Are you *insane*?"

Walsh tipped his blond head, laughing. He looked like an absolute lunatic. "I'm going to get your journal for you."

"Isn't there a path? Go the normal route, you psycho!"

"Nothing wrong with taking a shortcut," he said nonchalantly. "It's not like I'd die or anything. All I have to do is dodge the pointy rocks. It's too dark to really see them, but I *think* I remember where they are."

I tightened my grip. Fear of him falling and cracking his head open made my voice shake. "You're not funny."

"I'm trying to be chivalrous, not funny."

"You're *idiotic*." The hand clutching Walsh's wrist started to sweat. He was just joking—he wouldn't actually jump. Right? "That's, like, a ten-foot fall."

"It's twelve, actually."

I could practically *see* him lying on the beach with his head cracked open.

Walsh swayed further over the cliff, buttoned shirt pulling taut in my grip. "I'll probably be fine. Hopefully I don't break anything. Or die. That would suck. Especially at the beginning of summer. What would my mother say?"

"Or your adoring fans," I added. If I couldn't convince him with logic and reason, maybe I could persuade his ego. "They'd fall apart without looking at you every day."

"But could you imagine how huge my funeral would be?" His eyes closed as he shifted further over. A gust of wind bit across the two of us, and I could see goosebumps on his arms. "Would you write my eulogy, Sophie? Make it real nice."

Sophie. The nickname grated on my nerves. "What would I write about? Just how *perfect* your biceps are—or maybe your *beautiful* hair? Oh, no, I've got it. Your *stunning* eyes."

"All of those are suitable options, but you forgot to mention my near-perfect batting record. Imagine how many copies you'd sell."

I just stared at his serious expression. "You're so conceited. Has anyone ever told you that? People compliment you, and you lap it up. Like a dog."

His smile slanted. "Did you just call me a dog, Sophie?"

"It's *Sophia*," I snapped in response.

Walsh grabbed the railing with both hands again, leaning close enough that I could see directly into his blue-green eyes. His breath tickled my skin. *Too close.* "I don't know why you're yelling at *me*. I'm not the one who cheated on you."

A switch flipped in my brain, and any ounce of jovialness I'd experienced a minute ago evaporated.

But Walsh wasn't finished. "It was only a matter of time, though, you know? Girls like you and guys like Scott don't really mix well."

Yeah, I was *this-freaking-close* to changing my mind and shoving him off the railing. *This close* to committing murder and not even batting an eye. I could probably get away with it, too. We were separated far enough away from the party that no one would see, and no one would believe that a *girl like me* would be hanging out with Mr. Perfect. Let alone push him off a cliff.

Instead of committing homicide, I raised my hands from him, backing up. "You know what? Fall to your death. *Please.* You'll be doing me a favor." With my dress fluttering in the breeze, I stomped away.

Walsh didn't understand how it felt to be dumped. Really, how could he? Guys like him didn't get dumped, and that made his presence and his words that much more loathsome.

"Woah, hey. Hey! Wait up," Walsh called after me, but I didn't turn to see if he struggled back over the railing.

With his luck, he probably looked smooth trying to slide away from his death. Or perhaps his foot slipped, and he ended up falling. Either way, I kept walking.

"Sophia, wait! Wait!"

I stalled, and that hesitation was all he needed to catch up, gently snagging my wrist. My world swayed as I whirled to face him. "Wow, you actually got my name right. Alert the media."

"You *are* the media, aren't you?" He still wore his signature grin—why did he have to have a smile like that? So pretty, so perfect. What, did he practice it in the mirror every day? "And of course I got it right. I know you, Sophia Wallace. You were in my US Civics class. You're the junior editor of the school newspaper. Won an award for your article on straw recycling in schools." He spoke as if he'd been rehearsing it, playing each point over and over in his head.

I was speechless. I mean, yeah, *I* knew he was in my US

Civics class, but the fact that *he* remembered *me*? Weird. "There's no way you knew all that."

"Yeah, I had to ask someone what your article was about. I didn't read it." Walsh lifted a shoulder, unbothered. "Not really my thing."

"What, reading or recycling?"

"I'm not an animal, Sophie. Reading, of course."

I realized his fingers still curved gently around my wrist, the weight of his grip oddly grounding. And even though it was the most basic touch, it still shocked my skin.

Despite all that, I gave him a pointed look.

Walsh caught the hint and quickly let go. "Sorry."

I crossed my arms over my chest, glancing over my shoulder. No one noticed us standing together, too engrossed in building the bonfire higher and higher. The glow from the flames ebbed out toward us, and our shadows mixed together on the lawn. The sea breeze came again, harsher now, and pushed my hair around my face.

"Thanks for sticking up for me," I grumbled after a moment, even though it was hard to choke the words out. But I had to add, "Even though I didn't ask you to. It was still... nice of you." *Gag.*

Walsh's frown etched into the lines of his forehead. I didn't know him well enough to read his facial expressions, so I couldn't read what the sharp look in his eye meant. "Scott shouldn't have treated you like that. I maybe shouldn't have intervened, but that wasn't cool of him."

"Honestly, it doesn't matter," I sighed, the words ugly and honest in the air. "He's just one step closer to his achieving his dreams. Scott told me that he wanted to be better than you. That was his goal. To beat you at everything—popularity, baseball."

"Why?"

"He's been like that forever. So obsessed with beating you or looking better than you. Pretty sure that pretty girl down there is his way of getting a leg-up somehow. Don't ask me how; I don't know how to interpret crazy."

A line formed between Walsh's eyes as he watched me, listening closely. "That's the dumbest thing I've ever heard."

"I think he feels like you get everything handed to you. You got captain position. You're the most popular guy in school, all the girls love you, and he's only got boring, plain me."

"It's not like I *asked* Coach to give me the spot," Walsh scoffed, more under his breath than aloud. "And you're not plain or boring. Everything he said in there was completely out of line, so don't believe any of it."

Was it out of line? I mean, Scott wasn't *wrong*. I never did go to any of Scott's games. Never had any desire to. We didn't do anything as a couple. We were polar opposites. "It's whatever," I said at last, leaning my head into my hand.

"What were you two doing together anyway?" Walsh looked at me a little warily, as if fully understanding that this topic is what set me off before. "I just mean, he's such a jerk and you're so..."

I waited but he didn't go on. "So...?"

"Nice?" It wasn't a statement, but then again, I hadn't been overly pleasant to him.

But that was the big question, wasn't it? Why was I with

Scott? Scott, who apparently hated everything about me, even down to my glasses.

"I'm writing an article," I told Walsh, figuring there was nothing left to lose. "About baseball. Scott was giving me information for it." *Even if he hadn't known it yet.*

"What's the article for?"

To get my funding back. "It was for the Back to School article," I said instead. "Just detailing the baseball team's winnings from the summer. But without him, it's not going to work."

"Well, why don't you use me?"

"Use you for what?"

The corners of Walsh's lips twitched as he looked at me. "For your article. Now that we're together, I can give you plenty of insider information."

"I'm sorry, what? Together?"I blinked. Once, and then twice, his words echoing in my ears. It took three repetitions in my brain for me to understand what exactly he was saying. "We're *not* together. We're not continuing this—whatever *this* is." I gestured almost frantically between us, my hand waving in the air.

Amusement colored his tone, and I wanted to shake it out of him. "Why not?"

Why *not?* Was he serious? I could think of a million "why nots." And for one— "Uh, because it's lying?"

"Is it really? Or is it just acting?" Walsh considered it while looking off in the distance, "I always thought I'd be a great actor. I mean, I did pretty great in there, you can't lie."

"No. My answer is no. Heck no." This guy was delusional. He seriously was. Walsh Hunter, my *boyfriend?*

"Thank you for sticking up for me—you didn't need to, though, because I didn't ask you to—but no. I don't need a fake boyfriend."

"Don't you? It'll keep Scott's mouth in check. No way is he going to be a jerk to you if you're my girl."

My girl. Those words made me nearly shudder. "No one would believe it."

"Sure they will. I can be pretty believable. I fell so in love with you that nothing else matters."

Jeez, just hearing him *say* that... Dude was off his rocker.

Just as I went to vehemently reject the lunatic idea again, Walsh's other words rang a little clearer in my mind. Using him for the article. Using the *team captain* for my article. Fake dating him would give me the perfect in for my undercover journalism scheme, exclusive access to insider knowledge, and Walsh wouldn't be the wiser.

I didn't need Scott if I had Walsh. And with the captain of the team, the article would practically write itself.

It sounded horrible, sure, but was it wrong? Truly? This guy got everything he wanted without having to work for it. Using him for my article was only fitting.

"Why do you want to do this?" I asked, trying to straighten out the last threads of sanity. A fake relationship was a whole other ball game. This was dirtier, messier. I knew my motivation, but what was his? "I get why you did it back there, impulsively helping me out because you thought it was right. But why draw it out?"

"Hey, telling the truth would make me look bad too, you know. Do you really want me to go back in there and tell Scott we were lying?" he asked, raising his blond eyebrows. "I can do that, but I can't imagine that'd go over very well."

He had a point, of course. I could just imagine Scott's mocking laughter now, ringing in my ears.

"You can always dump me a week later," Walsh suggested. "Just long enough to make it believable."

I glanced back toward the house. The shadows blended together, smoke billowing high from the fire.

Maybe it doesn't have to be so bad, a voice whispered in my head. *Use it to your advantage.*

Could I do it?

Walsh seemed to think so. "It wouldn't have to be much. Just in public, we'd act like a couple. Hand-holding and things like that."

My fingers curled into fists as if he'd already started reaching. "Hand-holding?"

"Uh, *yeah*. What kind of couple doesn't hold hands? You and Scott held hands, right?"

"Of course we did!" *Sometimes.*

"Well, that's what we need to do," Walsh said. He had an enchanting smile on his face now, like we'd already signed our fake relationship contract. "Hold hands. Hug. Kiss. Do couple-y stuff."

Ha. *Ha-ha.* I was in over my head and we hadn't even started yet.

"Don't worry, I'm good at couple-y stuff. You can just sit back and enjoy."

I stared at his mouth, his full lips, the idea of kissing him filling my mind's eye. A sharp sensation flipped my stomach, akin to the feeling one got before puking, and I swallowed hard. "No, no kissing, Walsh." To reiterate that fact, I stepped back. "That's a rule. No kissing."

Walsh's lips twitched as he fought a grin. "Fine. But the other stuff—pretend I'm Scott."

Pretend Walsh is Scott. I wasn't sure I could. "When are we even in public together?" I asked, folding my arms over my chest. "How long are you thinking, anyway? Until my article is done?"

If that was the case, I'd be working on it ASAP.

Walsh, though, probably knew what I was thinking. "It needs to be believable. Let's say until the final baseball game of the season."

"The middle of July?" I demanded, my voice echoing. "You want to keep this going for a *month?*"

"I'm not *that* bad, sheesh. A month would make it more believable."

A month. One whole month, fake dating Mr. Perfect. A month sounded like *forever*, but really, would it be that bad? It wasn't like we'd be hanging out every day. And besides, I might need that long to get my article written and perfected.

I looked away from him, everything running through my mind. So many things about the situation felt wrong. We were lying to others by faking our relationship and I would be lying to him to get inside information.

In all actuality, there was no choice. I needed to nail this article. And Walsh represented the very essence of baseball, even down to the pretty bleachers. He could survive this article; I couldn't survive *without* it.

I was dooming myself, but I took in a deep breath. "I'll do it. For one month, and then I'm done."

"Well, don't sound so enthusiastic. I like it when a girl plays hard to get."

Yeah, this is a bad, bad idea. I already wanted to smack him.

"I'd *love* to be your girlfriend, Walsh Hunter." The words were filled to the brim with sarcasm, and I added an eye roll to help punctuate my annoyance. "Yes. A thousand times, yes."

Walsh grinned—the sort of grin that lights the stars in the sky—and it was clear that the twisted game we'd both agreed to had just begun. "That's more like it."

five

*A*t first, I didn't know what woke me up.

It could've been sunlight, blinding and intrusive, my own personal alarm clock. Or it could've been the headache stamping into my brain, about to crack open my skull.

But after a moment of lying still, nearly falling back to sleep, I heard it.

"Amber, come on. You're mad because I didn't make you breakfast. You didn't make *me* any!"

"The wife never makes the husband breakfast!"

"What? Who made up that rule?"

I pressed my face into my pillow, groaning into the fabric. The warmth of sleep was quickly fading, the sharpness of lucidity shaking it away.

"Yeah, that's right. Walk away, just like you always do!" I heard my dad say. A door slammed in answer.

Since I was awake and I had to hear them arguing, I made the choice to do it with orange juice from the kitchen. My head felt stuffed full of cotton, everything foggy and clouded.

Pushing up into a sitting position, I glanced around my room. It wasn't very messy, though pencils and pens were scattered all across my desk. Just above my desk were several realistic-looking butterflies painted on the walls, still there from when Mom decorated the room as my nursery.

I looked away from them, rubbing my eyes.

I must've slept like a rock last night, because I couldn't pinpoint my last memory, at least not clearly. Did I even take my makeup off? Had Edith gotten a chance to hang out with Zach? Had I found—

Scott.

I froze, breath stalling with me. I *had* found Scott. Holding that girl in the middle of the party. Scott broke up with me. He told me I wasn't fun enough, that he couldn't fix me.

He dumped me.

And then—oh. Oh, gosh. *Walsh.*

I looked over at Shiba, the gray cat that sat on the edge of my window seat, giving me judge-y eyes. Granted, judge-y eyes were the only kind she had, but they did nothing to help me feel better.

"You're lucky you're a cat," I told her, swallowing hard. "Don't have to deal with stupid boys."

She just blinked at me, and when I slipped from the room, she didn't follow.

The TV was on in the living room again, but instead of Mom's soaps, a sports anchor spoke quickly. No one even sat around to watch it. Dad was too busy sitting at the kitchen table, pretending to be engrossed in his newspaper, but I knew better. He didn't have his reading glasses on.

I stumbled past him, trying to catch the headline of the paper as I did so.

"You're up early," he greeted, not looking. The lower half of his face was obscured by the paper. "I would've thought the first day of summer you'd be sleeping in. Especially since you were out late last night."

I made a soft noise in response, finally giving up trying to read the headline, making my way to the fridge. Yeah, *out late*. After the nightmare that was Walsh's party, I went back to Edith's place and we spent the time drowning ourselves in ice cream. She took pity on me, though, and didn't say a word about the party, about Walsh or Scott, or her conversation with Zach. We just ate our ice cream.

"Did Mom go to her room?"

"No, she went to the studio."

Mom rented out a studio downtown, where she held morning and afternoon yoga classes. Every moment she could, she was there. Her clients probably saw her more than I did.

I downed my drink fast, enjoying the sting that the OJ gave, and thanked the stars Mom remembered to buy pulp-free this time. "Well, I'm going to go shower. Save the paper for me, okay?"

"Don't forget to clean Shiba's litter box," Dad spoke to the pages. "It's getting full again."

Right. Shiba and her full litter box.

I groaned as I walked past him, pressing my fingers to my forehead, hating that my thoughts went back to last night. Try as I might, there was no shutting out the gory details of the stupid party.

It was official. Last night had truly been from my nightmares. I found out I'd been cheated on just before I got dumped, and then the school's most desirable bachelor declared his love for me in front of the entire county of high schoolers. And instead of just leaving it at that, Walsh proposed a fake dating scheme, to which I so stupidly accepted.

I was never leaving the house.

Edith had this strange habit of claiming my bed whenever she came over. She laid stomach-down on my bedspread later that afternoon, desperately trying to push her dark hair from her face with the back of her hand. Her wet nails prevented her from holding it back for long. "I just still can't believe everything that happened last night. I mean, Scott's a jerk, but what Walsh said? I couldn't believe my own ears."

I frowned at her, my desk chair squeaking as I turned. Our unspoken agreement of not talking about the party must've reached its expiration date because it was all she could talk about now. "Can you at least be mad at Walsh with me? Him stepping in was...ugh. Annoying."

"No," she said quickly. "It was *chivalrous*."

Ha. Sure.

"So are you going to do it?" Edith asked as she blew on her nails, kicking her heels together. "Fake date Walsh Hunter? I vote yes. The opportunity to date the most popular guy in school only comes once in a lifetime."

I'd told her everything, of course. Though the idea crossed my mind to keep it a secret from everyone—to minimize the utter humiliation of anyone finding out the truth—there was no way I could keep this secret from my best friend.

But really, a once-in-a-lifetime opportunity of dating Walsh Hunter? Yeah, I totally wanted to pass. "We didn't even exchange phone numbers. I doubt anything's going to come from it."

"Did you tell him about the article?"

My fingers rose to my lips to hold the truth inside. "Uh, well, you see—"

"Sophia! You can't use him to get information on the article and not tell him."

"Hey, he knows! I told him about it." You know, well, kind of. "You had no problem of me doing it with Scott."

One of her dark eyebrows raised as she gave me a look. "That's because Scott's a jerk."

It wasn't like I didn't feel guilty for not telling Walsh the actual topic of the article. The feeling ate through the lining of my stomach, but I needed to get used to it. I'm sure all the major reporters didn't let the guilt get to them when they reported on juicy stuff. Conflicted emotions came over me at the thought. On the one hand, I didn't want to go lying to everyone, but I couldn't deny that Walsh would definitely make my article that much more interesting.

At the very least, I'd sell more copies by name-dropping him.

"How are you feeling about that, anyway?" Edith asked, her tone falling to a more serious note, looking into my eyes. "About Scott? I know that must've been horrible. I'm so sorry he did all that in public."

I gritted my teeth at the wave of anger that passed over me, the heat creeping into my cheeks. Thinking about Scott elicited all those not-so-fun emotions and brought back every ounce of humiliation I'd felt. "I don't even want to think about him ever again," I said, stubborn and hurt.

She capped the nail polish bottle, rising up onto her knees. "Good riddance."

"Whatever happened with Zach?" I asked, trying to change the subject without being obvious about it. Probably a fail. "How did talking to him go last night? Hopefully your conversation improved once I left."

She bobbed her head slowly, up and down. "We're hanging out tomorrow."

"Like, as in a date?"

"I don't know." Her teeth worried at her lip. "Maybe?"

"That's a good thing, isn't it?" This new development made me feel a little bit more at ease. She'd have something fun to keep her mind away from sports for a little while, but her expression wasn't as excited. "Why are you frowning?"

Edith let out a sharp sigh. "A part of me thinks he's still dating Celia Lemons. He brought her up last night. I can't tell if he sees this as a date or just as friends."

Celia Lemons was another girl in our grade, a girl who was also on the volleyball team. I wouldn't have gone as far as to say that she was Edith's archenemy—that title belonged to Eloise—but Edith and Celia didn't see eye to eye often.

"It'll work out," I said, turning my gaze to the ceiling. "Just take it one step at a time."

A noise filtered from downstairs, something that sounded

like footsteps, and both Edith and I stilled. Her eyes lifted to mine. "I thought you said your parents were gone?"

"They are." Dad was out with a buddy playing golf and Mom was down at the studio. Neither one of them should've been home.

I pushed up from my desk chair and went over to the window, pinching the curtains to pry them apart. Mom's silver car sat in the driveway, headlights still on.

"It's just my mom," I told Edith, trying to figure out why she would've been home. It wasn't even one o'clock yet. "I'll be right back."

She flapped her hand around. "I'll be here, waiting for this polish to dry. You should've bought the quick-dry kind."

From the top of the staircase, I had a straight-shot view of the front door, and how it was cracked open. Mom's bedroom door was also swung wide, the glow emanating into the hallway. Shiba sat on one of the steps on the staircase, tail swishing back and forth, and I ran my foot across her side gently.

Part of me wanted to go and see what was going on, what Mom was doing home so early, but I held back for a moment. How many times had she chosen to keep watching her TV shows instead of checking on me? Why should I intervene now?

A rattling sound had me moving, though, forward enough to push open her bedroom door as wide as the hinges allowed.

"Mom?" I called hesitantly, immediately taking in her figure facing the closet. She still wore her yoga pants and had her hair knotted into a bun. "What are you doing home?"

Mom turned around, the lines by her mouth seeming deeper than normal as she pressed her features into an epic frown. "Have you seen your father today?"

"Not since this morning." I folded my arms across my chest, bracing myself for whatever her response would be. "Not since he went golfing."

She folded her hands over her heart, and her eyes were shaded, glassy. "Do you think he left us, Sophia?"

My brow furrowed immediately, and I blinked at the sudden question. "Left us? Why would he have left us, Mom?"

Though not a frequent play in her book, Mom did fret about their separation more than once. Not so much worrying to me directly, but in mutterings that would resonate through the walls and floorboards, or during conversations over the phone with her friends. She was afraid that one day her nagging would send him over the edge.

Today, as she pressed her hand to her lips, I'd never seen her so dejected. "I checked his closet, and it's missing clothing, Sophia. Do you think he's grabbed his stuff and left? I know we argued this morning, but you don't think he'd leave, do you?"

I glanced back down the hallway toward where Shiba sat on the stairs. Her eyes gleamed with sympathy. "I'm sure he hasn't left us, Mom. He just went to play golf; he does that every Saturday. As for the clothes, maybe he's just doing laundry."

Mom's cell phone in the pocket of her leggings rang, causing her to jump. She fished it out immediately, posture sagging in relief as she looked at the screen. Quickly, she raised it to her ear. "Richard," she exhaled, lips twitching into an almost-smile. "Yeah, it's me. Hi. How's golf?"

Clenching my jaw, I backed out of Mom's bedroom before I could hear more. When I moved to pass Shiba on my way upstairs, I paused, looking down at her. "Why am I the only sane one?"

Shiba blinked at me, as if replying, "You're the one speaking to a cat."

Six

$\mathcal{M}$y bike groaned as I pedaled up the Main Street hill Sunday morning, the sun burning into my back. I was hoping a change in scenery would help this giant block clogging my emotional toilet. Yesterday was so unproductive. I hadn't left my bedroom all day, and no new information was hiding underneath my pillows.

To get that information, I had to get out of the house and face Walsh Hunter, who I hadn't seen since the party. A fake couple had to get together *sometime.*

Or maybe all that was done now and what I'd told Edith was true—this would all fall on the wayside.

I wasn't sure how to feel about that. Yes, it probably would've been for the best, but my future in journalism at the *Blade* would've been nonexistent. Then again, I didn't know if it was a good idea to place the fate of my journalism career into the hands of Walsh Hunter. Probably not.

As I continued down Main, I rode past the baseball field, spotting bodies moving around the diamond. My sneakers crunched against the gravel as I dragged to a stop, squinting

against the sun. A figure in uniform and baseball hat stood at
the pitcher's mound, not seeming too interested in the practice itself. He ran his feet through the dirt while his teammates tossed the ball around them.

When the player lifted his head, I saw that it was Walsh.

His baseball cap was turned around backward,
completely ignoring the benefits of wearing it like a *normal
person*.

And as much as I hated to admit it—and I never ever
would've admitted it aloud—his uniform looked good on him.

Scott stood out on the field too, leaning into a squat.
Something inside of me sharpened when I saw him, to the
point where drawing in a breath hurt. It didn't feel much like
heartbreak—what was that even supposed to feel like?—but
something more like unease.

I tried not to let myself grow angry, but it was hard. All I
could remember was how he made me feel at the party. It just
felt nerve-wracking to be so close to him after everything that
happened not even forty-eight hours ago, to be so *public* after
the whole story from the party had, no doubt, spread like
wildfire. Everyone had to know by now.

Focus, Sophia, I told myself sternly, swallowing hard.

I'd shown up at the baseball field at the perfect time,
because the coach called in the players to the dugout, ready
to end practice. Even from this distance, I could hear his
reprimanding voice. "If you idiots play that pitifully tomorrow, we can kiss that championship goodbye. And do we
want to kiss that championship goodbye? Do we *want* to
throw away four years of wins?"

"No, sir," came a chorus of low-toned replies.

"Didn't think so. Now get your sorry faces off my field. Walsh, stay behind."

The boys started to disperse, grabbing their bags and pulling their baseball mitts off. Walsh lifted his hat from his head to run a hand through his golden hair, trying to straighten his spine. He still hadn't seen me hovering by the fence, hadn't even glanced my way.

You're such a stalker. Watching him without him knowing it. Watching Walsh Hunter. *How has this become your life?*

I winced when the coach clasped a hand on Walsh's shoulder, trying to shake the tension from him.

"Sophia, are you even wearing any sunscreen?"

I didn't notice that Scott came up to me at the fence, hooking his fingers through the metal rungs and leaning into it. Sweat pasted wisps of hair to his forehead, streaks of dirt smudged along his cheeks.

"Hey," I said awkwardly, leaning back on my bike seat. "Good practice?"

"The best," he replied with a voice drenched in sarcasm, frowning at me. "What are you doing here?"

The confrontational energy seeping from him put me on edge; I *so* wasn't wanting a round two of Friday night. But this time, I wasn't sure I'd stand there gaping like a fish. No, the shock had worn off, and he wasn't going to talk to me like that. "What, I'm not allowed to bike past the baseball field?"

"You hate baseball," Scott pointed out. "What, are you meeting your new *boyfriend*?"

Heat sparked in my ears at the word, at the way it fell like a swear word from his lips. I almost screwed everything up right then, almost jumping to deny it. *Gross, no!* The words were on the tip of my tongue. *As if!*

But Scott's response clued me in on one thing: he was jealous. The mere idea of it was startling, almost stupid. It made me furious. What right did he have to be jealous when he dumped me in front of the entire student body?

"Yeah," I said after a moment, forcing myself to square my shoulders. "I am here for him."

"You two put on quite the show Friday night. No one believed you guys though. It was so obvious it was an act."

"Come on, Scottie," a voice chimed in. "I just think you don't know what real emotion looks like."

Walsh had walked around the side of the fence and came to my side, his hat still turned around backward, bag over his shoulder. He rested his hand along the back of the bike seat, arm grazing my lower back.

Scott's eyes locked on it. "Do you have to butt in on all our conversations, Hunter?"

"Only when you're being an idiot," Walsh tossed back casually, unaffectedly. "Though, that's pretty much all the time, isn't it?"

There was a vein I'd never seen before on Scott's forehead, and it began to throb. "Good effort, you two, but you can drop the act."

"No act," Walsh said, looking down at me. His hand lifted from my seat to snake around my waist. The movement rucked my t-shirt up ever so slightly, his arm brushing against the bare skin of my back. I jerked at the sensation, tensing all over. "We just hit it off."

Even though I gripped the handlebars like my life

depended on it, I forced my lips to curve into a smile. "You know what they say about chemistry."

Without allowing myself to think about it—not for a *single freaking second*—I reached up and pressed my lips against the top of Walsh's cheekbone. His skin was warm underneath my mouth, smooth, soft.

Two thoughts shot through my mind. *Are my lips chapped?* and *Oh my gosh, I'm kissing Walsh Hunter—with my mouth.*

"We should get going if we're going to meet my parents on time," I told Walsh, pulling away, my face no doubt on fire. The words came from my mouth so quickly—too quickly for me to censor what exactly I was saying—and I just hoped Walsh could think fast on his feet.

And of course, Walsh took my words in stride, fishing his car keys from his pocket. "I'll move some stuff around so your bike can fit into the trunk." He tossed a final glance towards the boy at the fence. "Later, Scottie."

"Good luck," Scott called back to us, even though we didn't turn. I hopped off my bike so I could walk it alongside Walsh, and he immediately slung his arm over my shoulders much like he had Saturday night. The weight felt lighter this time, more comfortable. "With her parents, you're going to need it."

I gritted my teeth but refused to turn around, refused to give him that satisfaction. I could feel Scott's eyes burning into our backs, but that only made me settle into Walsh's embrace more. With his relaxed posture, Walsh was practically declaring *she's with me and I'm proud of it.* Even if it was fake, I couldn't deny how great that feeling was.

And I wanted Scott to mull over it.

Once we were a safe distance away, Walsh glanced over at me. "That was really perfect, you know. The part about your parents especially. I think you might be better at acting than me. And that *kiss*—"

"Don't get used to it," I said immediately, lifting my chin. "It'll never happen. Ever again."

My words did nothing to erase his grin. "I thought we had a no kissing rule."

"I refer to my previous statement."

Laughing, Walsh dropped his arm, walking over to a banged-up SUV in the middle of the parking lot. He tugged on the handle of the trunk, fighting to pull the hatch open while I frowned. "What are you doing?"

"Uh, putting your bike in the back?"

I looked at the rusted bumper, the squeaking of the hatch as it swung up. The car looked so old that it shouldn't have been on the road anymore, like it was more of a safety hazard than anything else. "That is so not your car."

Walsh stood back and appraised the hunk of metal, rubbing his palm over the front of his Royals jersey. "Why not?"

Was he serious? When he glanced over his shoulder at me, gaze completely blank, I realized he was. "No reason. I thought you'd drive something...shinier."

"Something more expensive, you mean," he said on a sigh, reaching forward and laying his hand on the handlebars. "Don't diss my baby. She's an oldie but a goodie."

"Not dissing just...surprised is all."

Walsh lifted up my coral bike with ease, contorting the

wheels so that it would fit inside his car. He shoved his bat bag in alongside it, dusting his hands together. "So, what are you doing here, anyway? Did you miss me that much?"

My eyes shifted to his, actually looking at him for the first time since he'd approached. There were deep circles underneath his eyes, and when he blinked, the movement was slow, unhurried. He didn't sound tired, but he looked it, exhaustion living in his bones. The sight of him caused me to falter with a response.

"We're dating," I told him, feeling stupid saying it out loud, for having to remind him. "You're supposed to see someone when you're dating. Plus, I have an article to work on, remember? But, hey, if you want to stop this whole thing early, it's no big deal. I can figure out something else to write about."

"I'm thinking we could get ice cream," Walsh said lightly, reaching up and rubbing his eye with one knuckle. He didn't even seem to think about what I'd said before he began talking, like he'd already had this idea in his head. "I'm really craving some rocky-road."

Even though I realized he hadn't directly answered me, I made a face. "Rocky-road is your go-to?"

"Well, we could always get slushies," he offered, unknowingly hitting my sweet spot. "And besides, it's a hot day, and I could use something cool. How about you?"

I narrowed my eyes at him, totally knowing I looked like a sweaty mess. "That sounds like manipulation."

"No, it's called being strategic." Walsh ducked his head to peer into my eyes. "Up to you, Sophie, but what kind of monster could decline a slushy?"

"It's *Sophia*," I corrected him automatically, trying to ignore the way my lips relaxed the longer I looked into his eyes. Dang, he did have a compelling gaze. But I was *so* not affected. "And you're buying."

I heard the deadbolt flip over a little after seven o'clock that night, one earphone plugged into my ear, the other dangling next to me. The drumbeat of the song I had on repeat for the past hour was echoed by the familiar tapping of my pen on an old notebook, and I probably did more head bobbing than actual writing.

For the past hour, my nose had been stuck to these pages. I'd managed to find a notebook with a few blank lines in an old drawer and used it for plotting out my article paragraphs.

More than ever, I hated myself for throwing away my prized possession—my writer's notebook. Mrs. Gao would've had a heart attack. I missed the familiar texture of it, the stickers that covered the front. It was like I'd thrown away my best friend. But it was gone, and I'd have to get used to its absence.

I always found this method of plotting fun. First, I worked on a hard-hitting headline, which ended up being *The Curveball Truth Behind Bayview Baseball*. It was always fun playing with the phrasing, trying to get enough of a unique, eye-catching header.

After I got the headline down, I moved onto the hook and the thesis. They had to be enticing enough to attract a person who didn't normally read.

Basically, I needed to attract a Walsh Hunter. With 'baseball' in the headline, I doubted I'd have much trouble.

Once I thought of Walsh's name, my train of thought snagged on earlier this afternoon. We'd gone to a small little ice cream place by the bay, where I could order a slushy and Walsh could order his rocky-road. Strangely enough, I had a nice time. But that could've been from the fact that Walsh didn't talk much, what with trying to keep his ice cream from dripping down his hand. Still, it was...nice.

Weird.

Mom's signature sigh sounded as she walked down the hallway, a harsh exhalation that hinted at a long day. From the corner of my eye, I saw her figure drift into the kitchen.

We were soundless partners in this house. Despite that, I still strained with the one ear free of music, listening to the sound of the fridge opening.

"Of course!" Mom shouted from the kitchen.

I reached up and pulled the other earphone from my ear. My mouth shouldn't have opened, but it did. "What's wrong?"

Mom came back through the open kitchen, stepping into view. She still wore her workout clothes, sneakers loosely tied. Her hands were on her hips, her signature *your father is irritating me* stance. And, sure enough— "Your father ate *my* portion of dinner that I've been saving. And it was leftover spaghetti. I love spaghetti!" She threw her hands into the air. "Now, I have to cook, and it wasn't my night to. Ugh!"

Of course she immediately blamed Dad. Did she ask *me* if I'd eaten her spaghetti? No. I mean, I *hadn't* eaten it, but still.

Mom turned back into the kitchen and started slamming cupboards loudly, huffing under her breath. Open and shut, open and shut. A symphony of anger.

"I can make you something," I said slowly.

Mom jumped at the chance, as if she'd been waiting for my offer. She pulled off her headband. "Oh, Sophia, that'd be great! Maybe some sandwiches? I'm going to go take a hot bath, wipe off the grime from the studio. Come get me when it's done."

With that, she turned on her heel and disappeared toward her bedroom.

I sat still on the couch, looking at the words I'd written down, but now they hardly made sense. What had I been expecting? Her to offer to help out? That we'd have a mother-daughter bonding moment over stolen spaghetti? Of course that wouldn't be the case.

That would've required Mom to actually wake up and remember she had a daughter.

Slamming my notebook closed, I pulled the blanket off of my legs, wishing I'd never opened my mouth.

Seven

Most kids had summer jobs at their uncle's farm or served at the downtown burger joint. I'd tried the whole waitress thing once, last summer at Mary's Place in Greenville, the next town over. It went really well, up until I dumped a tray full of greasy French fries on this ancient man with more lines on his face than I could count.

The funny thing was that he didn't even realize I'd dropped them onto his lap until I scrambled, face flaming, to pick them up before they burned him. He then threatened to call the police on the "groping waitress."

My job there didn't last long.

To compensate for my failure, I walked dogs.

Two feisty, blood-thirsty dachshunds currently tried to pull my arms from my torso, weaving in and out and wrapping the leashes together. The plastic retractable leashes that Mrs. Vasquez owned were broken, so the lead didn't retract, leaving just knots of tether to trip over.

"Come here, pretty puppies," I cooed to them, hoping my

tone sounded soothing enough to calm their craziness. "Hold still—ow!"

A laugh bubbled through my frustration, and I looked up to glare at Walsh, who seemed to enjoy the view of me struggling. He had his hands in his sea-foam green shorts pockets, utterly relaxed.

Yeah, sea-foam green. I didn't know they made such monstrosities. "I know you said you didn't need help—"

"If you helped me, it wouldn't be fair." I blew a stray hair from my face, trying to pull dachshund number one, Dina, away from her sister, Tina. Dina took a sharp left and nearly pulled my arm from its socket; Tina didn't like Dina's proximity and bit at her collar. "Even though these are hellhounds, I can manage."

"I don't mind, really," he insisted for the tenth time, trying to grab a leash.

I tugged the dogs away. "No, Walsh, I mean it. My job, my responsibility."

"But—"

"*Mine.*"

He continued to reach, but his hand bypassed the dog leashes. His fingers caught ahold of the strand of hair that'd been bothering me, tucking it underneath my headband. I didn't want to even think about the sweat he must've felt at my hairline.

Walsh's eyes met mine, tone teasing. "You're welcome."

"My hero," I quipped, trying to be lighthearted. "This must be the perfect place for you, Walsh. Among your own kind."

"You know, I wondered why I felt so comfortable."

I finally managed to get Tina's teeth from Dina's collar, but their leashes still tangled together. They'd manage to wrap themselves around Walsh's ankle, but he didn't seem to notice. In fact, he seemed well at ease in this moment, in this company.

As much as I struggled to understand it, I had to admit that I felt much of the same.

This wasn't a park I frequented often since it wasn't really a dog park, but Walsh had suggested the route. Asking him to come walk dogs with me was a foreign compulsion, one that I had no idea where it'd come from. Maybe it was because I wanted to see if he'd know anything for my article, or maybe I just wanted to get out of the house and wanted company.

We'll go with the former.

"Smile," Walsh said, and I realized he'd pulled his cell phone out, aiming the camera at me.

"What?" I immediately looked down at the dogs, averting my face. "No. I'm gross and sweaty."

"No, you're *glowing*." He pulled his cell phone down and peered at the screen. "I'm going to caption it '*Puppies aren't the only thing I love.*'"

Uh, wait, wait. "You're going to *post it*?" I did not sign up to be plastered on Walsh's social media page. Especially looking like an armpit. "You're not seriously doing that. You're not posting that."

He glanced up from his phone, gaze innocent. "How else are people going to know we're dating?"

"*Fake* dating," I corrected, grabbing onto the words and launching them at him. "And no one needs to know. We're only carrying this on for a month before we're breaking up."

Or fake breaking up. Or real breaking up our fake relationship. Ugh. So confusing.

I found Walsh smiling. "A month is a long time, Sophie. And if no one needs to know, why did you invite me to come with you this morning?"

"Because I'm just *dying* to hang out with you," I said as sarcastically as possible, trying to hide the truth.

Quite honestly, I'd been surprised Walsh even agreed to come out with me today. Scott never went with me; he said he wasn't really an animal person. Having company felt strange, but not unwelcome. Crazy as it sounded, spending time like this with Walsh was easy.

Someone alert the media: Sophia Wallace could stand next to Walsh Hunter without exploding into annoyed comments or angry eye rolls. Go figure.

I squeaked as the leashes constricted against my wrists, clenching tighter even though I fought to separate the two. Dina's own legs tangled with it, tripping her as she tried to avoid her sister's teeth. "Okay, you know what? I changed my mind. Take Tina. She's evil."

"Oh, sure, give me the mean one," he sighed dramatically. "I see how you are."

Us spending time together, alone, still had my brain in a blender because never in a million years would I have seen this coming. Like I'd been plunged into an alternate universe. On Friday, I'd been nothing but annoyed with him. Patting my shoulder in the hallway, misusing my name, butting in at the party. And maybe that had something to do with Scott.

Scott always hated him, rolled his eyes at the mere mention of Walsh's name—it must've rubbed off on me at some point.

But here we were, mere days later, doing our first outing as a couple.

Fake couple.

Gosh, have to remember that fake part.

"I was just thinking of your article, you know." Walsh took a step away from me to pull Tina back, reaching down to scratch her head. "You're going to write about the baseball team, like you said, so I'm trying to rack my brain for any amazing tidbits of information."

"Uh-huh." I didn't tell him that my article was actually going pretty well without his tidbits. But he was right— sooner or later, I was going to need him to spill his juicy little secrets.

Before I had a chance to say anything else, Walsh reached over and took my sweaty hand in his—*am I destined to constantly be sweaty around him for the rest of our time together?* The gesture was casual but determined. He tugged me closer, nearly causing me to trip over Dina.

Nearly causing my heart to skip a beat. "Uh, what are you doing?"

"That girl over there. Redhead, with the Pekingese." He looked ahead, expression calm and collected. It was annoying. "She was at the party. We want to show her we're a real couple." Walsh raised our joined hands slightly, as if saying *this is us bonding. We must show off.*

I kept my voice casual, though my insides were chittering with nerves. "A real couple, huh? I could jump you if that makes us a bit more believable."

Walsh's head snapped toward me, eyebrows high. "Uh—"

"I'm kidding."

"*Gosh*. How am I supposed to know when you're being serious?"

"I roll my eyes when I'm serious."

He gave my hand a squeeze. "You're ridiculous."

"Fancy seeing you two here," a voice interjected, one that was immediately familiar.

Okay, how the heck did we keep running into him?

Scott stood a few feet away with his arms folded over his chest, basketball shorts pulled up high on his waist. I gripped Walsh's hand tighter in response, practically grinding his bones together.

"Hey," Walsh greeted with the perfect dose of nonchalance, so much smoother than I would've been. He looked ahead, expression calm and collected. It was annoying—no way I could even fake that amount of indifference. "What a surprise, Scottie. Enjoying a stroll too?"

"Playing basketball." Scott jerked his thumb over his shoulder. A basketball court was several feet behind him, and a few guys bounced a ball back and forth. "I come here a lot to play with some guys from the basketball team."

"Oh, that's right," Walsh said, nodding.

I glanced between them, the tension thick in the air. Yeah, we were fake dating, but I never entertained the idea of having to show it off. Holding hands in front of strangers was one thing, but faking in front of people we knew? In front of Scott for the second time? Beyond weird.

I couldn't get myself to speak, even though I knew I

should've said *something*. Dina and Tina pranced around in the grass, completely oblivious to everything going on.

"How was meeting Sophia's parents, Walsh? Were they at each other's throats or overly mushy gushy? They can never really decide."

Even with the summer breeze, heat crawled over my skin, up my neck and making me feel like I was burning. That knotted sensation in my stomach returned with a potent twist. The words felt wrong in the air, especially with Walsh being right in earshot. Fake dating was one thing—he didn't have to know all my secrets.

Scott's lips curled into a mean smile, and the fact that the curve looked familiar shocked me.

"They were happy as could be after breakfast this morning," Walsh told Scott easily, not missing a beat. "We had to eat early so they could go to work, but it was nice."

Jeez, Walsh hadn't been lying. He *was* a great actor. "Yeah, they're doing great, Scott," I said. "Thanks for asking."

Dina tugged on the end of the leash as she strained to walk on, Tina coming to gnaw at her heels. "We should get going," Walsh told him. "These puppies can't walk themselves."

"You two coming tonight?" Scott asked just as he'd begun to turn.

Walsh nodded, slow, eyes darting to mine for a brief second. "Maybe just for a minute or two."

I wanted to ask where he was going, and now where *I* was going, but I didn't know if that would mess with our game. Wouldn't a fake girlfriend know where her fake boyfriend was going to be? Maybe, maybe not, but I didn't risk it.

Scott ended up just nodding his head once before heading back off toward the basketball court, barely glancing in my direction.

I released a heavy breath as soon as he was out of earshot, my lungs on the brink of bursting. Leftover tension caused my fingers to tremble, and the hand that held the leash tightened its grip. "That was—"

"Brilliant." Walsh smiled, letting go of my hand. Cool air brushed my skin, and I wondered if my hand felt clammy to him. Ugh, what if it *had*? "Did you see his face, Sophia? He's totally buying it."

How could Walsh tell by merely looking at his face? "Really?"

"Totally."

I pursed my lips, not completely sold. "You're trying way too hard."

"What? How?"

With him looking at me like that, the urge to smack him was so strong. "We're supposed to convince people that we're dating, not planning a wedding."

He laughed at that, saying nothing in response.

We walked together in quiet for a moment, a little girl on a tricycle pedaling past us. Dina tried to get in the path of her wheel, and I pulled her back at the last second. "Thank you for coming with me," I told Walsh quietly. "It's nice to walk with someone who can speak to me for a change."

"It's what fake boyfriends do, right?" His voice was

gentle, and as was the hand that lifted, pushing my glasses up my nose. I hadn't realized they'd fallen low.

Staring at his face, I noticed a faint, silvery scar underneath his right eye, as small as my thumbnail. I reached out with my free hand, tracing my fingertip along his skin. A featherlight touch, barely there. "What happened here?"

His gaze never left mine. "Baseball cleat. Fourth grade. One of my teammates threw it at me."

"Some little league kid threw their *shoe* at you? *Why?*"

"I told him that he couldn't bat very well." Walsh shrugged. "He couldn't take the truth."

I snorted. "You were *that* kid? The dream crusher?"

"Well, someone had to be." His small smile was unapologetic. "Ask me who the kid was."

I looked at him for a moment before tipping my head. "No way. Scott?"

"Who else would be that aggressive as a fourth-grader?"

Dina pulled at my arm as I laughed, shaking my head at the thought of miniature Scott throwing a shoe at small Walsh. I stepped out from the tangle of leashes at our feet, glancing down. "Oh, your poor rich-boy shoes."

"What?" Walsh looked at his feet. "*Oh.*"

Brown smeared the side of his expensive-looking shoe, probably coating along the bottom. "With dogs around, you should probably watch where you're walking."

Walsh let go of my hand to switch the leash and proceeded to try and smear the offensive substance onto the grass. "Now you tell me."

"Should we clean the poop off your shoe together? Is that romantic?"

His response was dry. "Ha-ha."

"What? Shouldn't we get a photo and caption it, *'This might've been an accident, but falling in love wasn't'*?"

"Watch it, or I'll wipe it on your ankle."

I jerked back just in case he tried it, nearly tripping over Dina's wealth of leash. "So, what's going on tonight that you're hanging out with Scott?

"Ryan's just having a small party." Walsh's voice was hesitant as he rose. "He's a guy on the baseball team."

"He's having it on a Tuesday?"

"His parents are out of town. It's a real small thing." Walsh slipped his shoe back on, stepping away from the pile. "Did you want to come with me?"

Ah, it was *that* kind of party. The "no adults, just friends" kind of party. Most of the time, those included alcohol. "You should know that I don't drink." I don't know why I blurted it out like a complete loser, but the words hung in the air anyway.

Walsh made a noise in the back of his throat. "I don't either."

I wanted to call him out on it, but he'd said it so simply, so quickly, that I couldn't be sure he wasn't telling the truth.

"If you don't want to go tonight, that's okay. Sometimes they're fun."

I probably wouldn't have used the word *fun*. More like horrifying. Going to a party on my own free will without Edith? Ew.

But wasn't that what fake dating Walsh was for? Getting access to this insider kind of thing? Getting exclusive information on things that I would've missed out on originally?

Ryan's party was a prime example. Without Walsh, I never would've been invited to this. And it was an excuse to get me out of the house. A win-*win* scenario, resting in the palms of Walsh's hands.

"Would my *boyfriend* like that?" I prodded with heavy sarcasm, peering at him underneath my lashes.

Walsh didn't look at me when I spoke, my words hanging between us, the question left unanswered and weighing in the wind. *Boyfriend*. Weird.

He took his time smearing every inch of brown off his shoe, making sure it coated the grass before slipping the shoe back on.

When Walsh looked up, he looked at me with a challenge in his eye. "Tina and I will race you to the end of the park."

"Poor Tina doesn't know that she's saddled with a slow runner. I've heard your run on the field is a mom-jog at best."

This time, both of Walsh's golden eyebrows rose. "A *mom-jog*?"

"Plus those awful shoes have you at a disadvantage. You'll be slipping on the grass the entire time."

Amusement glittered across his gaze, though he tried to hide it. "Sheesh, woman, you're attacking me left and right."

One of my shoulders lifted as I stretched my legs. "I talk a big game, what can I say?" I shortened Dina's leash, gripping the bundle tightly in my hand. "You backing down?"

"I guess you don't know me very well," Walsh replied simply, and then took off running. Tina, surprised by the sudden movement, had no choice but to chase after him, barking loudly.

Dina started toward them first, leaving me kicking up

grass as I lunged forward. "Whoa, wait! You're such a cheater!"

Even with his back turned to me, I could see Walsh tip his head back into the sunlight, his musical laugh echoing throughout the park. "Who's got the mom-jog now, Sophie?"

eight

I had time to kill before meeting Walsh again to go to Ryan's party. Too much time. I couldn't help but overthink the prospect of tonight, the looming doom hanging over my shoulder.

Ugh, looming doom? What was I talking about? It was just a high school party. Sure, my last one had sucked bad.

Real bad.

I needed to distract myself, so I buried my nose in research for my article. I borrowed Mom's personal laptop that she kept in the living room, powering up a search browser.

Being in the journalism class gave me all kinds of access to the school's information. By state law, Bayview was required to post its annual budget sheet for the public to see, and using my old credentials from class, I logged onto the server.

One of the major points in my article was focused on unfair funding, so I crossed my fingers that something interesting would pop up.

The first option read *"Bayview High School Treasurer's Reporting"* and I clicked on it with lightning speed. A page with a whole lot of numbers loaded up, with two columns of *revenues* and *expenses*. Most of the rows were common things, such as Instructional Costs, Operation and Maintenance, Taxes.

None of the numbers seemed out of the ordinary. Not that I knew what those numbers *should* look like, granted, but everything at least resembled the other sections in the amount.

However, when I looked at the Athletics row, that number nearly doubled any other column. At the bottom of the page, I saw that there was a *"Where the Money Comes From"* link.

"Honey?" Mom asked sleepily, moving from the hallway. "What time is it?"

"Not sure." I didn't glance at the clock on the computer. She must've been napping—she had come back from the studio early this afternoon nauseous. I guess I hadn't realized she'd been asleep this entire time.

A bar chart pulled up on the page, with several different colors creating it, showing the athletic department's budget from the past three years. The first year was lower than the last two, and the last two had a significant amount of blue to the bar. Much more than any other color. When I looked for the key, I read that the blue indicated *Fund Modification*. What did that mean?

"I'm not feeling too great," Mom went on, and I glanced up to find her pressing a hand against her stomach. "Can you get me a glass of water, Sophia? I'm going to go lay back down."

"Uh, yeah, just give me a second."

I had no idea what Fund Modification was, but it sounded sketchy. I wasn't an expert in numbers or anything, but it wasn't hard to use deductive reasoning. Changing the amounts in the funds. Transferring money to different spots. Could they do that? Were they allowed to transfer funds from other accounts like that? Maybe I was just making an assumption.

After I hit the print button, I stood up from the couch, heading toward the kitchen to grab Mom her water. More information would have to be looked up for sure, but it was a step in the right direction.

"Should you be sitting that close to the fire, dude? You're going to burn off an eyebrow."

The "party" at Ryan's house turned out to be small, just like Walsh said. But by small, he meant *small*. Ryan's house wasn't nearly as big as Walsh's, and neither was his gathering of people. Mostly baseball players showed up, all chilling in Ryan's living room. No obnoxious music, drunken high schoolers, or alcohol.

Well, there was a little bit of alcohol, not that I drank anything.

Ryan had lit the fireplace in his living room and pressed his face as close to the flames as possible, letting the heat warm his face.

"I doubt you're going to be able to get girls with one

eyebrow," Zach continued from where he sat on an armchair, shaking his head of dark hair. The width of his shoulders made him look more like a linebacker than a baseball player, but it wasn't hard to see what Edith liked about him. He *was* pretty cute. "You can barely get them now."

"You've never seen my charm at work, Balker." Ryan pulled back from the fire to take a drink. "Walsh, you think I could rock a one-eyebrow look?"

Walsh and I sat on the couch together, one of his arms draped across my shoulders. He'd cleaned up since earlier, replacing those horrible shorts with chinos. The fancy shoes were missing, replaced with black sneakers. "It would look a little funny if you ever tried to raise your eyebrows," he replied without hesitation. "So I vote no."

Ryan looked to me. "Sophia?"

I pressed my lips together to hide a grin. "I think I have to side with them. If anything, I'd burn them both off."

Walsh laughed at that and nestled me closer. "It's unanimous. Move away from the fire, nimrod."

"I don't know if we're going to win tomorrow," a different player said, lounging on the adjacent sofa. I couldn't remember his name, but I thought it started with a T. "Walsh, your game has been off. I blame your new relationship mojo."

"Sophie isn't the reason we're losing games," Walsh said immediately. "It's because you think it's a wise idea to come to games hungover."

For some reason, hearing him use that nickname now —*Sophie*—had me nearly smiling, no annoyance in sight. Not that our banter about it held much heat before, but hearing it roll off his tongue now made it different. Maybe it was the fact that we were in front of all his friends, and he wasn't trying to make me invisible. He'd spoken it like an endearment, and that was something I could get behind.

Wait. *No.* Not acceptable.

"Or pre-hungover," Zach added, grinning at Walsh.

"No, it's definitely Walsh," a new voice added, and we all turned toward the entrance of the living room.

Scott, the girl he'd been hanging onto at the party, and Celia Lemons walked into Ryan's living room, coming around the corner from where the front door was. The girl who'd been with Scott wore a pair of sweatpants and a workout shirt, her curly hair wild around her shoulders.

Part of me was surprised she'd shown up to a party in sweats—the other part of me was jealous. I wish *I'd* worn sweats and not a fancy top and jeans.

Celia glanced around the room, eyes resting on Zach.

"He fell asleep at the game against Northwood last Friday," Scott went on, not caring that no one replied, that no one greeted him. "Right there on the bench. Coach reamed him out for it."

"I wouldn't talk, Scottie," Walsh replied just as casually, unbothered. "I'm not the one who strikes out every game."

Scott just ignored that, though, brushing the words off so easily. "Sophia, have you met Jewel? Jewel Branson?" Scott gestured to the girl that was practically on top of his heel. "My *new* girlfriend?"

Of course it had to be a unique name like Jewel. Unique, pretty, and I hated it. Okay, maybe not really. But I did hate that he'd moved onto someone *prettier, better,* and all the things that I wasn't. And he was rubbing it in my face.

"Hi, Jewel," I told her, forcing myself to find a genuine smile.

She showed her own set of sparkling teeth. "It's so nice to meet you, Sophia. I've heard so much about you."

Yeah, and I was certain that she hadn't heard good things.

"Find a seat, guys," Ryan told them, gesturing to the open spaces. There was a couch kitty-corner to Walsh and me, where the other baseball player sat. "We're just about to start a game of M.A.S.H. and paint each other's fingernails."

Celia laughed at that, moving to sit on the arm of Zach's chair, resting her legs along his. She leaned comfortably against the edge of his arm, hip pressed against his side, and Zach didn't look like he was about to move.

Disappointment welled. Was Edith right? Were they back together? I hoped not.

"Ooh, really?" Celia glanced around. "Whose nails can I paint?"

"You can paint mine," Zach said from beside her, wiggling his fingers. "Only if it's pink."

My gaze shifted over to where Scott sat with his own girl-friend. The air stalled in my lungs when I found that his eyes were already on me, noting where Walsh's arm was slung over my shoulders.

Guess I'm desirable now, huh? I thought at him, pressing up closer to Walsh, holding my breath so his scent wouldn't fill my nose. The way the couch sagged put us pretty close together anyway, unable to escape the sinking cushions.

Walsh used his free hand to reach over and trace designs on my knee. "What's the point of buying jeans with holes in them?" His voice was soft underneath the conversations mingling around us.

"You sound like a grandma."

His grin came easy at that. "I'd make a pretty grandma."

I leaned into his side, appreciating how comfortable I felt. It was easy to touch someone when it meant nothing. Easier when there was no pressure. And I surprised myself for playing along so well. It was almost like I was a better fake girlfriend than a real one. Sitting here in front of all these people, most of whom I hardly knew, I didn't feel awkward. There was no pressure to be someone I wasn't. I could just be me.

A soft buzzing noise filled the air, and Walsh leaned away from me just enough to pull his cell from his pocket. He peered at the screen. "My dad's calling me," Walsh said, pulling his arm from me. I didn't miss the tight expression on his face. "I'll be right back."

I wanted to reach out and snatch his wrist, forbid him from leaving me alone. Not with Scott and his pretty new girlfriend. But I didn't. Instead, I smiled, but it was tight. "Okay."

The space next to Walsh sunk in slightly in his absence, the warmth of his body disappearing as he left me on the couch alone. I pressed my hands into my lap, looking at my fingernails. The blue polish was chipped—always chipped.

"Yo, Taylor," Ryan murmured, voice low in the mix of the music and talking. If I hadn't been laser-focused on picking up any small details, I would've missed the interaction entirely. "We're missing your cut for the payout. I need to give it to the guys at Hampton."

The player from the couch—Taylor—shifted quickly, reaching a hand into his front pocket. "Sorry, sorry, I have it."

Hampton. Hampton High? They were giving money to Hampton High? What did Ryan say? *Payout...I need to give it to the guys at Hampton.*

Wait. Wait, wait, wait. Why were they giving money to a rival school?

I tried to be discreet as I watched Taylor pass over a thick wad of cash to Ryan, who quickly stuffed it in his jacket pocket. I wasn't discreet enough, apparently, because Ryan's eyes locked onto mine. "Graduation money," he told me after a beat. "We're pitching in on a gift."

It wasn't hard to realize he was lying, but there was no way I'd point that out. I decided to play dumb. "Looked like a big chunk."

"I'm just a giver," Taylor said, nodding, totally confident. "We're buying the guy a ball launcher."

"So, Sophia," Zach said from his chair, drawing my eyes over to him. There had been more to that money conversation, I was sure, but Zach effectively changed the subject with his friendly grin and easy voice. "You and Walsh Friday night—no offense, but I didn't see that coming. I'm a little hurt that I wasn't let in on your secret."

I swallowed hard, glancing off in the direction Walsh disappeared. "He made it sound more dramatic than it really was. We were just...talking. Here and there. Him saying all those things definitely came out of left field."

Zach laughed genuinely at that, causing Celia to shift against his frame. "Baseball pun, nice. He's already converting you."

Ew, I *had* done a baseball pun. Cringe.

"That's the thing I don't get," Scott piped in. "I mean, Sophia, you were talking to him while we were together? And Zach, you're his best friend. Did he tell you that?"

Before I could call out Scott for being a hypocrite, I felt the air *whoosh* from my lungs in one harsh exhale. Had Walsh talked to Zach about this just as I talked to Edith about it? Surely Walsh told Zach the truth so he could vouch for us. Right?

Wrong. Apparently Walsh had kept his mouth shut, because the amusement melted slowly from Zach's face as he tried to think. "Ah, no. He never said anything to me."

Crap.

Seriously, Walsh?

"Then again," Zach went on, expression clearing as he settled back in his seat. "Walsh and I don't spend too much time talking about our love lives."

"Good thing, because that'd be awkward," Celia chuckled, reaching over and running her fingers through his short hair. He jumped a little at the touch. "What kinds of things would you say, anyway?"

Zach's gaze immediately went to mine. *Oh, he might have more to say than you think,* I thought to her, fighting the urge to lift a challenging eyebrow at the boy Edith was crushing on.

Even though I didn't give him a look, he seemed to have caught onto my thoughts, because his cheeks pinked.

"We'd talk about our feelings, of course." Walsh's voice was smooth as he walked back into the room, but I didn't miss the edge to it. He stopped just in front of me, hand stretched out. "Come with me."

I tentatively wrapped my fingers around his as I rose to my feet. "Where?"

"Outside. Let's get some fresh air."

Walsh lifted our hands up to his mouth, pressing a kiss against my knuckles. *Too much, too much*, I wanted to tell him, but the only way I could convey it was by squeezing his palm. The hand on mine was a big flag of *look at our lie!*

"Ugh, you two are gross," Ryan said from where he sat, watching us, but I didn't miss his teasing smirk.

"You're just jealous," Walsh replied, not missing a beat, leading me away.

The night air was clear as I stepped out into it, drawing in a deep breath. Crickets chirped somewhere in the night, and from here, I could see where Walsh's car was parked at the curb. The way one of the street lamps hit the metal illuminated a dent on the hood, another sign of how old it was. For some reason now, knowing Walsh drove a normal car was almost endearing. He wasn't stuck up enough to need a shiny convertible. He was just as fine driving a dented SUV.

I reached down and slipped my fingers into my purse. My writer's notebook wasn't there, long gone now, but I'd stashed a paperback in there before I left. Even though I couldn't see it, I slid my fingers along the pages, wishing the rotten feeling in my chest would start to ebb away.

"You ready to head out?" Walsh asked from behind me, voice quiet.

"What?" I glanced over my shoulder, frowning a little. "Why? Are you?"

"It's getting crowded."

I crossed my arms over my chest and turned back around, looking down the empty street. "Scott's so infuriating. Pointing fingers at *me* for talking to someone else before we even broke up. Um, *hello*, he was talking to that random girl in there before he dumped me! He's such a hypocrite."

Walsh wrapped his arms around my waist quickly and quietly, a light pressure, as if he were unsure whether or not I'd push him away. He still put on a show, nose brushing along the whispers of my hair. "Don't let him get to you," he murmured. "He's just trying to rile you up."

Yeah, I knew he was. He was trying to get me to expose our fake relationship because he *knew*. To him, it was obvious. He knew me, knew how completely opposite Walsh and I were from each other.

That thought, that Scott knew the truth, made me feel like I'd been coated in mud.

Walsh shifted behind me, his chin a soft nudge against my shoulder.

"You're having fun, aren't you?" I baited, staring at the dark road. "Being all lovey-dovey in front of everybody."

"You're not?"

"I'd rather pull the book out of my purse and read." I turned in his embrace, looking up into his eyes. The blue was dark, subdued. "Better than lying." *Way better than lying.*

"We're being watched," he whispered.

Something inside of me tightened, and I couldn't interpret it as a good or bad emotion. I held my breath, afraid to breathe in or out. *We're being watched.*

When I agreed to this fake dating thing, I hadn't expected

to feel this bad about being dishonest. It wasn't like I knew these people personally. What did it matter what they believed? And yet, here I was, guilty.

I hated that feeling. "Is your dad okay?"

"My dad?" He sounded confused.

"He called you."

Walsh let out a soft sigh, shaking his head. "It was nothing."

Before I had a chance to ask more, Walsh shut his eyes and leaned his forehead against mine, looking like he just wanted to bask in the silence of the moment. I found myself watching him, studying the way his golden lashes fluttered over his warm cheeks, the way his golden hair curled delicately over his ear. My own arms were still at my sides because I couldn't will them to move, to lift, to return this fake embrace. I couldn't deny the warmth that came from being in someone's arms, and each second that ticked past my insides felt calmer and calmer.

For a moment, my thoughts shifted to the wad of cash Taylor passed to Ryan, and Ryan's excuse. Were they *paying off* the other team? Was that what the money was about? That would explain Zach's quick diversion, pulling my attention away. Was he in on it, too?

Was *Walsh*?

"Don't listen to Scott," he whispered. "He just thinks he's cool because he knows how to be a jerk."

Yeah, no kidding. But this side of Scott was new to me— or maybe it wasn't. Maybe he was always like this and I just never thought about it. All the times he wanted me to wear my contacts, put on makeup, wear certain clothes—it all made sense now.

"I think I've made enough of an appearance," Walsh said, unaware of my thoughts, pretending to push up the rim of my glasses even though I wasn't wearing them. His fingertip brushed the curve of my cheek, as delicate as a sigh. I blinked quickly, torn between wanting to pull back and lean forward, closer to the soft caress.

"Yo!"

I jerked at the sudden shout, nearly knocking my head against Walsh's. I looked over to find Ryan standing in the doorway, leaning against the jamb. "If you guys are going to make out on my lawn, you can leave. I don't need the cops called for public indecency."

"I'm sure it's happened before," Walsh called to him, but pulled back a bit, still watching me. "We're going to head out."

"What? You two haven't even been here that long!"

"We've got things to do."

Ryan put his hand on his hip and raised his eyebrows at Walsh, causing a laugh to escape my mouth. "I can read between the lines. Fine. Go kiss your girl in the back of your crappy car. Have a better night than me." He paused, briefly, before he asked, "Did you invite her to the fourth of July party down at the bay?"

Right. Every year, the bay's boardwalk did a huge fireworks display, inviting out street vendors and face painters and all sorts of fun things. It totally slipped my mind.

I hadn't realized next week was already the start of July. Granted, less than a week had passed since we started this fake relationship, but time felt like it was moving way, way too fast. I had to get this article going.

The thought of the article resurrected the sharpness of dread in my stomach, especially since I was wrapped in Walsh's arms. I couldn't figure out why it came so powerfully, so potent, but there it was, rearing its ugly head.

"You should come," Walsh said, voice loud enough to carry. "I'd love it if you came."

Meaning: *it would look really good if we went as a couple.*

I wasn't as good of a performer as he was, but I wasn't terrible. My lips pulled at the corners, and I tried to slip on a happy persona. "Sounds like a lot of fun."

Walsh lifted his hand to his friend before capturing my own, squeezing my fingers. "We can flip on the overhead light in the car and you can read to me on the drive home."

I narrowed my eyes at him. "Are you making fun of me?"

"Of course not. I think that sounds fun." Walsh's nose grazed the crown of my head in a perfect end to our show, and I found myself basking in the heat his body provided, in the comfort his nearness gave me. "You can try to convince me to like reading."

I couldn't even explain *why* this moment made me feel so calm, so quiet on the inside, but I couldn't shake it.

I just found myself nodding, hoping he was serious.

nine

"'*Some schools prefer football, but at Bayview High, they like to* play ball. *And they're good at it.*'" I stilled, the pen cap caught between my teeth. "No, maybe not. Um, '*Though football is the choice of many, baseball still remains America's favorite pastime, as well as Bayview's'*—ugh!"

Nothing was coming out right. No combination of words had the right flow when I wrote them down. Not even in the slightest. Or maybe I was being too hypercritical of myself, judging every tiny thing. Maybe I just needed to write everything out and see where it led me.

If I'd had my writer's notebook, I was sure things would've come out smoother. Those pages were magic. But, instead, I was writing in some crappy journal with no stickers and no clippings, and I didn't have a single ounce of inspiration.

The sheet of bar graphs that I printed off sat off to my side, numbers highlighted and sticking out at me. One of the most important things about information articles was to have actual facts. I couldn't get proof of bias in any other form than this, with the athletic funding bar shooting through the roof. I'd researched what *Fund Modification* meant, and all my searches gave me the answer of *"a transference of funds between other non-specific funding accounts."*

That sounded shady, right? Wasn't that what certain accounts were for? And again, Ryan taking that money from Taylor was super sketchy. For a graduation gift? Yeah, I really didn't think so.

I had my outline nailed down, and it looked good from the bullet points. Since the whole goal of the article was to prove how toxic the baseball team *really* was, I had to focus on its most atrocious parts. But translating my bullet points into concise, catchy paragraphs felt harder than usual. Usually this stuff came easily to me.

I blamed it on baseball. It was near impossible writing about something I hated.

"*'Though the choice is inconsequential, Bayview High students'*—nope, that sounds a little offensive, doesn't it?"

For my mental roadblock, however, I blamed Walsh. After we left the party the other night, he let me pull my book from my purse and read it to him in the car, parked in front of my house. The conditioned air filtered from the vents as he tipped his head back, listening to my words.

And he *was* listening. He'd interject almost every time the main boy spoke—"Oh, come on, she falls for *that* line about how her eyes shine brighter than the sun? Ridiculous"—but judging by the way his shoulders slumped when I told him I had to go inside, I had a feeling he enjoyed our little book club.

Or maybe I was just projecting onto him because it was the best fake-date I'd had.

But a night like that made writing this article hard.

I shouldn't feel guilty. The school board *was* changing around the funding. Seeing that the article written might spur them to give me back my class, rather than face backlash.

Okay...so that *sort of* sounded like blackmail, but it wasn't. Not really. It was the key I needed. The blockade keeping me from my future would be removed, and I could go back to happily knowing at least one thing in my life was set. My relationship with my parents was still crazy, but I had my writing class and the opportunity to build my résumé. Article, internship, career in journalism.

A good reporter is unbiased, I told myself, steeling against the icky sensation. *Just keep going.*

"So if everything's organized from least scandalous to most," I said aloud, tracing my pen along my bullet points, trying to reorganize my thoughts, "I need to figure out a way to smoothly connect them all. Teacher bias leads into school board bias, then money wiring—"

Again, I cut myself off, dropping my pen onto the piece of paper. Why was this so hard? Why was nothing *feeling* right?

I slouched in my chair, expelling a harsh breath. All my ducks were in a row, but nothing was coming out right. Garbage word after garbage freaking word. What was that about? Me, Sophia Wallace, having trouble *articulating* my *thoughts*?

Ridiculous.

My cell phone started to ring, effectively cutting off my thought process. I almost ignored it, knowing that I needed to force my mind to focus, but found myself grabbing it up. "Hello?"

"What's the score? Are we close?" Edith greeted from the other line, words coming quick, barely giving me any time to catch them. "Gosh, we'd better be kicking their butts or else I owe Zach five bucks."

I massaged the spot between my eyebrows as if that would help me process her words better. "The score? What are you talking about?"

"It's Friday. *Hello.* Baseball-game-Friday?"

'Cause that's a popular term, I thought to myself. Besides, don't they have games other than on Fridays? "I wasn't invited."

"Sophia, you're dating the team captain. If you don't want people to suspect anything, you should probably go to his games, personal invite or not." She let out a harsh breath that morphed into a groan. "I can't be there because I'm stuck babysitting my dweeb of a brother—who, by the way, has done nothing but play his stupid video games for the last two hours. Why he needs a babysitter is beyond me."

"Uh, because he's nine?"

"He's *boring.* And zombie-killing obsessed. Anyway— baseball. Whatever you're doing, it can wait until you get back from the game."

Combing my fingers through my ponytail, I really, *really* tried to take her words seriously. I even tried to envision myself getting up from my chair, pushing away my papers, and going out to watch a baseball game. Sitting amongst other people, cheering on the players as they swung their bats and ran around. It was a horrible image. "Edith, you know this is fake. Whatever Walsh and I have, I mean. I'm not *obligated* to go to his games."

She adopted a sing-song-like voice. "Zach said you were cuddled up *real* close at Ryan's party the other night. And don't worry, I didn't blab. He just said you two were super adorable."

I blocked out almost everything in that sentence but one thing. *Zach.* Zach, allowing Celia to lean up against him. Zach, who looked at me guiltily.

"Can I ask you a question?" I said slowly, debating my words. "Has Zach ever mentioned...cheating?"

"Cheating? What do you mean?"

I traced my pen along my page. "The team, I mean. Whether or not the baseball team cheats. At the party, Ryan asked another player for cash so he could give it to Hampton."

"Hampton," Edith repeated, voice sounding strange. I strained to listen closer. "You're sure that's what he said?"

"Yeah. Why?"

"That's the team they're playing today."

My grip on the phone loosened a little as I stared at my sheet of paper. They were playing Hampton High today, and Ryan asked for money to pay them. And that wasn't all of it, either. Ryan said they were missing *Taylor's* chunk, meaning other people—other *players*—had pitched in.

"They *are* paying them off," I murmured, more to myself than to her.

Quickly, I started drawing arrows onto the sheet of paper, reorganizing the bullet points in their new order.

I found myself standing from my desk chair before I even realized it, reaching for my purse. "I think I might go catch the end of that game after all," I told Edith, snatching up the notebook from my desk and shoving it into my bag. "I'll let you know the score."

For the second time in my life, I pedaled my bike to the baseball diamond, but this time I did it like my life depended on it. I needed to catch the tail end of the baseball game. I had to at least *see* how people were playing. Batting. Running. See if any of the players sucked more than normal.

But then again, what *was* normal, anyway? I had no idea how Hampton played, or even Bayview for that matter. So maybe my thinking was flawed. Come on, though. It's going to be obvious if someone was trying to throw the game, right? Maybe?

My bike barely stopped rolling forward before I hopped off it, shoving it into a bike rack. I quickly looped my lock through the spokes and clicked it into place. A bead of sweat slipped between my shoulder blades, the sun not being kind to me as it glared down.

I was so late to the game that there wasn't anyone selling tickets anymore—I walked right through the entrance without having to fish a five out of my pocket. Which was super helpful because the idea of contributing to the madness that was Bayview High Baseball made my temples ache.

Here I was, the girl who hated our team, showing up to catch the tail end of it. Who the heck was I becoming?

As soon as I stepped past the empty ticket booth and deeper into the baseball area, it took me a minute to just get a glimpse of the field. Because there were so. Many. People. So much purple and gold loitering around, our school colors a scream to my senses. One person even had a *flag* with the school logo on it.

Did everyone have to be so energetic about baseball? Yuck.

The nauseating obsession of baseball in Bayview was also a major contributor to my aversion. I never understood why people would sit in the blazing sun, burning their butts off, just to watch boys swing a metal bat at a ball. Whoop-de-do.

But after sidestepping around the bodies, the baseball diamond came into full view, giving me an eyeful of everyone standing around it. The Royals were in the outfield, dots of purple jerseys against green grass. My gaze roamed over their faces, explicitly avoiding looking at the pitcher's mound. No way was I going to lock eyes with Walsh, who was no doubt winding up a perfect throw. Didn't need to be distracted.

After reading together in the car the other night, the idea of seeing Walsh now had my throat tight, my stomach fluttery.

No idea what that was about. So I refused to search for him.

That didn't stop me from stepping closer to the chain-link fence though, bypassing the bleachers, crossing my arms over my chest. As I passed, I couldn't help but glare at the metal contraptions. They were beautiful! Not a trace of rust in sight and yet Bayview High wanted to replace them? They cut my program to replace something that was practically new?

The scoreboard said that we up by eight in the sixth inning, with just one inning to go. Or something like that, right? Either way, we were winning. Now it was just time to determine if we were winning legitimately.

"Sophia!"

I whirled at the sound of my name, so totally thrown off.

"I thought that was you. I can't believe you're here," Jewel said from the bleachers off to my side, sitting at the edge of the front row. She smiled when we locked eyes, wide and genuine. "Here I thought I'd be stuck watching this boring game by myself. Well, I mostly did, but now you're here!"

"I am," I said haltingly, glancing around at the people behind her. No one seemed too interested in us talking, but they really should've been. Scott's ex-girlfriend talking to his current girlfriend? Weird, weird, weird. "Uh, you here to see Scott?"

She nodded quickly, scooting further over on the metal bench. "Come sit by me. I can give you the low-down on how this game's been going."

I racked my brain for a polite way to turn her down—that I see better from the back or that I don't want to sit on the bleachers sucking my newspaper funding dry?—but eventually, I just moved to sit by her.

"He hasn't pitched at all today," Jewel said to me, angling her chin toward the field of players. "Walsh, I mean. Coach hasn't put him in at all, but I saw him out practicing before the game started. Do you know what's up with that?"

I looked at her sharply, frowning. My mind immediately

switched from thinking about the article to thinking about why Walsh might be doing poorly at his game. Though I was supposed to interview him for my article, I never got around to it. I knew almost nothing about him. Did he have any pets? Were his parents together? Scott said that Walsh fell asleep at the game against Northwood—but why did he fall asleep?

All these questions were left unanswered and made me a terrible girlfriend. Or fake girlfriend. Whatever.

"I'm not sure," I said finally, turning my gaze to the pitcher. She was right, of course—it wasn't Walsh up there; it was Taylor, rubbing a baseball against his mitt. "Maybe he wasn't feeling well today."

"Well, hopefully he feels better by tonight."

"Tonight?"

A corner of Jewel's mouth lifted. "No offense, but Scott was right when he said that you don't get out much."

Despite the obvious rudeness of that statement, I strangely didn't feel offended. It was weird—like the way she said it really just had me lifting a shoulder, thinking, *true.*

But it also triggered another thought—the two of them talked about me? *Why?*

"The guys on the baseball team organized an after-party down at the bay after the game. There's going to be a volley-ball tournament and everything. I'm pretty sure Walsh is even signed up."

"Oh, right," I found myself saying as a player stepped up to bat. "The after-party."

The after-party no one told me about, down at the bay by the ocean. What, did that just elude Mr. Perfect's brain, inviting his girlfriend to a party where there'd be people to show off to?

He wasn't out on the field to witness my death glare. He was safely hidden by the dugout's walls.

Taylor steadied himself for his pitch, taking time dragging his foot through the gravel, trying to intimidate the batter. He held his mitt up in front of him, stepping off to the side and leaning onto his back foot.

Even though sitting next to Jewel was weird, being at a baseball game was weirder. Scott begged me to go ever since the season started, but I'd avoided the games like the plague. I think it was always because he played the *good-girlfriend* card. "Good girlfriends support their boyfriends" or "Good girlfriends do what their boyfriends ask." When that card was pulled out, I did everything in my power to perform the opposite.

I found Scott in the outfield, and though he stood a distance from us, I saw that his eyes were in our direction. No doubt wondering what Jewel and I were doing sitting so close to each other. Wondering what we were saying. *Good*, I thought to him, drawing in a breath. *I'll put on a show then.*

I plastered the friendliest expression on my face that I could muster. "Are you going after this?" I asked her. "We should hang out together at the bay. Watch the volleyball tournament together."

"I'd love that! I have a blanket in the back of my car we can sit on."

As the teams switched sides, the Royals stepping up to bat while the other team went into the outfield, I found myself a little unsure. Did Walsh even want me at that party at the bay? If he wanted me there, he'd have invited me. Right? Or was I overthinking this?

But honestly, what did I care about what he thought? If he didn't want me there, too bad. I wasn't going to base my actions off of him.

Besides, a party at the bay would be the perfect place for more inspiration for my article.

The baseball game ended with the Royals winning by a long-shot. Jewel offered to drive me to the bay herself, but I told her that I would just wait for Walsh to come off the field. "I'll see you at the bay," she said, backing away from where I sat on the bleachers. "I'm going to go find Scott."

"See you there," I said, pulling my cell phone out from my purse, shooting Edith a quick text.

Me: *We won.*

Edith: *Ha! Zach owes me five bucks. You see him anywhere?*

Before I had a chance to lift my gaze, a certain noise sounded right in my ear. "Psst."

Jumping a mile, I turned my head to find Walsh leaning against the edge of the second-row bleacher, baseball cap brim low over his eyes, fully decked out in his baseball attire. Even though I hated it, the air punched from my lungs at the sight of his purple jersey and pants and the way they seemed to morph to his frame so perfectly. As if it'd been tailored for him. And the way his golden hair tucked out from underneath his cap, strands catching by his eyes, just made me...

Focus. "Hey." I grabbed nonchalance by the ankles and

forced it to be my best friend. "You did great today. Really gave them a run for their money."

Walsh snorted, shoving to sit beside me in the first row, leaning his elbows onto his knees. "Yeah, definitely."

One of the benefits of Walsh not playing today meant he wasn't sweaty—which meant he didn't stink. I looked up at his profile since he was looking away from me, trying to discern any emotion. Dirt smudged one of his sharp cheekbones, and his jersey was untucked from his pants. The half-smile covering his face was luminous, but his eyes were tired.

"Why didn't you play?" I asked. "Why didn't you pitch?"

Walsh opened his mouth to speak, but someone beat him to the punch.

"Hey, you guys going to the bay?" Zach asked as he walked up to us with his bat bag slung over his shoulder, his purple pants streaked and smudged with dust from the diamond. His light eyes glanced between us. "Hope I'm not interrupting something."

"You're not," Walsh said, rubbing a hand over his face. "I think I'm going to pass on the bay."

"Dude." All jovialness on Zach's face vanished as he stared down his friend. "You are *not* bailing on me. You're the one who made me sign up for that stupid tournament. No offense, Sophia, but I called dibs first."

I fought a grin as I pushed to my feet, standing over Walsh. "Let's go to the bay," I told him, reaching down and picking up his hands. I didn't tug on them, didn't draw him to his feet, just held them. The strangeness of the moment hit me: I was holding hands with Walsh Hunter. In public. "It'll be fun. I'll watch you play volleyball and I can get a slushy. We can even take cute *pictures*."

I wasn't sure that pictures would've even been an incentive for me, but Walsh's lips twitched ever so slightly. "Can't turn down the slushies," he said eventually, rising to his feet. He tugged on my hands firmly enough to pull me closer until my chest hit his. I couldn't help but let out a sharp breath, the sudden proximity jostling my insides. "Can't say no to you."

My lips smiled, my heart skipping a beat. "No," I said. "You really can't."

ten

$\mathcal{I}$ didn't go to the bay all that often, mostly because it was always packed with people. Either with families milling about, trying to enjoy a beach day, or teenagers running around and surfing in the ocean waves. I wasn't big on people, so I frequently steered clear. However, when I showed up to the bay just as the sun began to set, I felt a little surge of excitement.

A plan was developed shortly after Walsh agreed to go. He wanted to go home and change, and I wanted to go home and get a swimsuit. Edith, as it turned out, was relieved of baby-brother-babysitting-duty, and she ended up grabbing me from my house and driving us over.

By the time we got to the bay, people were roaming around by the droves, and the volleyball nets were all in use. "I don't see Walsh," I said to Edith, straining onto my tip-toes.

"He might not be here yet. You rushed out of the house so fast I didn't even have time to get my own swimsuit on." She held up her bag. "It doesn't look like they've started building the fire yet—probably giving the baseball players enough time to show up."

"Yeah." I glanced over to where the volleyball net hung, rubbing my bare arm nervously. "I'm going to go get in line for a slushy."

"You and those slushies." Edith shook her head. "I'm going to run to the bathroom and change. I'll meet you in five."

The sand was soft and warm, my sandals kicking up flecks of it as I walked. Food trucks and stands lined the sides of the sandy beach, all open and ready to serve. Their bright colors were beckoning, accompanied by the signature smells for each designated booth. I, however, gravitated toward the one that didn't have a distinct smell. *Slushies.*

I glanced around the open beach, searching for a particular head of blond hair.

"Sophia, there you are!" Jewel called as she came towards me, a blanket thrown over her arm. She'd changed into a pair of white shorts and a blue halter swimsuit top, her dark hair curling over her shoulders.

She looked gorgeous. Figured. It made me feel a little more than frumpy in my one-piece.

"It's been lonely," she went on, reaching up and fluffing her hair over her shoulder. "Which is funny, because it's so crowded here. Scott's been playing volleyball for the past twenty minutes, and I've just been so bored."

Which probably isn't a bad thing, I thought bitterly. "Have you seen Walsh?"

"Haven't seen Walsh, but I did see his friend, Zach. He

was talking to Celia over by the pier." She paused, tilting her head. "Are those two together? I can't tell."

Honestly? Neither could I.

A quiet lull fell over the two of us for a moment as I stepped further up in line. "So, Scott said that you were working on some sort of article for school." Jewel burrowed her toe in the sand, overturning it in a grainy clump. "What are you writing about?"

"Baseball," I said before I really thought it through, my thoughts snagging on what she'd said before that. Scott told her about my article? "Just...focusing on the season, I mean. Nothing too exciting."

"That's fun. And I bet it's been cool interviewing Walsh for it, now that he's your boyfriend and all."

I turned to look at her, squinting against the orange sun that shined just over her shoulder. "I'm sure Scott had something to say about *that*."

"Scott has a lot to say about a lot of things," Jewel said lightly, though her expression didn't quite match her tone, "but you and Walsh *do* tend to be a frequent topic."

"Hey, can you tie the strap behind my back for me?" Edith said as she came up to me, lifting the hem of her shirt a little and turning around. "I couldn't reach."

I picked up the red straps of Edith's bikini top, double-knotting it. "There."

"Thanks, it was kind of—oh. Uh. Hi."

Edith's eyes snagged on how close Jewel stood off to my side, expression going from calm to tense in an instant. Jewel's first impression with Edith wasn't the best—nor was her first impression with me—but part of me felt strangely defensive of Scott's new girlfriend.

Jewel, though, acted like she didn't notice the sharpness to my best friend's gaze. She stuck out her hand. "We haven't officially met. I'm Jewel."

"Edith." She didn't offer her hand. "Interesting to find you with Sophia."

"Oh, she's one of the familiar faces that I know. We were both at Ryan's party on Tuesday. Celia and I went with Scott."

A shade of darkness washed over Edith's expression, starting with her eyes. *Celia.* Crap, I never told her about that. When I opened my mouth to say something, anything, I got cut off by the girl behind the slushy stand.

"How do you know Celia?" Edith asked, folding her arms over her chest.

"We're family friends."

Had I been a bad friend for not telling Edith that Celia had been at the party? For not telling her how Zach seemed a little too friendly? Edith hadn't really said anything was going on with her and Zach, but was that breaking girl code? Gosh, what even *was* girl code?

"Why did you two run out so fast the other night, Sophia?" Jewel asked after I ordered. "You and Walsh left almost as soon as we got there."

"That's because Ryan's parties are lame," Edith said on a huff, turning her gaze away. Yeah, probably a bad sign.

"Just had some things to do," I said to Jewel politely. *Like reading together in the car.* In all honesty, that was *way* better than Ryan's party. I turned to Edith as the girl handed over my slushy. "Are you playing in the tournament? Get your practice in?"

She hoisted her bag higher up on her shoulder, watching Jewel trail after us with a distrustful gaze. "I'm in the second round."

Without warning, two arms wrapped around my waist and pulled me backward, startling me so badly that I nearly dropped my slushy cup.

A soft voice accompanied the embrace, warm words close to my ear. "Found you."

The quickness of my pulse didn't lessen as my brain registered the voice as Walsh's. In fact, it almost started to beat faster. I tried to catch my expression, to morph it into a look of elation.

Get your game face on, Sophia, I thought again, and gave a small, feigned gasp. "Walsh." My voice was so high, and I fought off a cringe. "You scared me."

When I turned to face him, I faltered at the view, at least on the inside. I'd seen him an hour ago, but for some reason, the sight of him now had me doing a doubletake. Probably because he was shirtless.

His dark navy trunks and blond hair both were dripping as if he'd just jumped into the bay, dripping water droplets onto his skin. My back had just been against his bare and tanned chest, and I couldn't get past that thought.

"Sounds like it," he said with a grin. "Is that a slushy?"

I could feel Jewel's eyes on us like a physical weight, bouncing back and forth. Gosh, was I paranoid now?

Paranoid or not, I made sure not to let it show. "Of course."

Walsh swiped the cup from me, his mouth closing over the straw, taking a long pull. I tried to breathe normally, watching my slushy in his hands, jittering with nerves. He smacked his lips together. "Mm. A little syrupy for me."

I couldn't stop looking at his mouth. "Syrupy is the best."

"Shouldn't you be on the court?" Jewel asked Walsh, gesturing to the volleyball players. "Weren't you signed up for the first round?"

"Some girl named Eloise stepped in for me. I'm not feeling too great tonight."

It didn't take me long to realize why the name sounded familiar. Even from the corner of my eye, I saw Edith stiffen, and her eyes narrowed. "Eloise Xiang? Tall, dark hair?"

"Uh, I didn't catch her last name, but yeah, she was tall. She's from Greenville, I think."

Edith grabbed Jewel's beach blanket, the one Jewel clung to. "Come on."

Jewel glanced back at me. "But Sophia—"

"I'll catch up," I told her, but Edith already dragged her away toward the volleyball net, out of earshot. I turned back to the bare-chested Walsh, forcing my gaze up to his eyes and totally not on all that golden skin. "Hey."

"We've already done that part," Walsh teased, teeth biting at his smile.

I glanced at where a bead of water dripped from his hair onto his collarbone, tracing a line across his tanned skin. "Why are you all wet?"

"Jumped in the water to cool off," he said with a slight chuckle, like *duh*. "You know, I'm going to be honest. I'm surprised you wanted to come to this."

"Why?" I raised an eyebrow at him, slightly offended. "Is that why you didn't ask me to come? You didn't think I'd be fun?"

Walsh reached out and wrapped his arms around me, loosely at my waist. In our time together, I'd come to learn what the sudden embrace meant. *He sees someone.*

This time, though, I didn't have to force myself to relax against his chest. My body did that all on its own.

"I didn't ask you because I wasn't really feeling it tonight myself. I'm not much of a partier."

"Walsh Hunter, the introvert?" I teased, reaching up and tracing my free hand down the side of his neck. *Whoa, why am I touching him like this?* His pulse fluttered underneath my skin, and the feel of his heartbeat made this moment turn warmer, feeling like someone dialed up the temperature. "You never answered my question earlier. Why didn't you play tonight?"

Walsh smiled a little, looking down at me with a gaze that could've made any person weak in the knees. "Just tired," he said, and then changed the subject. "Is that a swimsuit I see underneath that shirt?"

I arched an eyebrow. "Are you seriously trying to look through my shirt?"

His grin split wider, and he looked off to the side. If I didn't know any better, I would've thought he was blushing. "I'm not—no. *No.*"

Teasing him like that sent something of a thrill down my spine, especially when I was so perfectly in his arms. My feet were in the soft sand, a slushy in my hand, and I was pressed against Walsh's naked chest. I couldn't tell if it was a very good world I'd been thrown into or a very bad one.

I took a drink from my slushy to cool down my insides, the cool blue-raspberry liquid covering my tongue. Walsh watched where the straw stuck in my mouth. "What do you think? Too syrupy?"

All at once, the realization hit me. *He just drank from this. His mouth was just on this.*

"I don't have cooties, I swear," Walsh chuckled as if reading my thoughts, gaze shifting toward the volleyball net. "You showed up with Jewel, huh?"

"She found me in the slushy line. She wanted us to sit together." I held my cup between us, between his bare chest and my face, a small barrier that gave me a semblance of clarity. "That's weird, right?"

"That your ex-boyfriend's new girlfriend wants to sit by you?" He lifted a bare shoulder. "Does she know that he cheated on you with her?"

I looked over to where Jewel now sat in the sand, Edith on the blanket next to her. Jewel had her hands in her lap and her sunglasses on, a relaxed smile on her face. Edith was just the opposite, strung tight, arms crossed.

"I don't know. I doubt Scott told her the truth. He probably just told her I was a friend."

"She seems nice."

Yeah, she did. So what's a nice girl like her doing with a guy like Scott? I looked up at Walsh. "I didn't know you played volleyball."

"Oh, I don't. Not well, anyway, which is why I backed out. Ryan had signed me up."

That made sense. Seemed like Ryan liked to push Walsh out of his comfort zone.

I backed up out of Walsh's embrace and ran my tongue over my lips, making sure there was no trace of syrupy slushy on them. Lifting my head, I looked him in the eye. "Take my picture."

Walsh blinked once, and when he looked up and met my gaze, I realized he'd been looking at my mouth. "What?"

"Take my picture. I give you permission to post this one."

Walsh hurried to get his cell from his pocket, fumbling to raise it. "Say, 'Walsh is the best.'"

My smile faltered just a little bit. "No."

"'Sophie is the best'?"

"It's an *A*, Walsh. Is it really that hard to replace one vowel?"

Walsh gave me a look that was a cross between playful and exasperated. "Fine, just smile."

I forced my features into a somewhat relaxed expression, trying to look as happy and cheerful as I could without looking like I was trying too hard. Which was difficult. But Walsh, who was looking at the screen of his cell phone, smiled a bit as he snapped the photo, and I knew I must've done something right.

"You know, I've been thinking," I said as Walsh slipped his cell back into his pocket. "Shouldn't we be convincing people we're growing apart? Not getting closer?"

"No, it's too soon. We need to drag it out a bit more. Make it more believable. Our honeymoon phase wouldn't be over yet." His response was quick as he tossed his phone into the sand, grabbing my hand and pulling me after him. "Come on, let's go for a swim."

I blinked, nerves fluttering. "A swim?"

"I already know you're wearing a suit."

I yanked my hand free, folding my arms over my chest. "So you *were* looking through my shirt."

Walsh stopped just on the edge of where the ocean met the dry sand. "You know, you haven't asked me many questions for the article. It's the perfect time to. Swim a little, interview a little. It'll be fun." Walsh grabbed my purse strap, tugging. My grip on it tightened and for a moment we just grappled with it. "Do you not want to swim, Sophie?"

"I'm not...like the other girls here, you know." Ugh, I *so* shouldn't have been insecure, but everyone was wearing their pretty bikinis with their beautiful bodies with their flowing hair. Realistically, I knew me in my swimsuit was not a big deal—so many people on the beach wore even less—but I couldn't shake the feeling, nor the heat in my cheeks. "All cute bikinis and flat stomachs. I'm not—"

Walsh placed a hand over my mouth, his scent filling my senses. The sharp scent of ocean water clung to his skin, smelling familiar, mixing with his natural earthy scent. "If you say you're not as sexy or amazing as anyone on this beach, Sophia Whatever-Your-Middle-Name-Is Wallace, I'm going to throw you in the bay."

It was the perfect moment for a snarky remark on my part. Dang, at least a freaking eye roll, because I had to do something other than gape at him, his hand on my lips, holding my jaw from falling to the ground. He'd called me *sexy*. No one ever called me that before. The word drew my eyes to his own naked chest, tightly toned from all the years of playing sports, a little unevenly tanned from his jersey.

When his hand fell from my lips, I had the strangest urge to reach out and touch him again. Not on his neck this time, but lower, along his flat, muscular stomach, to feel his smooth skin underneath my fingertips. What would he do in response? Would he laugh? Gasp? Reach out himself and trace a fingertip down my bare skin? Would he—

Mentally smacking myself, I forced myself to fill my mouth with slushy until my brain froze. Where had *that* come from?

"It's Vanessa." The words were barely there, breathless. "My middle name is Vanessa."

He didn't have to say that he liked it, because the sparkle in his eyes said it all.

Walsh tugged my purse from my grip, dropping it against the dry ground beside his cell before taking off toward the water. I stared after him, his bare back, hating the fact that my lungs refused to draw in air.

"Come on," he called, turning around with a wide grin. The sun was a backlight behind him, filtering around his body. It made all his edges look soft, almost golden. "Last one to the farthest buoy buys the next slushy."

eleven

*P*eople always say "Tell me something no one knows about you," and I never understood it. I never understood the significance of knowing the little things about someone, things that no one else in the entire universe knew. I used to think stuff like that was wasted knowledge, useless facts that cluttered up brain space.

But as Walsh and I paddled through the water together, dodging the waves and floating on our backs, I learned his little things.

His favorite color was brick red because that was the color of the truck his dad taught him to swing a bat on. It was an old truck, no engine, didn't run, and Walsh's dad took him out to practice his technique on the sides of it.

He had a chef/housekeeper/nanny/therapist—his words, not mine—named Janet, and they sometimes played poker before she left for the day. And according to him, she always kicked his butt.

He only drinks one brand of water, because all of the other brands don't taste as good.

He box-dyed his golden hair black when he was thirteen, because he knew it would make his mother mad.

Small things, useless knowledge, and with the setting sun falling lower and lower on the horizon, I found that I could've been with him for the rest of the day, just to hear him talk.

And though I would've thought it'd be hard for me to open up, I told Walsh a bit about myself. I told him how my one passion was, above all else, writing. I told him that I could sit for hours writing. That had been why I joined the school newspaper, because I absolutely loved the craft of it.

"I want to be a journalist," I had told Walsh decisively, smoothing my wet, auburn hair from my face. "That's why this article means so much, why this *class* means so much. It opens so many doors."

And Walsh had listened to everything I said. The idea that my words meant something to someone was almost jarring. To be heard when I spoke was a rarity for me. My parents didn't pay attention; Scott never cared. But when I spoke, Walsh watched me the entire time, eyes doing that soft-melty thing that made me look over my shoulder. We'd been far out enough in the bay that even if people were watching, no one would've seen the look in his eye.

Had to hand it to that boy—he knew how to smolder.

When we'd been talking about baseball uniforms and helmets, how often the school purchased the team new equipment, he'd let the words slip.

"Ryan's parents donated some money back in March for the team," Walsh had said while he looked up at the sky, lips slanted into what almost looked like a frown. "The school's not really allowed to take direct funding for stuff like that—I mean, yes, it goes into the sport's fund, but not for a specific team. I don't know why they allowed that."

I couldn't even remember what I'd replied with because my brain was too busy connecting dots. Though the money graph I'd found online meant a lot of gibberish, there *was* a spike in baseball funding in the beginning of spring.

That's where it'd come from—Ryan's parents. What a perfect bullet point to add once I got home.

No sooner than I'd thought that, my insides flinched. This was the point of everything—I'd ride out this fake dating thing with Walsh, and I'd write the article on the baseball team. That was the entire plan.

Then why did I feel so guilty?

The sun was fading fast as Walsh slowed to a stop in front of my house now, his brakes squeaking horribly. Walsh had draped towels over the seats to soak up any water that seeped through our clothes, but we were both mostly dried off now. My hair still was a little damp, dripping water onto my shorts.

When Walsh spoke, I realized that we'd both been quiet for a long time—long enough for me to get used to the silence while looking out the window. "Hey, you okay?"

"Yeah." I'd left my bedroom light on and could see the outline of Shiba sitting on the windowsill. "Just lost in thought."

It didn't look like I was the only one either. The driver's seat made a creaking noise as Walsh leaned his weight against it, hands slipping from the steering wheel to fall onto his bare knees. The way he slouched made me remember what Jewel told me earlier, saying that he didn't play tonight. Walsh had said he was tired, and now as we sat in the quiet of his car, the energy seemed like it had been zapped out of him.

"You look exhausted," I whispered in the quiet, thankful for the dimness of the cab and his closed eyes. Being so close in a small space seemed less intimate with him not looking at me, making me feel more relaxed. "Are you okay?"

"I didn't get much sleep last night." Walsh tipped his head to face me, the dashboard lights casting a haunting look across his features. "Coach put Taylor in today because I wasn't in any shape to pitch."

I thought about Scott's comment about him falling asleep at one of the games. "Has that happened a lot?" I asked him. "Coach putting Taylor in?"

"Only when I ask. Today, I asked. Lately, it's been more often than I'd like." Walsh's face screwed up as a surge of weariness crept across his features, shoulders wilting. Exhaustion coated his body and made him less guarded. "I love the sport. I could spend the rest of my life playing baseball. It's just lately...it's been tougher than usual."

"How come?"

Walsh was a much more pensive guy than I'd previously given him credit for. His silent pauses rivaled my own in length, and I found myself almost eager for him to open his mouth, to speak, to confess to me. I wanted to know what was going on inside his head so badly.

"Family things have been making things rougher and..." He let out a sigh. "I'm different than those guys."

"Oh, please," I snorted, immediately shaking my head. "And you call my romance books clichéd."

That got his lips curving upward, just a tiny bit. "I meant

that they're more competitive than me. It's all cutthroat to them. Do or die. I don't...I don't play that way."

I tilted my head to the side ever so slightly. "You play for fun."

"Like I said, I love the sport." Walsh tipped his head to meet my gaze. "But I hate the game."

I wanted to say something supportive, but words eluded me. I wasn't used to comforting others. Especially Walsh. Because even though we were in this fake relationship, moments like this had me feeling like I hardly knew him. Like there was a whole other side of him that I couldn't see— and I found myself wanting to uncover it.

"I'm sorry," he said softly. "I should be giving you positive stuff for your article."

"It's okay." My words came out immediately. "You can always say whatever you want."

We sat in the quiet for another moment, and I knew I needed to get out of the car. Heck, he might've even been waiting for me to get out and go inside, but I didn't want to. Not yet. I wanted to pull my book out of my purse and open up to another page and read. I wanted to turn on the radio and find a song that he would sing along to. I just wanted to stay in this moment of time a little longer.

Walsh reached over and placed a hand on my bare knee, his touch gentle. "We have another game on Sunday. You should come to that one."

I mimicked the way he sat, my head against the cushion, slouching. My damp hair felt chilled against my neck, the air conditioner making it frigid. "I don't know."

"You don't like baseball?"

Ha. "That's an understatement."

"Why?"

"A lot of reasons, I guess." I traced where his hand rested on my bare leg with my eyes. "It's long."

"Football is long. Golf's long."

True. "I hate golf, too."

The hand on my knee squeezed ever so slightly, trying to coax out a genuine answer. "Sophie."

My eyes slipped shut, and I focused on the turned down music filtering over the radio, not recognizing the faint song. I listened to my breathing for a moment, to Walsh's own inhales and exhales mixing with mine. With my eyes closed, it was easier to pretend I wasn't talking to the infamous Walsh Hunter, Mr. Perfect and captain of the baseball team. He could be somebody else, anybody else.

"Everything revolves around baseball," I said finally, biting my lip.

"Baseball *is* life, you know."

I couldn't help but roll my eyes, prompting Walsh to say, "I saw that."

"Everyone in this stupid community praises you players like gods. That's enough to turn any sane person's stomach. I guess I'm just...sick of it."

For a moment, I wondered what I was doing. This relationship was fake, and I shouldn't have been baring my soul. But today, just the two of us spending hours together, made things feel different.

I opened my eyes, but he wasn't even looking at me. Walsh was staring at the roof of the car, eyes open but unseeing. The ends of his hair were still damp, curling ever so slightly. Something was wrong, something he wasn't telling me. But there was no way I was going to force information out of him.

I didn't know how to make him feel better. "Are you okay?"

"Ask me a question," Walsh murmured to the roof. "For the article. Ask me something."

"Does Bayview High ever cheat to win?" The words came out of left field, blurting from my mouth before I even had a chance to screen them.

Walsh chuckled at that, and quickly, too. As if the idea was absolutely absurd. "I know it might seem like it, but no. We're just that good."

I sat in his answer for a moment, mulling it over. Was it possible that his teammates were cheating and he just didn't know? "Do you think you're a good fit for captain?"

Walsh turned his head and was quiet for a long time. So long that I thought I'd imagined asking the question. Blue eyes looked at me intensely, deeply, like if he looked at me hard enough, he could see into my soul. "Next question."

"But—"

"Next question."

I knocked my sandals together, racking my brain for something else to ask. The deep questions were pushed out of the way, answered and ignored, and I had to come up with something. "When did you know that you wanted to play baseball?"

Walsh's lips curled into a smile, but this time it looked genuine, authentic. "My mom took me to a baseball game when I was seven. Bought me a foam finger and a baseball from one of the insanely over-priced gift shops. Ever since, I've been obsessed."

There came the mention of his mother again. I couldn't hold back this time, my curiosity getting the better of me even though this was supposed to be for the article. "You said you had a rough night. Something about your parents?"

"It's more my mom. We just haven't been seeing eye to eye. It's not a big deal."

I looked out of my window to my house, staring at the collection of dark windows and the empty front porch. His words connected with me in a way that he couldn't have known. I considered the idea of saying "I know the feeling," but my mouth clamped shut. It had been a while since my parents and I saw eye to eye on something.

Little voices came from the dark of the cab, hostile and echoing. *You're not good enough for Scott, not good enough for your parents. You have to force Walsh to fake date you. This article, no matter how good you think it is, won't be enough.*

A thinness took over the air, for the breaths I pulled in weren't enough to satisfy my lungs. *Don't think like that*, I willed myself, swallowing hard. *It'll be enough. You'll be enough. They'll see.*

I didn't even realize how firm my grip was on my leg until Walsh's hand slipped over mine. "Hey. Where'd your mind go?"

"I'm okay." I didn't look at him but rather at our hands, trying to breathe through the dread that was welling in my chest. Rough patches lined the skin at the tops of his palms, callouses from how hard he gripped the baseball bat, I guessed. "It doesn't matter."

"Anything that goes on in that head of yours matters."

I wanted to roll my eyes at that line, shaking my head in the darkness. "I'm just thinking about the article."

"You can be honest with me, Sophia."

"I am being honest," I lied.

"Just letting you know." He gave my hand a squeeze, expression softening. "I've been told that I'm a good listener."

I tried to shrug off his serious, kind words, but failed. They were already burrowing deep inside of me, nestling their home in my heart.

"Say you'll come to the game on Sunday," Walsh said, backtracking to that conversation. "I could play the guilt card and say you're the only one that comes to watch me."

"Except you'd be lying, because we both know half of the people in the bleachers are there for you. They probably even make cheesy signs."

"Yeah, but you're the only one I care about." One side of his mouth tipped up, looking none too modest. "Will you make me a sign?"

"Oh, no. Nope, totally not doing that. I'm bad at signs. Besides, what would it even say? '*He stole second base and my heart*'?"

Walsh tipped his head back, giving the first genuine smile I'd seen since we left the beach. "Please do that, Sophie. I'd love you forever."

I drew in a sharp breath, pulling my hand from his. My skin still felt warm, even without his fingers against mine. "I'll think about it," I told him finally, reaching for the door handle.

If I was going to be honest with myself, part of me

wanted to go and watch Walsh pitch. But I was really good at lying to myself, so I was convinced that if I went, it'd only be because I couldn't risk missing anything newsworthy. No other reason.

I slipped free of the car, stretching my legs. We'd been sitting in there for a long time. "Goodnight, Walsh."

"Goodnight, Sophia," he responded, and when I turned around to shut the door, I saw that Walsh's hand rested on his seat buckle, as if he'd been just about to pop it free.

twelve

Sunday morning, my phone chimed with a text from Walsh mere minutes before I headed out the door for the baseball game. I managed *not* to get lost in article-writing, to keep an eye on the clock so I could make it to the field before they started.

My eyes scanned my phone's screen. *I'm not playing today. Home sick. Text you later.*

Much to my surprise, disappointment tugged my insides. Not about missing the baseball game.

I wasn't going to see Walsh today, and *that* was what was bothering me.

I wondered how sick he had to be to miss a baseball game. For how much he loved playing, I imagine he'd have to be pretty sick. Or did he really ask Coach to put the other pitcher in? There was no way of knowing, not unless I asked.

An idea burst through my mind, and before I gave it a second thought, I headed out the door to get my bike.

. . .

Walsh's house from the night of the party was a haunting fairytale, with lights like pixies dancing around his property, lulling music leaking from the foundation. In the daylight, it was much less dramatic, like somehow the life had bled from the walls.

I realized, as the breeze whisked across my sweaty skin, that I probably should've called. I didn't know why this felt different. After our conversation in his car, something changed. Or at least it felt that way to me. And whatever that change was, it left me wondering where we stood.

Which was dumb, because this was a fake relationship, and I shouldn't have even been caring, but here I was.

My tires skidded on the concrete when I slowed to a stop, sliding off the seat. I took the tin can out of the basket and laid the handlebars down along the pavement, turning to stare up at his house. No faces peeked out from any windows, and no doors opened. No one was coming to greet me. I guess I'd have to pull on my big girl pants.

Stepping up to the door, my breathing went shallow. The idea of knocking made me nervous—why had I done this? Putting myself out there wasn't my thing. I should've just sent back a text with a frowny face and went about my day.

I pressed the little doorbell that was set into the brick, my heart jumping as the sound resonated from the other side of the door.

Not even a minute passed before the oak swung inward, revealing a short woman with graying hair. "Hello, can I help you?" She looked up at me expectantly, her voice soft.

I rolled the tin can in my hand anxiously, the contents sloshing around inside. There wasn't any resemblance to

Walsh in her features, and she wasn't as young as I'd been expecting. She looked like she was in her early sixties. "Hi. Is Walsh home?"

"Walsh?" The woman quickly touched the hem of her shirt, straightening it almost uneasily. "He's at his baseball game, dear."

Uh. Did he lie to me? Had he changed his mind about wanting me to come? "I-I'm sorry. I was told he was home sick."

"Well, hmm." She rubbed her arm, looking around the porch. "I don't know—"

"Hey."

I looked up at the sound of a low voice, conjured by the mere mention of his name.

Walsh looked—off. Like he'd just rolled from bed. He really did look sick, with purple circles under his eyes, hair tousled and sticking up. He was wearing sweatpants and a graphic tee that had a hole near the collar. His skin was pale, his pale hair washing him out.

I'd never seen him so un-put together in his life. "It's okay, Janet. I know I said not to let anyone in, but Sophie's got clearance."

I blinked. This was Janet, his chef/housekeeper/nanny/therapist, not his mom. She let out a little squeak, her entire expression transforming. "*You're* Sophia! Come inside, please. Oh, gosh, I've been keeping you on the doormat this whole time. Can I get you something to drink, sweetheart?"

She ushered me into the entryway, which was much prettier without the red cups and dancing bodies littering around. Smaller too. It seemed homier now, warmer.

I slipped my tennis shoes off, not wanting to dirty the carpet. "Maybe some water?"

"Why don't you two sit down in the family room and I'll bring out a tray?" She looked between Walsh and me for a quick moment before going off in the direction of the kitchen.

Walsh watched us from the bottom stair, leaning against the railing, expression unreadable. Inexplicably, my tongue decided that words were overrated, and I just stared at him. Mute. Awkward.

Without a word, I shoved the can at him, totally aware that I'd been clutching it like a lifeline.

He looked at it guardedly. "What is it?"

"Chicken soup." I cleared my throat. "It was either that or tomato. Chicken soup actually has less sodium than tomato, so I thought this would be better. You said you weren't feeling good."

Walsh stared at the can for several more moments before plucking it from my fingertips, setting it on the flat part of the staircase newel. "My favorite. Thanks, Sophie."

"It's Sophia," I corrected him, but my lighthearted tone fell flat. I was too unsettled by his worn-out appearance to be properly sarcastic with him.

He hopped down from the last step, leading the way into the family room. "Come sit down."

I trailed after him, but at a distance. "I smell."

"What? You do not."

"You haven't gotten close enough. Biking all the way to your house in this heat was an awful idea."

Walsh fell onto the couch, lining his arms along the back of the gray cushions. He looked exhausted; if he were to relax, he could've fallen asleep. "It can't be as bad as sweaty baseball players."

I rolled my eyes. "Totally worse."

Walsh's gray expression broke, the clouds in his eyes parting to show a ray of light. The sun on a rainy day. A surge of triumph came over me, knowing I was responsible for this break in the weather. "Is it sad when you rolling your eyes at me makes my entire day?"

I plopped down next to him on the couch, deciding that I didn't care if I smelled or not. "Rough night?"

"Are you that good or are the circles under my eyes that dark?"

"Both."

Janet's socks made no noise as she moved into the room, carrying a tray with a water pitcher and two glasses. She set it down on the coffee table, and Walsh leaned forward to stop her from pouring. "Let me get it, Jan."

She allowed him to take over, pressing her palms together. "You're very beautiful, Sophia. As pretty as Walsh said you were."

That sentence startled me, but I tried not to let it show. Instead, I looked at Walsh accusingly. "I haven't been talking to people about you. Now I feel like a bad—"

My mind seized on the word and choked, forbidding my mouth to speak it. I'd never said that word in reference to him before.

"Girlfriend?" Walsh covered smoothly, leaning back and handing me a glass of water. "Don't worry. You haven't hit the red zone yet."

Cue my second eye roll.

"Be nice." Janet swatted his arm. "I'll give you two a little privacy. It was great to meet you, Sophia." She shot me a little smile as she headed back out of the room.

Walsh leaned deeper into the couch, moving so his inner elbow was brushing the skin of my neck. Ugh, I hoped I wasn't as sweaty as I felt. "You told Janet about us?"

"I figured if I'm going to be living a lie, I might as well practice it everywhere I go. That way I won't screw up, right?"

A sour feeling simmered under my skin, hot and itching. I moved out from underneath Walsh's arm, letting it drop to the seat of the sofa with a *thunk*. "It was *your* idea."

His eyes went wide, clearly caught off guard. "*What* was my idea?"

"'Living a lie'? I never asked you to. You were the one to start all this."

At that, his eyebrows slammed together. "I'm not mad about it, Sophie. I just thought if I'm being consistent then—"

"It's just one vowel, Walsh. How would you feel if I called you *Welsh*?"

"—I'd be less likely to accidentally say the wrong thing to the wrong person."

"Does this bother you?" I set my drink down, even though my throat was dying for a sip. "Lying, I mean."

Walsh rubbed his eye with a closed fist. "No, it doesn't. It's not really a lie, anyway. It's like acting. A stretched truth. We *have* been hanging out more often."

"Because of the lie."

"So you asked me to go to the dog park the other day just because of who we might've run into? And the bay?"

No. "Yes."

Walsh's face screwed up as if he'd tasted something incredibly bitter. "Well, I didn't think about it that way."

Sometimes, I wondered if Walsh was just playing me. If I was part of his acting scheme. Because he'd go and say things like that, say things that made me feel *warm*, and I couldn't figure out why. I wasn't an interesting person, and it would only be a matter of time until Walsh figured it out. Scott tried to change the uninteresting things about me, but it didn't work. I was still a nerdy girl obsessed with her article.

"You're not really sick," I said, looking at him closer. "Are you?"

A surge of weariness overpowered his features, and he spoke to his glass of water, eyes downcast. "I had a really—" He dropped his voice, "—*really* bad night."

"If you keep skipping out on games, aren't you going to get cut from the team?" My words sounded rude, but I was genuinely curious, and couldn't figure out a different way to phrase it.

"Coach knows what's been going on."

"What *is* going on?"

Walsh shook his head, a muscle in his jaw popping. "I had a fight—a *disagreement*—with my mom last night. And as stupid as it sounds, I don't want to talk about it."

"I'm a good listener, too, you know," I said, kicking his socked foot with my own, echoing what he'd said the other night.

He didn't say anything in response to that.

I didn't want to see him like this for a moment longer—upset without speaking about it—but there wasn't much that

I could do. There was no way I was going to force information out of him, but I didn't know how to make him feel
better.

"Let's do something," I said on impulse, trying to pitch
my voice high and cheerful.

"Like what?"

I glanced out the window, seeing the cliff in his yard.
"Swimming."

"Swimming," Walsh repeated, finally looking up. His
blue eyes were treading with a sea of emotion, but the first
one I recognized was amusement. Good. That was good.
"Again?"

I nodded, latching onto that positive look. "Swimming.
It's summer. We can swim more than once this summer."

"You don't have your suit."

I glanced down at my denim shorts. "Yeah, but I didn't
wear white undies today, so I should be fine."

Walsh seemed to stop breathing, blinking up at me like I
spoke a different language.

"That was a joke," I deadpanned. "I'm going to keep my
shorts on."

The back of his head touched the couch cushion as he
stared up at the ceiling, pressing a hand to his chest. "Oh my
gosh. I think I'm having a heart attack."

I swiped my water from the coffee table, sliding past
Walsh's legs and heading for the back door. He still wore the
startled expression when I glanced back, eyes wider than I'd
ever seen them. I couldn't hold in my laugh. "Get your mind
out of the gutter, lover boy, and come on."

· · ·

My tennis shoes still squished when I got home, my thighs itching from how my shorts chafed at the skin. My movements were quiet as I slipped off my shoes, but the house was quieter, and I attracted attention.

"Sophia, can you come to the kitchen, please?" Dad called to me, and I followed his voice.

Mom and Dad were opposite of each other in the room, both trying hard not to catch the other's eye. It made sense, then, why I hadn't walked in on voices if they were both in the cold shoulder phase. Dad was busy trying to *not* look at Mom while she sat at the table.

"I know it's my night to cook," I said. "Can I change first?"

"We ordered pizza," Mom said in a level tone.

I looked between the two of them. "Dad hates pizza."

"Your mother was craving some." Dad pulled back from the fridge with a soda in his grip, eyes tired. "It should be here any minute."

"Don't pretend like it was only my idea," she quickly said, giving him a look. "You knew Sophia would want some, too."

"I can't read our daughter's mind and know if she wants pizza."

Mom transferred her focus from him to me, her eyes still holding leftover anger. "We have something to tell you, Sophia."

"Over dinner, Amber. Like we talked about."

"Can this wait until after I change?" My shirt was suctioned to my skin, making me feel like a soaked sponge. With the air-conditioned chill of the house, I started to shiver.

Mom acted like the pair of us hadn't breathed a single word. "Your father and I are separating."

All three of us had different reactions. Dad's face practically fell into his hands, a muffled groan coming from him. Mom looked at his reaction with a triumphant smile.

I...wasn't sure how I felt. "Like a divorce?"

"Yes, like a divorce," Mom said, and this time, when she looked at me, her gaze was a little less steady. "We understand this may be tough to hear."

"Sweet," I said with absolutely, completely *no idea* why I said it.

It was almost comical how quickly their heads whipped towards me. Mom was the first to speak. "What did you say?"

Honestly, that probably wasn't the smartest response, but I couldn't help it. And sparking their anger was something that happened very, very rarely, and I found myself uncaring if I evoked it further. "I said 'sweet.' I'm going to go change."

Dad's eyes were bright and filled with a terrible emotion, a bottled mix of anger and pain. "You think your parents' marriage falling apart is something to celebrate?"

That question made my insides shift, like a hand reached into my stomach and clenched its fist tight. But I wasn't going to feed into their drama by giving them a reaction. I'd save it for my bedroom and Shiba, who would just sit and listen. "I'm going upstairs."

Neither one of them thought of an appropriate response until I was halfway up the stairs, Mom calling after me, "Good! Stay there, because you're grounded, Sophia!"

Taking a cue from my mother's playbook, I lifted my

hand in a thumbs-up. The only difference was that where her hand had been steady, mine was shaking.

A separation. An actual divorce. A myriad of emotions battled inside of me, negative and positive, but I couldn't latch onto a single one. It left me disoriented, unsteady in my thoughts, as if the earth was tipping on its side. I felt the exact same way when I realized Scott was holding Jewel the night of the party, the realization that something *wrong* was happening sinking into my bones.

But I recognized this—their announcement of a divorce—for what it was. Mom used to fear separating from Dad. Dreaded it. I couldn't imagine anything changing her mind, and that's how I knew this wouldn't stick. It was like a board game, where someone draws a card and reads off a command for them to do. Sometimes they plucked up "Start Fight Over Dinner" or "Watch A Movie Together," but they'd picked up a new one for them: "Divorce." They were just playing their game.

I fell back onto my bed, hair still damp from swimming. Through the floorboards, my parents' voices were silent.

I couldn't deal with the idea of them right now, the pain or the thought of a divorce or any more theatrics. I had too much on my plate. The article, the fake relationship with Walsh, the internship—all that needed my focus.

My parents and their never-ending drama would have to wait.

*M*y dreams that night weren't pleasant ones, filled with stress and anxiety that manifested as darkness. But what had I been expecting? I'd been looped into a soap opera of my own, following in my parents' footsteps. *The Young and the Overwhelmed.*

Totally me right now.

The next morning, a knock came at my door, and Mom and Dad stood on the other side, ready to dole out my punishment.

"We've decided to ground you until after the Fourth of July," Mom announced, her yoga gear all in place for her morning class. "Three days of grounding should do you good. And then maybe you'll learn to be more respectful."

Ha. More respectful, how funny.

"Plus, having you home will be better for us during this trying time."

Sheesh, "trying time"? Where'd they hear that from, a stupid pamphlet? *Getting Divorced and Bonding—How to Manage Both?*

I blinked at them, not quite believing what they said. "I have plans on the Fourth." Plans that I *really* couldn't cancel. Despite the fact that it was the biggest party of the summer, Walsh invited me, and I didn't want to let him down. Not with everything going on with him lately.

"I'm sorry." Dad's voice was totally unapologetic. "You don't get to be disrespectful without consequences." He looked down at his wristwatch. "I need to get going if I'm going to be out by a decent hour. You know how much I hate working on a Saturday."

"We're done." Mom drew in a breath, pressing her hands on her hips. "I'm sorry about this, Sophia. You know we hate taking away your freedom."

When had they ever taken away my freedom? And they decided to be actual parents *now*? When I actually have a *life*?

I wanted to say something snarky in response, but I didn't want to risk adding to my sentencing.

"I'm trusting that you'll stay home today while we're gone," she added, raising her eyebrows at me while Dad disappeared down the stairs.

"It's not like I have anywhere else to go anyways."

I'd opened the door wide open for her. *What about Scott?* she could ask. *Edith?* She wouldn't know to ask about my newfound relationship with Walsh, but I just wanted her to say *something*.

Mom just looked relieved, adjusting her workout top and moving toward the stairs. "Oh, I left some pizza for you in the fridge in case you get hungry." And she disappeared from view.

Shiba sat by my windowsill with me, keeping me company as the day passed into the next. Saturday rolled into Sunday, and then Sunday into Monday, and all the while, I sat at home. Doing nothing. I had to be the perfect child for my wishy-washy parents, displaying my best behavior so that maybe tomorrow, the Fourth of July, when I asked to go out, they would say yes.

Sure, it was a long shot, but it was my only shot. And I just needed to patiently wait to shoot it.

I sat cross-legged on my bed in the afternoon, a book propped between my knees. It was the one Walsh and I had sat in his car reading, and I took my time reading through the parts he'd commented on, trying to recall his exact words. It'd been two days since I left the house last, and two days since I'd heard from him.

The doorbell chimed, pulling me out of my Walsh-themed rabbit hole. I threw my legs over the side of my bed, tossing the book to the side. Shiba hopped down from the sill, following me out into the hall. She tried to weave in between my legs, nearly making me stumble down the stairs.

When I opened the door, Edith stood on the other side.

Her dark hair was twisted into a side braid, tight and professional, her green eyes wide and looking up to mine. "Your door was locked," she said, sounding confused. "If you're going to be locking your door, you've got to give me a key. You're lucky it wasn't raining."

Seeing her in front of me, hearing her voice—albeit, a

little snarky—took a heavy weight from my shoulders. "How did you know I was needing company?"

"When I'm not practicing volleyball, I'm practicing the art of reading minds." She winked theatrically.

"Where have you been?" I demanded, shutting the door behind her. "I can't even remember the last time I saw you."

"Don't be so dramatic," she said, tipping her head. "I've been... around."

"With Zach?"

She didn't even have to answer—her small grin told it all. "Not all the time."

"Boyfriends outdo girlfriends now?"

"*Not* my boyfriend." She started toward the staircase, leaving me to shut the door and follow after her. I thought she'd say more, but she reached her hand out to me. "Come on, let me curl your hair to make up for my disappearance. It could use some TLC, no offense."

We walked back into my bedroom while running my fingers over my head, feeling for any knots. "I haven't been out of the house in a few days."

Edith went over to my vanity and pulled out the curling iron, plugging it into the wall. She turned it to the middle setting before facing me. "Boys are a distraction," she told me, voice calm and nonchalant.

"Oh, please. It's summer. Prime time for distractions."

"No, summer is for volleyball training. For volleyball dedication. Nothing but volleyball."

In a way, I understood her dedication. How she felt about volleyball was exactly how I felt about my article.

I sat down at the chair and turned to face my reflection.

Edith was right; my hair *was* crazy, a downright rat's nest. I thought I'd brushed it the past few days, but I couldn't remember.

Edith snagged a lock of my hair and wound it around the barrel, focused. "Why are you here by yourself, anyway? You said you haven't left the house in two days?"

The sunlight filtering through my window caught along the lens of her glasses, reflecting in the mirror. "I'm grounded, actually."

Now Edith looked surprised and I couldn't blame her. The news was shocking if you knew my parents. "I don't even know what to say. Look at me, speechless. You struck me speechless. Why are you grounded?"

"They're getting a divorce."

Her silence was long and obvious as she searched for what to say. The heat of the curls was uncomfortably warm on my neck. In the reflection, her shoulders slumped a little. "I'm sorry, Sophia."

"Well, I'm not," I said, even though I wasn't sure if it was the truth or not. "And when I said 'sweet,' they got mad."

"You did not." Edith, after moving the iron a safe distance away, smacked the back of my head. "Sophia! You were asking to get grounded!"

"Ouch! I wasn't meaning to! But what was I supposed to say? I'm not like them, all theatrical and dramatic. And you know what, I *am* kind of glad they're getting a divorce. I'm just ready for things to be different. Is that bad?"

Edith didn't look me in the eye through the mirror; she just continued curling, no eye contact. "That *is* a little twisted. You could've at least shed a fake tear or two—you should know how to play their game by now."

But I didn't *want* to play their game. I didn't want to play a game at all. I just wanted to go back to the way things were before they checked out.

My cell phone started to ring from my nightstand, the noise making me jerk straight. Not expecting the sudden movement, the hot iron brushed along the skin of my scalp. "Ow! Edith!"

"Well, don't move!" Edith shouted back, pulling the barrel away.

The chirping noise continued to come from my phone, each ring twisting my stomach into tighter knots.

Edith already reached for it, scooping up the phone and pressing it to her ear. "Sophia Wallace's phone. Oh, she's right here, pretending not to be straining to hear every word you say."

Now I rolled my eyes.

"Yeah, one sec." She offered the phone to me, batting her lashes. "Some guy named Walsh Hunter? He wants to talk to you. Should I tell him you're busy?"

I took the cell from her before she said something else that he probably heard. *Now* he finally called me, after two days? "Hey."

"She lives," Walsh greeted lightly. "I was trying to play it cool and not blow up your phone, but I couldn't hold out any longer. I'm glad you're not dead."

"Yeah, me too."

"Edith's there. Does that mean you're too busy to come with me to get a few last-minute things for tomorrow night?"

He sounded hopeful. "Getty's General Store was sold out of inflatable floaties—apparently everyone wants one for the Fourth of July—but they still have some in stock at the Greenville mall, at least according to their website. A long drive if you're going by yourself."

Psh, "long drive"? Greenville was only an hour roundtrip without traffic. Not *that* bad. "What kind of pool float are you wanting?"

"They're the ones that fit two people. How cute would we be?"

Yeah, and Walsh probably wouldn't be able to resist the photo opportunity. And as much as I hated to admit it, I could imagine the two of us on a pool float, coasting around the bay lazily. Me splashing at him. Walsh grinning, his eyes the same color as the water.

"I wish I could," I sighed, disappointment welling. Disappointment at which part, though? The idea of missing the super fun pool float or missing out on spending time with Walsh. "I'm grounded."

"Nerdy Sophie, grounded?" I could hear a smile in his voice. "What'd you do, read past your bedtime?"

"Ha-ha." I wasn't sure if he'd actually get it if he knew the real story, and I was too afraid he'd see me as a spoiled little kid for what truly went down. Would he agree with Edith, that my response *was* messed up? "I, uh, forgot to empty Shiba's litter box."

"Seriously?" Edith whispered, eyebrows pulled together. She didn't look impressed. "Was that really the best you could come up with?"

"Jeez," Walsh said from the other line. "Until when?"

I inhaled air through my teeth, my insides feeling like mush. "I'm grounded for the Fourth. That means no fun pool floaties."

Walsh sighed dramatically on the other end of the phone, the sound theatrical and over-the-top. "I'm devastated, Sophie. *Devastated.* Shame on you for not cleaning her litter box."

"Do you want to walk dogs with me on the fifth?" It didn't feel weird asking him this time, not nearly as strange as it had originally. "Assuming they don't try to extend my duration in prison."

"I'll check my schedule and let you know," he said, then quickly added, "Oh, look at that. It's clear. And I'll bring better shoes this time."

"I don't know, I thought the boat shoes were a hit."

"Yeah, a hit in *dog poop*."

"If you two are going to flirt like this," Edith said, leaning down to talk into the phone, "then should I go in the other room? We were *trying* to have girl-talk."

I could hear Walsh laugh. "Sorry, sorry. I'll leave you two to it, then. I'll see you Wednesday then, Sophie?"

My lips twitched a little bit. "Wednesday it is. Bye."

When the other line disconnected, I realized by looking in the mirror just how red my face was, how hot my skin felt. I pressed my palms to my cheeks, hoping to cool them down.

Edith gave me a knowing look, moving onto the last section of my hair. "Cute."

I straightened my shoulders. "You know it's not like that. We're just pretending."

"For who?" she asked innocently. "Who's around to witness your flushed cheeks, hmm?"

There was no denying what she said. In the mirror, my red cheeks were completely obvious.

"So I've been working on my article," I said, changing the subject at breakneck speed. "It sucks because I don't have my original journal with any ideas, but I found a scrap notebook I could use. It's coming along. I've got the working title, actually. *The Curveball Truth Behind Bayview Baseball.*"

Edith stopped moving with a lock of hair wrapped around the barrel.

I didn't realize the silence between us was tense until I saw her expression in the mirror. It was pinched, almost disbelieving. "What? Too long? I could get rid of the word 'curveball.'"

"You're not still writing the exposé...right?"

"What do you mean? You've known about this." Heat started coming from the curler, little smoke squiggles wafting into the air. "Edith, my hair!"

She hurried to untangle the iron, yanking a few hairs in the process, and stepped around, looking directly in my eye. "You're not using Walsh to get more information, are you?" she demanded, studying my expression. When I remained silent, her eyes widened. "Sophia!"

"It's not like I'm spreading lies!" I threw my hands into the air. Half of my curls bounced around as I shook my head. "And I'm not *using him.* I wasn't the one to suggest this fake dating nonsense. If you remember, this was all his idea. They're cutting the newspaper, and if I don't have a good article, I can kiss the internship at the *Blade* goodbye—kiss jumpstarting my journalism career goodbye. Kiss my *dream* goodbye. How would you feel if you had to give up volleyball?"

Edith's anger seemed to dissipate slightly, hearing the distress in my voice. I didn't want to look at her in the mirror, my anger forcing me into an arm-crossed pout, but when she spoke again, her voice was softer. "Sophia, you are an amazing writer. I've read your stuff. Heck, your straw article changed the school board's mind before. You don't need to write anything mean." She kicked the edge of my stool. "That's not the kind of stuff you write, anyway."

Her words left me feeling icky on the inside, all over. Edith wasn't wrong. Undercover journalism *wasn't* the kind of writing I did. Take-down articles weren't my thing. Informative articles, maybe, or even personal ones, but never negative.

But Edith didn't understand. "Recyclable straws won't bring my class back."

"Well, what does Walsh think of your article topic?"

My silence was answer enough.

"You haven't told him," she laughed, but it held zero humor. "Sophia, when he finds out, he's—"

"Going to be furious," I finished, already knowing. And he'd have the right to be, but he knew about the cheating. As team captain, how could he not? He knew what he was getting into. That wasn't my fault. "I don't have a choice, Edith."

She started sorting through my hair again, picking up another piece and winding it around the tool. Gathering my courage, I lifted only my gaze to the mirror, finding the disappointment on her expression. All the denial and anger burst like a balloon in my chest and I felt *bad*—bad for lying, bad for scheming, and bad for keeping my mouth shut. But there was no other option.

"We all have choices," Edith eventually said, not doing a thing to soothe my conscience. "Some just have bigger consequences than others."

*I*ndependence Day gifted both of my parents time off of work, and they decided it would be in the spirit of the holiday to make a big family breakfast.

And it was bizarre.

Now that they'd decided to get a divorce, it was seemingly time to do parent things. Like grounding me and making family breakfast. What was next, a family vacation?

Quite honestly, when Dad came to my room to ask "bacon or sausage," it really almost seemed like things were back to the way they'd been. To life before starting high school; to life before we grew apart.

When I got downstairs, I saw that Mom had papers sprawled out in front of her at the kitchen table, sorting through them. Dad stood at the stove, stirring what looked like scrambled eggs in the pan. He still wore his pajama bottoms, the hems coming up above his ankles

Despite their separation announcement, neither one of them had packed up their things. They even still slept in the same room, unless one of them snuck onto the couch in the middle of the night.

"Good morning," I said.

Mom glanced up from the papers, smiling. "Morning, Sophia."

"What are you working on?"

Dad scraped the pan of eggs onto a large plate, voice peevish. "Divorce paperwork."

This time, I kept my mouth shut, and even mustered a somber expression. *Good behavior.*

"Do you really need to do that now, Amber?" Dad went on, not turning. "And at the kitchen table?"

"The lawyer needs them by the seventeenth and it's better to get things done early." She continued to trace the paper with her pen, reading the lines.

The ceramic plates slammed down on the breakfast bar, and Dad stepped away from them. "You should eat before it gets cold."

Mom acted like she hadn't even heard him, sorting through the paperwork with her ears turned off. Dad pretended like she *had* listened to him, moving to make a plate of his own food.

The doorbell chimed as I reached for a plate, startling Mom from her focused state. "I'll get it," she said, finish the line she'd been reading before standing. "It's probably Mariana. We're going out on her pontoon for the day. Isn't that fun?"

It *really* irritated me that my mom could have plans and I couldn't. *Good behavior.*

As I turned to start loading my plate with bacon, I

noticed that Mom stood at the edge of the hallway, her words hanging in the air while her eyes were on Dad. With his back turned, he hadn't seen her look. She opened her mouth to speak but disappeared off toward the front door.

I sat next to Dad, readjusting my glasses. "Do you have any plans tonight, too?"

"A few friends from the office are going down to the bay for the fireworks display. I'd invite you, but—" he shoveled a forkful of eggs into his mouth, "—you're grounded."

"About that," I said slowly, carefully cutting into my waffle. "I was going to ask—"

"No, you can't get off early." He looked at me like he knew where that question was going, which he did. I guess it *was* pretty transparent. "I'm sorry. I'm trusting you'll stay home the whole night."

I deflated. "Yeah, yeah." I was too much of a goody-two-shoes to sneak out, and he knew it.

"Sophia," Mom called from the direction of the front door, voice oddly cheerful. "You've got a visitor."

Edith again? She'd left after she curled my hair yesterday, pretending like she wasn't hard-core judging me. I was surprised she'd given up on the cold shoulder so soon, and quite honestly, I wasn't sure I was ready to give up mine.

But I walked into the hallway, with a clear view of the door, and I stopped mid-step. Definitely not Edith.

Walsh Hunter stood in the middle of my meager entry-way, hands in the pockets of his jeans, glancing around. And I stared at him with bedhead, no makeup, and my glasses on. Though my hair was still slightly curled from last night, I hadn't brushed it this morning, and it was a tangled rat's nest, all knotted in the back.

My heart stopped beating for a moment.

Walsh's eyes finally settled onto mine, and his lips broke into a bright grin. He pretended that he didn't notice my pajamas, my knotty hair, or my glasses. No, that smile ignored all of that and only focused on *me*. No hesitation.

"Hey," he greeted, sounding just as cheerful as Mom. "I just wanted to stop by for a little bit and keep you company. If that's all right with you, Mrs. Wallace. I don't want to intrude on a holiday."

Mom seemed charmed by him, though, his random appearance immediately welcome. "That's perfectly fine. Come on in. We were just getting breakfast set. What did you say your name was again?"

"Walsh," he answered, readily offering his hand. "Walsh Hunter."

"A friend from school?"

Walsh took great pleasure in speaking his next words; that much was obvious from his expression. "Sophie's boyfriend, actually."

Am I having a heart attack?

Dad spoke then, right behind me. "I thought you were dating that other bonehead."

Maybe it's a stroke.

"Steve?" Mom suggested unhelpfully.

"I thought it was Silvan."

I'm definitely dying.

My tongue started to work again, but the words sounded far away. "His name is *Scott*, and we broke up."

"Good." Dad shook his head. "I never liked him."

Unsurprisingly, Walsh chuckled. "Yeah, he's a stick in the mud."

Okay, ha-ha, that was enough communal conversation. That was enough of Walsh being around my parents, too. I wasn't going to give him any chance to see more of their weirdness, to hate them as much as Scott had.

I grabbed for Walsh's wrist. "We're going upstairs."

But Dad wasn't sold, holding a hand out. "Now hold on, young lady. You haven't eaten your breakfast, and I think we need to know a bit more about Walsh here before we let him go up to your room."

Well, you see, when Scott dumped me, Walsh told everyone that we had a secret love affair. Funny story, now we're pretending to be dating because Walsh was sticking up for me, but I'm using it to my advantage so I can dig up information for my article, which will save my writing career. Ta-da!

Walsh interlocked his fingers with mine, giving them a warm squeeze. "You definitely need to eat breakfast," he told me, sounding like a concerned boyfriend. Points to him. "It's the most important meal of the day, you know."

If my brain hadn't been short-circuiting, I might've rolled my eyes.

Even though my nerves were chewing apart my insides, I forced myself to sit back down at my plate of food and resume cutting up my waffle like everything was fine. Like Walsh Hunter *wasn't* in my house, wasn't bearing witness to my horrific hairdo, and wasn't sitting at the seat beside me. Dad must've taken care of his plate.

"Can I get you anything, Walsh? Would you like a waffle?"

Walsh pressed his hands on the countertop, and I just stared at them. For some reason, I couldn't help but wonder what they looked like holding a pencil, poising to write. "I actually just ate. But...do I smell coffee?"

"Would you like milk or sugar?" Mom asked, happy to serve our guest.

The whole exchange was bizarre to witness. Aliens. I blamed aliens.

I was really on a different planet. Or in an entirely different universe. With Scott, this situation had been completely different. Mom and Dad hadn't put on their best behavior for Scott. I'd brought him home the first time, and they just continued to argue over me trying to make introductions. "They seem...crazy," he'd told me, right in front of them. They hadn't even noticed.

I pushed a forkful of my waffle into my mouth, and it was slightly soggy from sitting in the syrup.

"How long have you two been dating?" Mom asked, standing by the counter opposite of us. She seemed almost enchanted by Walsh's appearance, at the idea of her daughter dating someone who didn't look at them with judgey eyes.

Dad set a coffee mug in front of Walsh, careful not to slosh any liquid out since he'd filled it to the brim.

Walsh took a long sip, and it took me a moment to realize it was on purpose. He wanted me to answer. "Oh, uh, about two weeks."

That earned me angry eyes from Dad. "You never mentioned him, Sophia."

"I know. My bad."

"She's been so busy," Walsh said, reaching over and patting my arm. "When she's not with me, she's so busy with her article, aren't you?"

"Article?" Mom glanced to me. "What article?"

I sliced the side of my fork through my waffle, tearing a small piece from the circle. Even though everyone's eyes were on me, I didn't want to meet any of them. I didn't want anything to do with the curiosity in Mom's gaze, the curiosity in Dad's, or whatever was in Walsh's gaze. Pity? Confusion? I didn't even want to know. "My Back to School article for the fall. I'm writing it on baseball."

"Baseball," Dad mused. "Strange topic for you to pick, Sophia."

"I may have influenced her a little bit," Walsh said. "I'm on the team and thought it could be fun—free publicity and all."

I pushed my plate away. It held less than half my waffle and only two pieces of bacon. "Thanks for breakfast."

Walsh stood up after me, although more hesitantly, grabbing his mug of coffee. "Wait, are you sure you're done? I didn't mean to interrupt."

"You didn't," Mom assured.

"Definitely not." Dad had moved closer to Mom as we were talking, and he was now leaning right next to her against the counter. She glanced up at him, seeming to notice their proximity as soon as I did. "I can take care of your plate."

Another parental gesture that made me a little wigged out. Did Walsh just draw out everybody's good side? I grabbed him again, not wanting the spell to be broken. "Thanks. We'll be up in my room."

"Keep your door open," Dad warned, as if reading a line from a play.

When we got to the stairs, Walsh smiled down at Shiba, who sat atop the second step. Her tail lobbed lazily against the railing. "You said you had a cat, but didn't say she was a Persian cat."

I frowned at her. "She has a bit of a temper."

Shiba meowed as she leaned against his outstretched hand, protesting my words.

"See?"

"Why are we rushing to your room?" Walsh asked once we reached the landing, concerning himself with steadying his mug. "I mean, I can appreciate your enthusiasm, but I'm just not that kind of guy, Sophie. I mean, your parents are home."

Oh. My. Gosh. I made sure to keep my jaw clamped shut in fear of it falling to the floor, taking a moment to compose myself in front of my closed door before I turned to face him. "Can you give me a second?"

Walsh raised a teasing eyebrow. "Have to make sure your undies are picked up?"

This time, my jaw did drop open. "No, I—just—*stay*."

"Yes, ma'am."

I grasped the door handle, opening it just enough that I could slip inside, and then I shut the door in his face. Thankfully, no undies *were* on the floor, but several pairs of shorts and a few shirts were, and I shoved them all into my hamper. The sheets across my bed were crumpled from how I'd left them this morning, and I hurried to maneuver them into a somewhat made position. There wasn't anything I could do about the butterflies painted on my walls, faded from the years. They weren't going anywhere.

I hurried back to the door, pulling in a reset breath so I didn't seem so winded. Without preamble, I pulled the door open.

Blue-green eyes lifted to mine, innocent and curious, but something about them caused my insides to shift. Like a tidal wave, I found it hard to draw in a breath, and it had nothing to do with me rushing to clean up my room. It was definitely just the sight of him standing in my hallway. That was so beyond weird.

Those eyes immediately went to the giant red and black butterflies painted on the wall, and amusement overpowered his gaze. "Don't," I said.

"Don't what?" Walsh walked into my room, over to my desk to where one purple butterfly was. "They're cute."

"They're horrendously embarrassing."

A lopsided grin peeked at me over the rim of his mug. "I like them. Makes me think I should paint butterflies on my wall." He picked up papers that sat on the desk, fanning them out. It took me a second too long to react. "Hey, is this the famous article?"

"Don't!" My heart and I lurched at the same time, and I lunged forward, practically tearing the papers from his fingers. The papers crinkled together, and I pressed them against my chest. I knew what was on these papers—all the bullet points I'd scribbled on the baseball team. Walsh's confession was on this paper. "I—it's not finished. I don't want you to read it until it's finished."

He merely chuckled, moving to sit on my windowsill while my heart was still coming down from its adrenaline rush. I slid the papers underneath a few books, letting out a breath. "Touchy, touchy. Don't mess with Sophie's writing, good to know."

I sat down on my bed, crossing my legs and pulling a pillow to my chest, shaking ever so slightly. That was a close call. From the expression on Walsh's face, I didn't think that he'd seen any of the words on the page. He probably couldn't even read my handwriting.

"Did I do okay down there?" Walsh asked, almost uneasily, glancing toward the floor. His fingers tapped the mug's edge uneasily. "I've never exactly...met parents before."

I never assumed that Walsh Hunter was a ladies' man, or whatever that was, but his words struck me as odd. "You haven't?"

"Not, like, a girlfriend's parents. Nothing was ever serious enough."

Even though I tried, I couldn't remember Walsh having a girlfriend. Before, I tried not to pay much attention to him in the hallways, but there wasn't even a faint memory of him holding hands with someone, never heard Edith talking about him being in a relationship.

"You did great," I told him, squeezing my pillow tighter. "I think they fell in love with you, actually."

Relief was evident, washing over his face and his posture. A genuine reaction.

"So, what are you doing here, anyway?" I asked. "And don't give me the parent version."

"The what?"

"You know, what you say to impress parents. Because you were totally schmoozing down there."

Walsh sipped at his coffee. "That wasn't the parent version. It was the *actual* version. I just wanted to spend time with you."

The look I gave him was skeptical, one eyebrow raised, probably a mock of Scott's *look*, only not as stern.

"I mean it, Sophia."

He *was* telling the truth. "Sophia" was the clear indicator. Huh. The idea of someone wanting to spend time with me just because was...nice. It made my insides feel warm. Made me want to smile.

I tried not to think about it too hard. "What time are you leaving for the bay?"

Walsh was admiring my butterflies, ignoring my gaze. "Soon. Do they have names?"

I flopped onto my back, staring at the ceiling, and the bed bounced with my weight. "My butterflies? Uh, no."

"That one looks like a Beatrice. Or Beverly. Definitely a B-name." Walsh hesitated for a moment, probably taking another drink. "Scott kept asking about you yesterday at practice."

As I stared at the ceiling, I found that I couldn't care less about what Scott asked. Not a single ounce of me seized up at the idea of Scott inquiring about me. Which was definite progress, and I would've patted myself on the back if I wasn't concerned that I moved on so fast. Maybe because I realized how horrible he was for me. But we were both happy with other people now. Or, you know, in my case, happy with other people in a fake way. "Oh?"

"He just asked if you were happy. Why we started dating. If I really liked you or if I was stringing you along."

Now my insides felt a little prickly. And *Scott* always got mad at *Walsh* for butting in? "And what did you say?"

"Yes, you're happy. We started dating because we just connected." He blew out a harsh breath. "And I really, really like you."

I really, really like you. Those words shouldn't have made my insides feel even warmer, shouldn't have made my fingers spasm on my pillow, but they did.

The space between us quieted for a moment as I thought about what he said, and I traced the air with my fingertips. It didn't really surprise me that Scott asked about our relationship. If I were Scott, I would've been suspicious.

I wanted to dance and sing *ha-ha-ha*. Go up to Scott and say, "See, I am good enough! Take that!"

I heard something *clink*, and in the next moment, Walsh sat on my bed, lying down alongside me. The bed shifted underneath his weight, causing me to rock toward him. "Told you it would work."

My foot nudged his, and I could feel his sock underneath my toes. "Does that mean we break up now? You know, since it worked, and he bought it. No need to draw it for two more weeks."

Walsh didn't look at me. "You want to break up?"

I snorted at the surprised tone of his voice. "Aw, you almost sounded like a real boyfriend for a second."

The smile he offered seemed stiffer than usual.

I rolled onto my side, tucking my hands underneath the side of my head as I watched him. "Hey, I know I was jerky about it before, but thank you for sticking up for me. I'm sorry you had to do all this." I gestured blindly at the space between us. *Putting up with me, putting up with Scott's inquisition, putting up with my deceit—which you don't know about, of course. But you will.* "Just...thanks."

Now Walsh's head did turn toward me, eyes darting to my own. "Don't listen to Scott. You should never apologize for being the rom-com loving, slushy obsessed, talented writing nerd that you are. Don't ever apologize."

The intensity in his eyes made my lungs confused—they seemed to forget how to pull in air. "I should embroider that on a pillow."

"You know, this has been refreshing. Having someone in my life that actually cares."

I placed my hand on the bed between us, shifting. Unintentionally, my body rolled closer to his on my bedspread, the space between us mere inches. "What do you mean?"

"You asked me to go walk dogs with you the other day, and I was genuinely excited, you know. When you came to check on me because you heard I was sick, you brought me soup, and you tried to cheer me up. I don't know how I'll go back to my meaningless life before this," he said with mock-despair. "You've ruined me."

"We can still be friends after this," I whispered, even though I hadn't meant to. I meant to speak normally, but the words came out soft and breathy, taking this moment and turning it into something...different. Something that made my chest tighten, my body warm to a degree that felt searing. "Can't we?"

At first, it was a hint of a touch, skin against skin. But Walsh moved his hand over my hand that rested on the bed between us, his fingers covering my own. Warmth from him jumped onto me, spanning along my arm until I was covered with it. I couldn't help but wonder what he was thinking, grabbing my hand when no one was there to see it. Slipping his fingers over mine, spreading them apart and tracing the knuckles. He wasn't looking at me, though, his gaze turned down to our hands.

The longer he remained silent, the quicker my pulse beat. Faster and faster and louder and louder until I could've sworn that he could hear it, feel it in my fingertips, know what my traitorous body was doing in response to his touch.

Stop that, I wanted to tell my heart. *Stop beating so fast. This is Walsh. This is fake.*

But those blue eyes lifted to mine and suddenly I was in the middle of the ocean, treading water but beginning to sink. Rapidly. Like I was wearing concrete shoes.

My words, though I tried to make them steady, came out barely there. "Why are you staring at me?"

The soft words broke the moment in half, and Walsh released my hand, curling his own into fists. His eyes moved from mine. "Your glasses are smudgy."

"They are?" I pulled them from my face to find them slightly speckled, and I used the hem of my shirt to swipe at the lens. My cheeks flamed hot. "I guess I'm just blind to it. Which is strange, since it's right in front of me."

The bed jostled as Walsh pushed to a sitting position. "I

should get going. There are a few things I need to do before heading down to the bay."

"Well, have fun. Drink a slushy for me." I sat up too, slipping my glasses back on. My face still felt warm, but I tried to ignore it. "I like blue-raspberry the best, so drink one of those."

Walsh smiled but didn't look at me. His gaze rested on my butterflies. "I will, I promise."

My fingers still held onto the residual warmth his skin gave off, almost a tingly sensation. I laced them together to try and make the feeling go away.

"Sophie?" he asked, still standing just in front of me.

This time, I didn't correct him. "Walsh?"

With a delicate touch, he slid a fingertip along the metal of my glasses frame, moving from the arm to slip a piece of hair behind my ear. "I really like your glasses," Walsh said. "Smudges and all."

And just like that, the tingly sensation from my fingers spread to my stomach.

fifteen

*M*om left around two in the afternoon with Mariana, Dad heading to the bay shortly after. It was strange being cooped up in the house on a holiday all by myself—this was the most un-Fourth of July ever.

I didn't even have the motivation to work on my article.

The problem about being isolated on a holiday was that there was no one to talk to. Edith, no doubt, was already down at the bay, soaking up the remnants of sunlight and playing some beach volleyball. My texts to her remained unanswered. I wondered if she'd be chatting up Zach or not— I hoped so.

I could've texted Walsh, but I doubted that he'd answer either, having to do his errands before going down to the party.

Would tonight be the end of our fake relationship? Would people wonder why we weren't together? Would they even notice? Scott would. And Walsh—would he say that I was just at home, or would he say that things weren't working out between us?

The thought of our ruse ending being up made me feel sad in a way. Maybe because I'd lose him as a source for my article. But then again, I did have a pretty good list running: the information I'd found on the school's site, the team paying off the other players—though I needed just a smidge more proof for that—and Ryan's parents' private donations to the baseball fund. With those points, my article was basically done.

Just the idea of letting everything fall apart, staging a public break up, probably never speaking again—none of it sat well with me. My mind went back to when we'd read together in his car and floated along the bay outside his house for hours, just talking. And the way he'd looked at me earlier this morning. All of it was...nice. Really nice. And other than with Edith, I hadn't had anything really nice with anybody in a while.

It had to end sometime.

The sun began to fall from the sky by the time my movie ended, and I stood up and stretched. Shiba laid on the end of the couch, sound asleep, her stomach facing the ceiling and her paws spread wide. She looked so uncomfortable. I really wanted to reach out and run my fingers along her stomach, but I knew what that would result in: claw marks, yowls, and probably tears on my part. I've learned the hard way that Shiba's sleep isn't to be messed with.

A loud knock came from the direction of the front door, startling me so badly that I let out a squeak. Shiba jerked awake, immediately shooting me a look. "Sorry," I told her, grabbing a blanket from the couch and wrapping it around my shoulders. "Blame whoever's at the door."

I made my way towards the door, wondering who would be stopping by at this hour. Maybe Mom or Dad, having forgotten their keys? When I got close enough, I raised my voice. "Who is it?"

"It's me," the voice said, pausing. "Scott."

I jerked away from the door as if I'd been shocked. What the heck was he doing here? Quickly, I reached up and took my glasses off, sending my world into a hazy blur. Then I ran my fingers through my hair, combing out all the knots. After readjusting the blanket, I tugged open the door.

Sure enough, Scott stood on the welcome mat, his sandaled feet covering the E and the C, though the letters were a little blurry. He wore a tank top with little American flags on it, and a red pair of swim trunks.

"I should've called," he said immediately. "I know I should've. But I saw that your parents' cars weren't home and your lights were on, so I thought I'd come knock."

I gripped the doorknob, trying to figure out why exactly he was driving past my house in the first place. "Oh. Yeah. I'm here."

"Why aren't you down at the bay with your boyfriend?"

"I'm grounded," I said, and my cheeks felt warm. I couldn't really pinpoint why. Maybe it was because we were finally alone together again, and it made me feel so uncomfortable. "Why did you stop by, anyway?"

Scott shifted on the mat, folding his arms across his chest. "I've been meaning to call you, catch up. We used to talk a lot, you know? You were a good listener."

My guard went up fast. He was *complimenting* me? Something wasn't right. "We didn't talk all that much when we were together, you know."

"Not as much as I would've liked," he agreed. And even though I didn't have my glasses on, I could tell when Scott's gaze dropped to my mouth. "I'm sure you and Walsh talk all the time."

I forced myself to swallow the annoyance that sparked and the urge to shut the door in his face.

"I'm surprised you two are lasting as long as you are."

"You're wrong about him," I said defensively. Heck, even *I'd* been wrong about him, but I wondered if I just let Scott's bias affect mine. "Walsh is a great guy."

Scott stuffed one of his hands into his swim trunks' pockets, chuckling. "You really think you and him are a good fit? He's way too self-absorbed for you. And entitled. And—oh, yeah—an idiot."

Yeah, and what are you? I wanted to shout at him, because all of his hateful words to me still played in my mind. The tone he used now replicated that which he'd used at the party two weeks ago. He hadn't come here to talk to me; he'd come here to try and convince me I was wrong.

"Irony is funny, isn't it, Sophia? I break up with you to find someone better, someone that could help me outdo Walsh, and then you go and become his girlfriend." Scott sighed. "Irony or a coincidence?"

Had he really come here to bash me some more? Seriously? Did we *really* need to rehash all this again? "It's called *karma*, Scott."

"I broke up with you because I needed someone *better*.

Someone that help me could beat him. Someone who could be the other half of a power couple, in a way. Someone people were jealous of. And he knew that. Don't you get it?" Scott's voice was so passionate, so fevered. I realized now that this was the way he always got when discussing Walsh, so vehement with anger. "Don't you see? Walsh is only dating you so he can mess with me. To ruin my life. That's what this has always been about. He and I have always been rivals, and you knew that."

Standing in the doorway, with Scott in front of me and an empty house behind me, it felt like I woke up from a dream. A dream that held Scott's and my past relationship, whatever feelings I had for him. All of that resided in that dreamworld, and now I woke up. I knew the truth about him now—I'd always known it.

I didn't even blink. "You sound crazy."

"You think he's so nice and charming and charismatic? He *wants* people to think that. He *wants* you to think he's got his life all figured out, but he doesn't. He's just as screwed up as the rest of us." He reached out and touched my hand sitting on the doorknob. "Sophia, come on. You and I make much more sense. I let all of it get to me—I shouldn't have let you go. I'm sorry."

It was hard to imagine there'd ever been a time where I basked in the rare feel of his skin against mine. Now the simple grazing contact made me sick to my stomach. His words now were hollow, meaningless. Apology as empty as could be. Because he was so transparent—he didn't want me back. He only wanted me because Walsh wanted me. That made me *desirable*. Not so boring anymore.

When Scott looked at me, though, he didn't see *me*. He saw me as something that Walsh wanted. To him, I was a toy that Walsh had, and Scott wanted it. And I didn't know what sparked this desire to have everything Walsh wanted, but now that I was included on that list, things were different.

Knowing that, knowing that Scott only wanted me because Walsh liked me, hurt. It hurt just as much as his words at the party hurt. "You should leave, Scott," I said, shaking his hand off and straightening my spine. "Now."

"Sophia."

"*Now*," I repeated, sharpening my tone. I wanted him gone, off my porch, away from my house. Heck, I wanted him gone from my *life*. He could go run off to his new girlfriend, though she deserved better than him. Anyone would.

Scott watched me for a moment, probably trying to gauge the severity of my attitude. But the straightness in my spine remained, and I didn't budge.

After a moment or two of silence, he backed away, flip-flops slipping off the welcome mat. "Go ahead, praise the ground he walks on," he called back to me. "You'll see."

I slammed the door shut in response, causing the pictures on the wall to vibrate. Who did he think he was? Coming to my house, insulting me, insulting Walsh. I couldn't even imagine being so stupid, so self-absorbed.

Angry tears burned in the back of my throat, and I glared at the wall, praying the feeling went away. The anger towards Scott morphed as I stared at the pictures, my emotions turning into something equally dark. The pictures that rattled when I slammed the door now hung immobile. I tried not to look at them too closely because it was only a testament to everything that ceased to exist, but I couldn't fully tear my gaze away. One was a black and white photo, and we were on the beach. Dad had his arms wrapped around both Mom and me, her hand curled over his shoulder. Squished in the middle stood me, the widest gap-toothed grin on my face, eyes squinted shut.

A thick emotion curled in my chest staring at the picture, because I wanted this back so bad. *So bad.* I wanted the ice cream nights, the beach trips, the weekends away. I wanted the family dinners, the "I love you's."

And instead, it all fell apart.

I found myself wanting to snatch up my phone and call Walsh, just to hear him speak. His voice had such a calming effect, one that seemed to chase away any worries that weighed me down. No, but I couldn't. He was at the bay, having fun, living his life. Who was he talking to now? A bunch of girls with tiny swimsuits?

You're not jealous—that's not jealousy, I repeated over and over in my head. I just wished he was here instead, saying some stupid joke or just reading with me.

Time passed as I stood at the door, enough for all thoughts of Scott to be scattered from my mind. So I jumped again when yet another knock came, lunging for the handle, ready to shout. "I swear, I will call the—"

But it wasn't Scott.

Walsh stood on the other side of the door with his blond eyebrows high up on his forehead. "Nice to see you, too?"

"What are you doing here?" I was ten kinds of disoriented, staring at his figure standing against the fading sky.

Did I conjure him from my thoughts? "Why aren't you at the bay? Aren't the fireworks starting soon?"

"I didn't go," he told me, slipping his hands into the pockets of his shorts.

"What? What do you mean you didn't go? Where have you been for the past few hours, then?"

Walsh reached a hand out to me, palm up. "I can show you."

As enticing as his words were, I hesitated, glancing at the picture on the wall as if somehow my parents could see me through it. "I can't leave the house."

"Your house," he said, eyes vivid with energy, "or your yard?"

Uh. "What?"

Walsh grabbed my hand and led me out onto my front porch, then down the two steps. "Close your eyes," he commanded, his other hand coming around to my other shoulder to guide me. "I promise I won't let you trip over anything."

"Walsh—"

"Shh. Just say 'yes, Walsh' and close your eyes."

I gritted my teeth but relented, swaying as my vision filled with black. "I hate surprises."

Walsh pressed firmer against my side, his chest touching my shoulder, a smile in his voice. "I think you'll like this one."

Grass crunched beneath my bare toes as he moved me along, but I remained a good sport and kept my eyes sealed. Though it was silly, my heart started to beat faster, the anticipation making me nervous. His hands that curved over my shoulders were gentle, the pressure steady, his body close enough behind me that I could practically *feel* his proximity.

"Relax," Walsh said, guiding me to a halt. "Your shoulders are so tense. I'm not about to kill you and stuff you in my trunk."

"Your trunk's huge. You seriously think you'd have to *stuff* me into it?"

Walsh was close enough that I could feel him chuckle.

"Can I open my eyes now?"

Walsh hesitated for a moment before he let go entirely. "Yes."

I blinked my eyes open, expecting to see my plain, boring backyard, the green grass and the decrepit garden shed pressed in the corner.

However, in the middle of the lawn sat a giant pink flamingo pool float, with throw blankets tossed over the top of it and pillows piled on. The pool float was made so that the body of the flamingo was two inner tube-like holes with a giant head poking straight up into the air. Beside the inflatable sat two clear plastic cups, and even from here I could see it was filled with something blue.

"I had to go to three different stores to find blue-raspberry. Every place had either cherry or cola. Apparently not everyone is as crazy about blue-raspberry as you."

I stared at the giant pool float, utterly stupefied. "Why?"

"I figured since you can't go to the bay, I thought I could bring some bay to you." When I looked over, I saw Walsh biting the corner of his bottom lip, pinching his fingers. Nervous. "I mean, if you'd rather just stay inside, that's fine too. Or if you just don't want company, that's okay. I just thought—I ended up getting the thing anyway, so I thought—"

I reached forward and pressed my hand to his mouth, much like he'd done to me once before, silencing him as I spoke in a rush. "This is singlehandedly the nicest thing anyone's ever done for me."

With his mouth under my palm, it was impossible to ignore how soft his lips were, unmanageable to pretend that I didn't notice. The pressure was like a shot of alcohol, thrilling and shocking and powerful at the same time, especially as I felt him smile. One corner lifted along the seam of my fingers.

In that moment, looking at him with the backdrop of the darkening sky, I felt a jolt as I realized how good-looking he was. I mean, I always knew Walsh was good looking—practically everyone in school raved about it—but it wasn't even just his looks. No, if it was just his looks, he wouldn't have gone out of his way to buy the pool float, the slushies, and put all this together in my backyard. If it was just looks, he would've gone down to the bay and hung out with his friends.

It wasn't just his good looks; his heart was just as beautiful.

I could write a whole article just on him—beautiful and unique and kind.

Electricity zapped my skin, every nerve responding at once.

Walsh's eyes were a little wide as I pulled my hand away, soft lips parted as he watched me. "Your eyes," he whispered, breath caressing in my ears, its fingers running down my spine. "I love them."

"First my glasses and now my eyes?" I shivered at the

intensity of his gaze. My stomach hollowed out at his words, and I couldn't figure out why he'd said them. Whether or not they were true was a whole other thing, but there was no one around to hear him. "You really know how to get a girl going."

A small smile rested on his face, so faint I wondered if he knew he wore it. "Come on, let's sit down before the fireworks start."

I followed after him, watching as he readjusted the pillows and blankets. In that moment, the dread and anxiety came back and hit me in full force. New words wanted to come from my lips, truthful but condemning. *I'm writing an article about baseball, but it's not what you think. And I can't tell you, because if you knew, you'd hate me. Drop me like Scott did. And you can't drop me, too.*

"So, my article is coming along," I told him instead, lying down on the inflatable. I propped myself up enough that I could sip my slushy. Walsh sat down, causing the air inside it to bob, settling beside me. "I hope Mrs. Gao likes it."

Walsh's body pressed up against mine, his hair tickling against the pillow. "Are you nervous?"

"Part of me feels...unsettled." *An understatement.*

"Pre-game jitters," he said helpfully, waving a hand at the sky. "I get them all the time, especially just before pitching. But they'll fade, and you'll be a rock star."

He sounded so sure when he spoke, full of certainty, and I allowed myself to relax a bit. Tension ebbed from me, if only slightly. "I hope so."

We both looked at the stars in quiet for a moment, finally the cover of the sun ebbing away so that they could shine. "I was thinking we could get breakfast before we walk dogs tomorrow," Walsh murmured to me. "There's this place in Greenville that makes the best crepes. Mary's Place, I think it's called. Have you ever been?"

"I worked there last summer," I said, taking a small sip from my straw. The rush of the syrupy-sweetness filled my taste buds, the right amount of refreshing. The straw made a clogging sound as it met resistance, and I cringed from how loud the noise sounded. "I've never had one of their crepes, though. But you don't have to do that."

"Do what?"

"We're not an actual couple who has to do dates and things."

Walsh shifted, his weight causing us to sink closer together by an inch. "I know. I want to anyway. Oh, but speaking of, we should take a photo," he said, pulling out his cell phone. "You know, to capture the moment."

"And so you can post it," I teased with an eye roll, settling in beside him so I could get in frame. "I swear, I think you're obsessed with social media."

I stared straight into the camera lens as he held it above us, his head coming in close. The soft scent of him washed over my senses, making me feel imbalanced.

Even though I knew this wasn't real, I found myself pretending that it was. Just for a second. Pretending that Walsh really liked me enough to buy this float and hang out with me on the Fourth of July. Only me. I pretended that Scott didn't exist, and the article didn't exist, and it was just the two of us.

I tried to push the mental image away. When he lowered

the phone, though, I looked over to find him already watching me, gaze steady.

Lost in the world of pretending, everything shifted. It was like I'd been looking at this situation with a pair of binoculars, and as I shifted the focus on it, everything become crystal-clear.

Electricity hummed along my skin, zapping me at each and every point our bodies touched. My arm and his arm, his ankle on my leg. And I just wanted closer, closer.

Kiss him, a voice whispered in my head, one that had been conjured by my "what if" thoughts, tempting and irresistible. *You know you want to. What would it hurt?*

My heart skipped a beat. What would it hurt?

A loud, earth-shaking *boom* exploded into the sky, and I jerked against Walsh's side. Quickly, I put my slushy down on the grass, leaning against the float as an even louder noise roared in the sky, color lighting the ground around us. The next firework burst in a colossal mass of blue and purple, screeching as it burnt out. As it reverberated, a shudder went through my entire body.

"That one was pretty," Walsh said softly from my side, raising goosebumps on my arms.

And we laid like that, listening to the fireworks boom overhead, watching the colors dance across our skin. If someone looked at us, they would've seen a couple lying with each other, enjoying the fireworks in the comfort of their backyard. No one would have guessed we were faking it all.

I added this moment to the list of things Walsh could never know. He couldn't know about the article and he could never know that this didn't feel fake to me. He could never know I'd thought about kissing him—if only for a moment.

But as Walsh shifted closer, his hand brushing mine, I allowed myself to entertain the idea that I wasn't the only one who felt those things, felt that way. If only for a moment.

My opinion on Mom and Dad's divorce changed drastically from how I first felt, and I was certain they would be happier with my amended response. No longer was this the best thing that could've happened to the family, not in my eyes. I found myself close to tears at the idea of it, weighed down by what could happen.

Things were always subject to change with them, but with the paperwork passing back and forth, I started to fear they were serious.

The other night, I'd inched downstairs to get a glass of water and saw something I wished I hadn't. Dad sat in front of the TV, still dressed in his clothes from work even though it was way past his usual bedtime. I opened my mouth to say something, to let him know that I was there, when he put his face into his hand and made a muffled noise, low in his throat. My chest tightened at the sound, the quiet sob, and I sprinted as silently as I could back up the stairs.

Yeah. I wasn't thrilled about the divorce at all anymore.

It'd been a week and a half since the Fourth of July, and Walsh and I had hardly seen each other. Last week, the team had two away baseball games and then something called "team bonding nights" in preparation for their final game coming up—which, according to Walsh, included bad pizza and crude jokes. Not something he was interested in but, as captain, was forced to attend.

We'd only seen each other twice, and those were the days that we walked dogs.

I tried to convince myself that it was okay. The Back to School newsletter was nearly complete. I had my body paragraphs written and was just waiting for the kicker. Something big that would really take people's breaths away and make them boycott the whole game for good.

Only ten days left until the article was due, and only a few days left of our fake relationship contract.

Was there even something bigger to report on? I mean, this was just the Bayview High baseball team, not some drama show Mom liked to watch on TV. Maybe the kicker *was* the paying off of players.

Surprisingly, and even more distressing, I missed spending time with Walsh to the point that I just found myself wanting to see those blue eyes and hear that voice. We texted back and forth, witty conversations included, but it wasn't the same.

The clock on our relationship was ticking. By the time August rolled around, by the time school started, this would all be over. A memory.

The dread inside of me grew.

But, breaking the monotony of the past week, Walsh

called me Saturday morning after he finished up practice. "I've been thinking about it, and I really want you to come over," he said, chuckling a little. "I want you to meet my dad. He's great. Kind of like me, but his jokes aren't as funny."

I smiled faintly as Mr. Denton's terrier squatted down in the city boulevard. "Will your mom be there, too?"

Walsh had talked here and there about his dad, but hardly ever about his mom. His parents were still together, I knew that much, but she didn't come up in conversation often.

Walsh's voice lost its amused edge. "Yeah, she will be. So, can I pick you up at eight?"

"Eight?" I got out a plastic bag, flapping it against the wind. "Isn't that a little late?"

"My mom likes to eat dinner late, if that's all right." His voice was hesitant. "You don't have to come if you don't want to. I just want to see you."

I just want to see you. He must've still been around someone, trying to show off. The words made my breath hitch anyway, and I hated myself for it. Even though the Fourth of July and Walsh's sweet gesture was over a week ago, things never normalized. At least not for me and my stupid brain. All those sweet things he said burrowed their way into my head and heart, refusing to budge.

"No, eight is perfect."

"You sure? Because we can do something else. There's that mini-golf place in Ashville that I've been wanting to hit up. I play a mean game of mini-golf." Walsh paused. "Or if you need to work on your article, you can. I know your deadline is coming up."

Ten days. "No, this is perfect. I want to meet your parents, since you forced me to introduce you to mine."

"I don't remember such a thing," he teased. "I'll see you tonight. Wear your sweatpants and your grungiest t-shirt."

When we hung up, my mind was buzzing with anticipation and nervousness. Him wanting me to meet his parents felt strange—less impromptu than him meeting mine on the Fourth, more planned. Meditated. Sure, I'd met Janet on the fly, but he was inviting me over for *dinner*. Why did that feel so serious?

All I knew was that using him for the article felt wrong now—way, way wrong.

It felt like the deepest betrayal.

Convinced Walsh was being sarcastic about the sweatpants thing, I found my nicest pair of jeans in the bottom of my dresser, pairing it with a blue striped shirt. Since I'd braided my hair after my shower this morning, there was a wave clinging to the strands. Pretty, but not trying too hard. At least, I didn't think so.

I dug through the bottom of my closet to find my black sneakers, well-loved with a hole near the eyelets. That was grungy enough for him, right?

It was seven-forty-eight when I decided that pacing around my room didn't pass time quickly enough, so I headed downstairs. Halfway down the steps, I heard the telling sign of my parents' fighting: Mom's soap operas on high volume, trying to drown out the tension that hung like smoke in the air.

"We need to talk about it, Richard."

"I'm trying." Dad let out a sigh, and the image of him scrubbing his hand over his face the other night, his stifled cry, came to my mind. "I'm trying to talk to you. I *have* been."

"How?" Mom's voice wavered. "You're never home! You're always at the office. Don't blame me—blame that stupid job of yours."

Sinking down onto the steps, I pressed my head against the railing, feeling like a normal kid. Hiding around the corner, heart racing.

"Oh, please," Dad said back at her, voice cracking. "Make this my fault for working too hard. We were fine until you went and rented out that new studio by the bay. The one on River Street was perfectly fine!"

Mom said something low and under her breath, and I couldn't catch it.

"Well, then, I'm sorry, Amber." Dad's voice got closer, but I was too dazed to move. "I'm sorry I ever wanted to help you, help this family, help—Sophia?"

Dad looked at me through the posts of the railing, his back curving with the posture of a defeated man.

"Were you eavesdropping?"

Mom appeared over his shoulder, eyes widening a little bit. I tried not to look too closely, but I could still see the tears in her eyes. "Sophia."

"Oh, I'm sorry," I said emphatically, using my anger to deflect my hurt feelings. Not that they'd know the difference. "When you're yelling the house down, I thought it was okay to listen in."

Dad frowned. "We weren't yelling."

Right, because when I could hear their voices through the floorboards, that still counted as a whisper.

I briefly closed my eyes, wishing that this would disappear if I refused to look at the situation. "I should be used to it by now, don't you think? Living with parents who yell at each other and ignore their daughter."

I should've been used to it, but I wasn't.

"Sophia." I didn't have my eyes open, but I could hear the hurt in Mom's voice, broken and chopped.

The gear-grinding screech of bad brakes hinted that Walsh pulled into the driveway, ready to pick me up. Practically jumping down the stairs, I moved past Mom and Dad, making sure they couldn't see how close I was to tears. "I'm going to Walsh's."

"Sophia, wait," Dad called after me. "Let's just talk, okay? Just wait—"

I hauled open the front door and whirled around. They'd stopped about a foot from me, an ironically united front. "I'm still here," I told them slowly, my throat tight and pained, "even though it's easier to pretend that I'm not."

They were words that were better off unsaid, words that only did damage, and I watched as they did just that. Mom's face crumpled in on itself, a look of sheer pain flitting across her features, and Dad's frown broke into a defeated look. I so badly wanted this to be their *wake up* moment, the moment where they saw the error of their ways and everything would change. But hoping for that burned me in the past.

"Don't wait up," I told them, and I hate, hate, hated how my voice cracked. Without giving them a chance to respond, I pulled the door shut behind me.

I half expected them to open it back up and yell at me while I hurried down the porch steps, maybe even try to ground me again for talking back, but they didn't.

Walsh was already out of his car and in the process of shutting the door when he spotted me cutting across the yard. He frowned, removing his sunglasses. "Those are not sweatpants, Sophie."

"Get in the car," I told him with a voice that was thick and splintered, my hand shaking as I reached for the handle. "And drive."

Walsh didn't hesitate, didn't ask whether or not I was okay, didn't look at me with a question in his eyes. He simply replied, with unwavering speed, "You got it."

Seventeen

*W*alsh remained quiet as he pulled into the attached garage, effortlessly maneuvering it around the sports equipment that cluttered the space. He didn't ask me what happened and I didn't offer the information up. I couldn't talk about it—not yet. So we sat in silence.

His fingers drummed against the worn steering wheel with a restless energy, knee bobbing up and down.

I couldn't believe it. Walsh Hunter was actually *nervous*.

I'd taken enough deep breaths to get the tears to subside from my eyes, to get my voice back under control. But that didn't mean that the emotions were gone; pain and hurt were still sitting just underneath the surface, simmering. "Wow, I would've thought you'd have a guy that parks your cars for you."

Walsh glanced over at me, his eyes still shielded by darkened sunglasses, popping open his door. "We give him Saturdays off."

I watched him as he slid from the car, moving effortlessly,

like he was being filmed for a commercial, leaving me sitting incredulous.

Just before he shut the door, Walsh poked his head back inside. "I'm kidding. Come on, let's go inside."

The urge to hit him upside the head worked its way over me. *Brat.*

There was a small mudroom/hallway that connected the house to the garage, walls completely filled with windows. It was beautiful, of course, and way nicer than the main entrance of my house.

The idea of meeting his family was starting to sink in, delayed from my fight with my own parents. Walsh opened the glass door that led inside, stepping back to allow me to go first. Even as I passed, I could see his eyes darting around, not resting on a single place for too long. "Let's go see what Chef Hunter is cooking up for us tonight, shall we?"

The little hallway deposited us in the formal dining room, with a crystal glass table that could fit twelve people. Four plates were set out with polished silverware, looking like a fancy restaurant setting. I felt so out of my depth.

As soon as I stepped over the threshold, I caught a whiff of sauce and melted cheese, like a gourmet pizzeria or a high-end Italian restaurant. I almost stopped in my tracks, the smell so good that my mouth instantly started watering. "Whatever that is, it smells like heaven."

"It's baked ziti with a cheese sauce, paired with garlic knots and a Caesar salad." A man came out of the kitchen, stained apron covering his nice shirt. It had what looked like tomato sauce smeared across the front, and more questionable stains near the hem. "Or, at least, that's what the recipe I printed off the internet said."

The resemblance to Walsh was striking. Mr. Hunter's hair was a bit duller than Walsh's, still blond but streaked with gray, and almost the exact same length. The only thing different about the two of them were their eyes—Mr. Hunter's were brown and framed by glasses.

"You must be the young lady my son is so obsessed with," Walsh's dad said warmly. Walsh's eyes closed as his dad extended a hand, dirty with flour. Mr. Hunter's face broke into a sheepish expression. "Oops, sorry. I've been cooking all day in preparation for this. My social skills are rusty."

I shook his dirty hand anyway, smiling. "It smells absolutely amazing, Mr. Hunter."

"I know it's very clichéd, but please, call me Wes." His smile was almost identical to Walsh's real one, the one he gave people when he wasn't trying to impress. The one he most frequently gave to me. "Well, please. Come in. Walsh, can you go upstairs and find your mother? She's probably in her study."

Walsh rubbed his hand over my back. "I'll be right back."

Wes reached his clean hand out to me. "You can help me mix the dressing for the salad."

Though I'd been to Walsh's house before, I hadn't gotten the chance to go through the kitchen. And seeing it now—it was picture-perfect. White glossy cabinets reflected the pendant lights that hung over the large island, parked in the center of the space. Near the sink, there was a large picture window that overlooked the backyard, and in full view, I could see the cliff, the one I'd gone out to after Scott broke up with me. The one Walsh nearly catapulted himself over to rescue my journal.

Oh, my journal. The wound still felt fresh.

Wes filled the island and nearby countertops with dirty bowls, containers, and measuring equipment. He gave a nervous laugh at the sight of it, hands opening and closing over the mess. "A tornado came through here. I—I'm not a good cook. Or a cook in general. Janet usually does this kind of thing."

I walked over and grabbed a few dirty dishes, moving them from the workspace. "Where is Janet?"

"Oh, her friend was hosting an event and asked her to help cater over in Hallow. Convenient, right?"

"Maybe she doesn't like me," I teased.

"How could she not? You're the only friend Walsh has ever brought home to meet us, besides Zach. She was bummed to miss this."

So many things caught my attention. How much did Walsh say about me? And wait, what did Wes say? I was the only friend Walsh brought over to meet his family? Surely Wes couldn't have been serious. Walsh had tons of friends. Have seriously none of them met his parents before?

Before I had a chance to analyze Wes's words any further, a sharp bang came from upstairs, like a door slamming closed.

A moment later, Walsh appeared from the other end of the kitchen, face tense. "She wants to talk to you."

"Okay. Can you pull the garlic knots from the oven for me?"

Walsh looked at me as Wes slid from the room, reaching

for a pair of oven mitts hanging on the wall. "So, listen," he said slowly, quietly. Shakily. His teeth grazed his lip. "My mom...she's a bit of a trip."

"A trip to where?" I joked, not really sure what he meant.

"Crazytown." His chuckle sounded a bit too breathy to be genuine. He grabbed the cookie tray, nudging the finished serving pan of ziti over so he could set it on the stovetop. "Just don't let her get to you. She'll say some things. Really stupid things. She does that. She's amazing at that, actually."

Again, his teeth bit at his lower lip, a small movement that let me guess how stressed he was. But meeting his dad was a breeze—how bad could his mom be? I thought of my own mother, my own family. "I can handle intense parents."

I wished I would've been prepared for what happened next. I wished I could've warned my heart not to try and jump out of my chest. Because Walsh leaned forward and pressed his mouth to my forehead, my breath catching in my throat. Those lips made me forget, for the briefest moment, what I was doing. Because *ohmygosh* they were *on my skin*. Why were they on my skin?

And why did I never want them to move away?

My brain was a traitor, beautiful words whispering to my heart, meaningless nonsense. *He's kissing you and no one's around to witness it.*

"She's right behind me." Wes came back into the kitchen with a cheerful expression, but it almost looked forced. He glanced between us, making a guilty face. "Am I interrupting?"

Walsh curved his arm around my waist, pressing me into

his side. "I was telling her to eat in small bites in case the food is poisonous."

"It won't be. Well...I don't think."

"You're the girlfriend, huh?" a new voice said from behind us.

I shrugged out of Walsh's grip to turn around.

Walsh's mother wasn't at all like I expected. I admit, I'd been stereotypically expecting a tall woman with long blonde hair and proper, expensive clothing.

But she wasn't at all proper and prim and clean. She was petite, maybe five-foot-one. Her hair, sheared short into a rough bob, was jet black, locks jagged and tucked behind her ears as best as she could. Her sea-blue eyes were rimmed with red, with deep circles underneath. She tied her oversized shirt into a knot at her waist, resting on the waistband of torn up sweatpants.

There was a glassiness to her eyes when she met mine, and they couldn't focus on me perfectly. Her voice pitched high and pretty, though it totally didn't match her image. Or her words. "Does she speak?"

Walsh straightened, a muscle ticked along his jaw. "This is Sophia. Sophia, meet my mom, Penny."

Penny made a face at his words. "*Sophia*. Sounds very sophisticated."

The words were right at the tip of my tongue: *And Walsh doesn't?*

"Penny, love." Wes's voice was chipper, totally offsetting hers. "Come sit down. Dinner's done and just needs to be laid out."

She pulled away from the doorway, moving like a little

fairy as she edged past me, and I didn't miss the scent she carried with her—the stale scent of alcohol. I pretended like I didn't notice.

Walsh's eyes followed her, and I reached down to grab his hand, giving it a squeeze.

"Well, don't just stand around like a statue," Penny called, heading toward the dining room. "Wes can take care of the food. Isn't that right?"

Wes nodded, unwinding his apron.

"Why don't you help him, Walsh? I can get to know your new girl here." She turned and eyed me. The color there matched Walsh's, and it felt disarming to see. "Sophie?"

"*Sophia.*" Walsh's voice was firm. "She goes by Sophia. And I think Dad can handle it—"

"Sounds great," I cut him off, letting go of his hand and following after his mother when she moved into the next room. My eyes sought his, trying to tell him *it's okay.*

Penny's footsteps were slow and uneven, swaying ever so slightly with each step she took. She went immediately to a china cabinet set to the side of the room, withdrawing a bottle of stashed wine. The red liquid sloshed inside as she poured it into her wineglass, and not a single drop slipped out.

"So." She dragged the word through the air, moving to fill the wine glass next to her. "How'd you two meet? You and my boy."

I moved to sit across from her, careful not to let the chair cut along the floorboards. "We met at school."

After filling the two glasses, Penny slammed the wine bottle down with such force I was surprised that the table didn't crack, or even the bottle. Her nimble fingers snagged her wine glass, eyes never leaving the swirling liquid. "So you met *at school*. What, you do his homework for him? Help him pass calculus?"

Ha. I mean, there was that time he cheated off my test.

Wes hurried into the room holding a covered dish of the ziti, placing the pan in the middle of the table. His eyes noted the full wine glasses at the table, and he paused before turning to go grab the other dishes.

"Look at him, playing the perfect host," Penny said, sniffing her wine. "Walsh is a lot like his father. Always looking for the best in people." She tilted her head. "I haven't heard Walsh say anything about you."

I had to admit, in some kind of twisted way, she did remind me of my own mother and how she interacted with Dad. I couldn't help but smile a little at that. "I could say the same thing."

"I'm not his favorite person." Penny's eyebrows shot up and down, almost like saying *I wonder why*, and she ran her hand along her chin. "That boy has no appreciation for his mama."

Walsh walked in then, holding a bowl with a towel folded over it, and set it down next to the ziti. "What are you talking about?"

Penny gave a wide grimace of a smile. "How my son is just the hero of the needy."

He took a seat next to me and also took in the full glasses of wine. "I take care of you, don't I?"

Wes came in with the last bowl of salad, now missing the apron. "Look at me! I think Janet would be proud. I should take a picture and show her."

"It does look really good," I agreed, really wanting to dig into those garlic knots.

Wes walked around the table and took the salad tongs, gesturing them toward me. "Sophia, put your salad bowl up here."

He helped Penny next, who sat back in her chair and watched him with lazy eyes. She ran a hand through her chopped locks, finishing off her first glass of wine. "That's enough," she said, putting a hand up.

"Any for you, Walsh?"

He shook his head. "I'm not much of a salad eater; you know that."

Wes looked at me, explaining, "I keep trying to cure him of his hatred for greens, but he doesn't seem to appreciate it."

"Carbs do an athlete good. We burn right through salad."

We got through the first course with no issues. Penny had poured herself another glass of wine but let this one sit for longer. Wes made small talk as he dished out the ziti, the perfect host with the biggest portions. He'd asked me what my parents did for a living and the other routine questions: whether or not I had siblings, how long we lived in the area, what my plans were after high school.

"Sophia writes for the school newspaper," Walsh told his parents, cutting his ziti with the side of his fork. "She did an amazing article last year about the importance of recyclable straws and how they're amazing for the environment. She's working on an article now about baseball."

I fought the urge to close my eyes. It was bad enough his parents were subject to our fake dating lie, but now I had to involve them in the article? I was a bad person. "It's nothing."

"Nothing," Walsh scoffed. "She wants to be a journalist. In the fall, she's going to be interning at the *Bayview Blade*."

"Maybe. I mean, they pick one student from each school, so it's not guaranteed." None of it was guaranteed—not even my journalism program.

I took a bite of ziti, all the tastes mixing in my mouth. It was the first time I'd tasted a meal cooked with genuine enthusiasm—usually my mother would heat up frozen meals or my dad would order Chinese for dinner—and it made my mouth water for more. "This is so good, Mr. Hunter."

Wes's eyes lit up at the compliment. "I'm glad you think so! I'll have to save some for Janet so she can taste my success. And package a plate up so you can take it home, of course."

"Yeah," Walsh said. "Janet never would believe it otherwise."

"Does your dad do a lot of cooking, Sophia?"

"We alternate the cooking between the three of us," I told Wes. "But he's definitely better than my mom. She can even manage to ruin macaroni."

A bug of guilt crawled its way into my stomach when I thought about how I left my parents today, scuttling around at the idea of what my parents were doing now, but I shoved it down. Squished it with the bottom of my shoe.

Wes nodded sympathetically. "Well, I'd love to meet your parents one day."

I tried to imagine that scene, our parents interacting. Dad would've liked Wes—they were a bit alike, both putting off the businessman-type vibe—and I think Mom would've, too. With Wes's infectious grin, it was hard to believe otherwise. It actually wasn't too bad of an image.

Penny laughed, holding her hand in front of her mouth to try and stifle it. Wes looked at her levelly, wearing something in his expression. It looked sharp. "Food go down the wrong pipe, hon?"

"It's just that—" she got out, shaking her head, reaching for her glass. "Oh, this is just funny. Meeting her parents? Please." Penny drank the last liquid from glass number two, pushing her plate of ziti away from her. "I think this is silly. This whole thing is silly."

A frown etched into Wes's features, though his voice was level. "That's enough, Penny. Why don't you eat some more ziti? I followed the recipe that you found for me."

"And I don't care what you think," Walsh responded, almost as if his father hadn't spoken. "Unless it's about this amazing food."

"Of course you don't." Her reply came cold, covered in ice. Her words sounded a bit wild now, the carefulness of her enunciation lessened by the effects of the wine. "You haven't cared in a long time."

Wes looked at me from across the table, speaking to me over them. "Please, ignore them. Walsh. Enough."

"I used to," Walsh argued back, and it was the first time that I heard his voice shake. It was a small tremble, one that I never would've noticed before we'd gotten to know each other. But as he watched his mother, threw words back and forth, I could hear it plain as day. "I used to care."

"*Enough.*" Wes's voice cut firmly between them, trying to build a wall in the middle of the table. But he wasn't building it fast enough, frantically reaching for supplies that weren't there. "I mean it, you two."

Penny glanced at her husband for a mere moment, taking a second of deliberation before deciding that he wasn't worth listening to, and she looked back to Walsh. "I don't know why you're introducing Sophie to us if you don't care what we think."

"It's *Sophia*," Walsh corrected again, "and maybe I wanted you to meet her because she's important to me."

For some reason, I found myself reaching under the table again and touching his knee, wanting to defuse the situation. Why was he getting so passionate about defending me, anyway? Was he really pretending about our relationship to this extent, or was it just to argue further with his mother?

"She seems way out of your depth, Walsh."

"And at least she isn't a drunk," he said loudly, exasperated.

At those words, Wes slammed his fork down, causing the table to shake. It made both the wine and me jump.

And for a moment, it was eerily quiet. No one spoke. Penny's back stiffened as if a board had been tied to her shoulders, propping her up straight. Her eyes got this faraway look, glazing over as her mind wandered.

Penny looked from Walsh to Wes, then down to her plate. I didn't know her well enough at all to read the expression that crossed over her features, barely there, blink-and-it's-gone. It reminded me of Walsh's hidden expressions, moments before he covered his feelings with a mask of a smile.

"I'm not hungry, as it turns out." She looked at me before she left the room, her eyes scanning me. In that moment, I could finally see the resemblance between her and Walsh.

She placed her hands on the table, ready to push to her feet. "I'm going back to my room."

As Penny abruptly stood, she upset the placemat that her wineglass rested on, sending it crashing to the floor.

The wineglass splintered with a scream onto the hardwood floor, the shattering ring echoing in the silence that followed. I felt Walsh stiffen beside me, but I couldn't look at him. My gaze was latched onto Penny, my heart pinching tight for her.

Her cheeks darkened with each second of quiet that ticked by before finally looking to me. The strength of her voice was gone, leaving it quivering as if she were about to cry. "Hope our introduction was impressive, Sophia."

Without another word, Penny hurried from the room.

After breaking from the state of shock, Wes grabbed his napkin and started cleaning up the mess. I moved to help him, my chair making a harsh noise as I pushed it back against the floor. With a napkin full of glass shards, he quickly said, "Oh, Sophia, please. I would feel even worse if you helped."

Awkwardly, I sat back in my seat.

"We had a guest and I wanted to make this special," Wes spoke in a low voice, speaking to Walsh but not looking up. "*Nice* for Sophia. You couldn't have held back, Walsh?"

Walsh looked at his father incredulously. "Are you kidding? She was insulting Sophia! What'd you want me to do, *agree* with her?"

"No, but you didn't have to provoke her. You didn't have to keep at it. You *know* she's like that when she's...well, when she's—"

"Been drinking? That's no excuse, Dad!"

Wes rose from the floor, clutching his now stained fabric napkin, filled with glass shards. "I know." He set the pile down upon the tablecloth, scrambling to put a garlic knot on his own plate and Penny's, scooping just a little bit more ziti to his pile to keep what was underneath warm. And then, he picked up both of the plates. "Sophia, it was very lovely having you in our home. Despite the evening, I hope you come back. I'm sorry we couldn't get through the dinner, but there should be some of Janet's cookie dough in the fridge if you two want dessert."

As soon as his father walked from the room, Walsh pushed his plate back, slumping into his chair and rubbing his hands over his face. Strained silence made the atmosphere in the room tense, almost tangible.

"Walsh," I began, but he let out a harsh breath.

"Please, I just..." Walsh didn't look at me but at his plate of food. "I'm sorry. I hoped she would be on her best behavior. She said—Dad said she'd try, but she never does."

"It's okay," I told him truthfully, mirroring the way he slouched in his seat. A sharp pain clenched in my stomach at the idea of him hurting, looking at where his cheeks were pink with embarrassment. Through the hair falling in my eyes, I met his gaze. "Are you okay?"

"What do you mean?"

"I mean about the stuff she was saying."

Walsh sat up, turning that incredulous look on me now. "Of course I'm not okay! She was awful to you—"

"She wasn't trying to hurt *me*."

His lashes kissed his cheeks once, twice. "Uh, were you present for that conversation?"

If the air weren't so tense, I might've smiled. "She wasn't lashing out at me, Walsh. She was lashing out at *you*."

Saying things to provoke him, to rile him up. It turned into a game. I couldn't imagine why, though. Why she'd been so cruel and antagonistic towards him. But I could recognize it in the way my own parents interacted with each other sometimes. When they were angry with each other, they used the other's weakness. Exploited it.

Walsh didn't respond right away, allowing my words to hang in the air, marinating for a moment. The way he looked at me made me wish, not for the first time, that I owned a direct line to his thoughts. Focused gaze, tightly-pressed lips. What could he possibly be thinking about, looking at me like that?

"She knew how important this was to me," he said after a moment.

"But *why*? Why was this so important?" What was I missing?

Walsh smiled instead of answering, but it gave me no comfort. It was his fake smile, smooth and practiced. Corners tight, teeth hidden, lips curled slightly. Half lifted, half arrogant, and totally faked. It eclipsed all his emotions, only showing the ones he knew looked good on him. "Let's get out of here."

I tried to brush it off, to swallow his subject change. Walsh sat so close, but he still felt a million miles away. "And go where? It's nine o'clock."

"So?" He stood up, grabbing onto my hands to try and

drag me up with him. "It's not even that dark yet. We need to do something other than baking cookies."

I put all my weight into leaning back against the dining room chair. "I was looking forward to cookies."

"Trust me," Walsh said, finally managing me to my feet. "You'll like this more."

eighteen

"*This* is better than cookies? You're insane."

Since Walsh lived out in the boonies, it took us thirty minutes to get to the place deemed better than cookies: the baseball field.

Yeah. He took me away from cookies to *practice*. Jerk.

Being team captain, Walsh had a key to the equipment shed that sat behind the bleachers, and he made a beeline for it when we arrived. The sun was setting quickly, but that didn't sway him from trying to pull some gigantic machine from the equipment shed to the pitcher's mound. And it didn't sway him from making me help.

"It's a ball launcher," Walsh said through a grunted breath, dragging his end to the field. He managed to hold his corner higher than me, taking most of the weight. "It pitches the baseballs so you can hit them."

"You took me away from cookies just so you could practice your batting?" I huffed, trying to not trip over an uneven patch of grass as I held up the other end of the machine. I had made an awful decision to wear jeans—even though the sun was almost set, humidity still clung to the air, and I was dying of heatstroke. Dying of heatstroke and about to be crushed by a stupid ball launcher. "You officially suck."

Walsh wasn't even dressed to practice, wearing his usual button-down shirt and signature boat shoes. His ghost of a laugh carried a musical tune that ran right through me, easing the tension out of me. "Not me. *You.*"

Once we set it up at a safe distance from home plate, Walsh handed me a metal baseball bat and helmet that was *way* too big. It smelled like head-sweat and sulfur.

"I don't know why you're dolling me up," I said as he positioned me in front of the home plate, a straight eyeshot at the machine. The metal monster looked ready to charge me and swallow me whole. Or impale me. "Because I am *so* not doing this. This is me, not participating."

The noise echoed as Walsh knocked his knuckles against the helmet. "You'll do great, Sophie."

I loosely swung the bat in the air, and Walsh ducked out of reach just in time, my aim nearly knocking him in the shoulder. "And what if I end up being better than you?"

He walked backward toward the pitching machine, grinning the whole way. "Then you can take my spot. Be team captain."

"I'll settle with co-captain."

"So generous."

I swung the bat again, my grip firmer this time, and a muscle in my arm screamed. Walsh fiddled with the machine for a moment, then loaded it with a few baseballs. "I'm putting on the lowest setting so it won't come at you fast."

I mock saluted him, knocking the helmet against my forehead. I guess I could humor him just a little bit. The machine came to life with a whir, and I squeezed the metal bat in my fists, trying to channel my inner baseball star.

If I'd blinked, I would've totally missed it. A ball whipped its way past me, the air fizzing as it zoomed by my head, and I jumped back.

"Walsh!" The machine threw another ball, shooting past me and smacking into the chain-link fence. "*That's* slow? Are you sure this thing isn't broken?"

Walsh—the little jerk—was *laughing*, leaning his hands to his knees and bending over. Even from the distance between us, I could hear him try and gasp in a breath, and it took him a moment to get his words out. "Okay," he said breathlessly. "Maybe that wasn't the best idea."

Even though all I wanted moments ago was to see him laugh like this, I now wanted to throw the baseball bat at him.

I whipped the helmet off, knowing my hair had to be terribly tousled. "Well, I'm glad nearly concussing me with a baseball makes you feel better."

Walsh turned the machine off. He held up a finger to me, jogging back in the direction of the baseball shed. "I have a better idea. One sec!"

"I don't trust your ideas!" I shouted back, my voice echoing in the night. "My ideas are way better than yours. They involve cookies!"

The landscape shielded the sinking sun, only a faint flame now that darkness moved in. This moment reminded me of the Fourth of July, sitting in my backyard with Walsh. As soon as the fireworks ended, I made Walsh deflate the float and head home. My parents could've been home any minute, and though they seemed to like Walsh enough, I hadn't wanted to take any chances.

Or, at least, that's what I told myself in the moment. But I also really needed space from him and his googly eyes, and sending him packing was the only way for me to breathe. For some reason, I found myself back in that headspace, my lungs unsure how to draw in a normal breath of air.

Walsh came back from the shed clutching a tee, the kind kids used in little league. He must've seen the look on my face. "No, you'll love this. This way you have total control."

"I'll look like an idiot. An idiot who doesn't know how to play baseball."

Walsh set the tee up over the plate, reaching down to scoop up a baseball. Brushing it against his shirt, he gingerly set it on the tee. "Have you ever played baseball before?"

"Unless you count that week we were required to play in gym class, no."

"Then this is perfect for you." Walsh took the helmet from my fingertips, placing it gently back on my head. His sea-depth eyes met mine under the lip, and he carefully adjusted how it sat. "This is how everyone starts out playing. They use a tee. And it's great because you'll hit it every time. Well, probably."

I swung the bat up from the ground, and Walsh edged back just in time to avoid being knocked under the chin. Oops. "I'm only doing this to cheer you up," I told him, moving to stand by home plate, "because I *really* think this is silly."

"Five bucks says you'll really like it."

"Doubtful." I hardly enjoyed *watching* baseball, and even that took effort.

Tightening my grip, I took a step to the tee and swung, the bat heavier now that I put power behind my blow, and the ball cracked loudly against the metal. It went left sharply, bouncing along the white line sprayed into the grass. The bat vibrated under my hand, and I lost my footing as I tumbled off-balance.

Walsh grabbed my arm to steady me, excitement already evident in his gaze. "Okay, we need to work on your stance. But that was a good start!"

I laughed at the shot of happiness and reached back to touch my shoulder as it throbbed. "I thought it was great."

Walsh moved to grab another baseball, setting it on the tee. "It *was* great. But, here, put your feet—" Walsh bent down and grabbed my sneaker, sliding it against the dirt. He pushed it out wider than my hip and then moved the other foot, so it was parallel to that leg, spreading them wide. "—like this. And put a bit more weight into the back foot, but when you swing—"

"Move onto the front foot?"

"Lightly." He got to his feet, brushing his hands on his pants. "It'll make sure you aren't tossed off balance when you put your little muscles into that swing."

"Please!" I scoffed, shoving him. "*Little muscles.* These bad boys are bigger than yours."

"Just swing." Walsh stepped back, far from reach. "And remember to put your front foot—"

"Light pressure. Yeah, yeah." I fell into position, a bit

more confident even though I was at little league level. "Eat
this, stupid baseball."

When I swung, the difference was obvious. This time
when my bat connected, the ball seemed to straighten out
more than before, going farther. It touched the ground almost
to third base, rolling past.

I whirled to face Walsh while grinning like a fool, holding
up the bat like it was a trophy. "Oh, my gosh! Did you see
that?"

Walsh's smile was so wide when he saw my genuine
delight, and my heart jumped at the sight of it, so vivid in the
dying light. In his hand sat another baseball. "Now do it
again."

We spent what seemed like hours switching turns, practicing our hits underneath the fading sun and soon the
glowing stars. Walsh even got me to step back and under-
hand-pitch a few baseballs to him, laughing like an idiot
when he "accidentally" missed. The more we joked around,
the more relaxed he became, his swings becoming wilder and
more theatrical.

I dropped the bat after I swung to put my hands around
my mouth, calling, "And it's out of here! Sophia Wallace hits
a home run! The crowd goes wild!" My voice echoed in the
field, loud. I mimicked an audience screaming an *ahh, ahh*
sound.

"I can't find the ball," Walsh called, wandering around.
"It's too dark; I can't see." And then all at once, Walsh
collapsed in the grass by the dugout, falling easily, landing
hard. I almost called out to him before he began to laugh.

Laugh and laugh, the sound plastered with happiness. "The sky is so pretty, Sophie. Come look."

"You're quitting? Walsh Hunter is a quitter?" I got closer, hovering over his lying form, hands on my hips. "Man, Scott's going to steal that captain spot from you if you don't put in enough effort."

Walsh's eyes shifted from the endless sky to me, but his gaze didn't change. He still looked at me like I held all the stars in my arms, brilliant and aglow.

Gosh, he shouldn't look at me like that, I found myself thinking, my lungs taking a shaking breath. *It's not fair.*

In the blink of an eye, Walsh reached upward and grasped my wrist, pulling me down to the grass beside him.

The ground was firm when I landed, but the laugh pulled from me was loud. We were close enough that I could feel Walsh's shoulder brushing mine, hear his breath pull in and push out. I didn't know why watching him breathe was so mesmerizing in that moment, but I became distracted.

For a long, silent moment, I stared at him and he stared at the sky, both of us mesmerized, both of us lost in thought. I wished I could be like him, caught up in the beauty of the night. His eyes, which had been glazed over with an excited sort of humor, bled into a more haunted look the longer we held onto our words. And the longer we were quiet, the harder the idea of talking became.

I tugged off the baseball helmet so I could see him better. "Are you going to play baseball after high school?" I asked, trying to fill the silence, wanting to hear his voice again.

"Don't know yet," he responded, not looking at me. His

fingers were splayed at his side. "There's a county league for Fenton—you've heard of it?"

I hadn't.

"It's kind of like your newspaper internship, just for baseball. They pick a few seniors from each school in the county to play for their league, especially if they want to go on to play for college." Walsh raised a shoulder. "They take their picks in the fall and it's hard to get into. That's why Coach drills us so hard about winning, why our team is so competitive. Last year, they only took one senior from Bayview."

"So that's what you want to do?" I asked, anxiety curling in my chest. "Play for that team next summer?"

"The county league has a leg-up for players to get on college teams. I have a better shot at it if we win the last game —it's the championship game in the entire county. It's us against Greenville."

I swallowed hard. *Guilt,* my brain whispered. *What you're feeling is guilt.* "But do you *want* to do that?"

"I love baseball," Walsh told me, voice almost sounding mechanical. I couldn't figure out why. "It would be a great opportunity."

I stared up at the stars as his words sunk in. Playing for the county league—that would be a great opportunity for him. He said that it'd be a good step if he wanted to play on a college team. But if I published my article and word got back to the county team about Bayview's cheating habits, they wouldn't want a player from a corrupt team. They wouldn't want Walsh, captain of that team, no matter how great his batting average was.

I blinked fast, feeling like I was fighting back tears, but

my eyes were dry. My brain was right—this *was* guilt, and it ate my insides, weighed down my body, turned my spine into lead.

Walsh turned his head to look at me, his hair rucking up against the grass, his bright blue-green eyes cutting into mine. "Are you cold, Sophie?"

Goosebumps dotted my skin, but I wasn't cold. The night stole my voice when I spoke, words coming in a whisper, "Why do you call me that?"

"It's your name."

"My name is *Sophia*. An *a*, not an *e*. I've corrected you how many times? And yet you didn't want your mom calling me that."

Walsh fell quiet for a moment, but I couldn't look at him. I was too afraid he'd see how desperately I wanted to know his answer or be able to sense how quickly my heart was beating. Rapid succession, *boom, boom, boom*, like stars falling from the sky and landing around us.

"I don't know." His voice was as rough as the gravel in the diamond. "I think I like calling you something no one else calls you. It makes it feel like I know you in a way no one else does, which sounds strange. It makes it feel...makes *this* feel real."

I closed my eyes, squeezed them tight. Real. It was a fake word between us, a lie.

"Do you want me to stop?"

"No." The word came out of my mouth before I even realized it, and there was no taking it back. I wasn't even sure I wanted to. "It's okay."

Walsh lifted his hand to run a single finger down the

length of my cheek, tracing to my jawline. His fingerprint drew a tiny shock along my skin, making the goosebumps worse. "I needed this, you know. Thank you."

I tried to go back to the joy I'd been experiencing moments ago, pushing all thoughts of baseball and articles and guilt down. "*I* needed chocolate chip cookies, but I'm here for you."

The bright moonlight shined down on his face, reflecting off his cheeks and igniting his hair. He'd never looked so beautiful. "You're a good girlfriend." He lifted his eyebrows. "A good fake one."

"Who would've thought?"

Lying next to him in the scratchy grass of the baseball field, I thought about how I would never do this for Scott. I wouldn't have helped him haul out the pitching machine, I wouldn't have let him put a helmet on me and make me swing at a baseball. I don't know *why* I wouldn't have; I just knew that there would've been no way.

But for Walsh, without question.

"I don't have a good relationship with my parents," I admitted quietly, suddenly, the words pulled out of me before I could think twice. He'd shared something personal with me—his mother—and now it was my turn. "I think they just want to give me space, but they gave me too much. We used to bake together, have movie nights. Now, I'm just... lonely. And they're getting a divorce—did I tell you that? I don't think I did." I took a breath, closing my eyes. "I thought I was glad about it, thought things would change, but now...I don't know."

The memory of the way I'd left my parents this afternoon

came back to me, but this time, I wasn't angry. The pain I'd been stuffing down rose to the surface, making everything in my body feel like it was tearing apart, nerve by nerve.

"What kind of kid is happy that their parents are splitting up?" I asked him. "That makes me the worst kind of daughter ever. But they just bicker all the time, like they're teenagers or an old couple who argue just to keep things interesting. And then I'm there, a little girl in a dollhouse, waiting to be picked up and played with. And that's..." My breathlessness caught up to me, my voice catching abruptly, like I'd swallowed a bug or something embarrassingly close to crying. "...sad."

I wanted to just sink into the rough grass, blend into the soil and disappear beneath the earth. A few crickets chirped in the distance, filling the silence between Walsh and me.

Like the brush of the breeze, gentle and tender, Walsh's fingertips ghosted across my cheekbone again. I fought a shiver at the touch. When his knee shifted against my leg, he kept it there, a comforting pressure.

I couldn't believe I was being so emotional in front of him. I couldn't even imagine what Scott would've said if he were here instead. Or if he would've even listened. "I didn't mean to make this about me."

Walsh's voice was as soft as whisper, raspy, like he'd been silent for years. "I love listening to you talk."

"Even though I'm a selfish spoiled brat? The one who is so consumed by her own joy in her parents' separation?"

"Look at me, Sophia."

It was because he said my name right—my stupid name—that I listened to him. Compelled, I turned my head and blinked my eyes open. All the crickets stopped chirping, and my heart stopped beating, and Walsh's leg touching mine became a much more prominent pressure.

Walsh's eyes were liquid pools of night, reflecting the moon, focused solely on me. "You aren't selfish for wanting to be in a home, not an empty house. Where your parents check up on you, bake cookies, have movie nights. Where you're loved, appreciated, and cared for. It's not selfish for wanting things to be different. It's your parents who are selfish. Not building up their relationship instead of tearing it down. Not building *you* up."

Walsh knew exactly what to say, when to say it. It was like he was taught from a young age what exactly to say, to win over someone with a bat of his eye and the glint of his teeth. If a class existed for it, I needed to take it.

"It's hard to remember my mom sober." His words were almost as breathless as my own, being dragged from the pits of his soul. "It used to be an occasional thing, her drinking and getting drunk. And now—it feels like it's been so long since it's been her. *Really* her. I stay up at night until I hear her go to bed. Until I know she's not wandering around the house, drunk—won't fall down the stairs or something stupid." Walsh's jaw tightened as he stared up at the stars. A rough exhale ripped from his lungs, voice dropping low. "You're not selfish for wishing things were different, Sophie. If you were, I'd be selfish too."

The wind shifted across the baseball diamond and found us lying in the grass. Tears tugged at the corners of my eyes, but I desperately tried to blink them away. Walsh's words, they unlocked something inside of me, opened part of my heart that made me feel warm and cold at the same time.

Walsh's eyes darkened to the color of the deepest part of the ocean as they traced my face, and it was then that I realized how close his face was to mine. Mere inches separated us, and I couldn't stop thinking about it. Any other thoughts dried up instantly, my body warming to a sharp degree.

Walsh sat up, pushing to his feet. He stretched a hand down. "We should get the equipment put away before it gets too dark to see."

I rocked my head back in disappointment, allowing him to pull me up. But I didn't stop moving, not until my arms were wrapped around his neck. It took him by surprise, and he rocked back a bit by the weight of my sneak attack. I hung on, needing him to ground me, the firmness of his shoulders and the strength of his arms as they swept around me.

Breathing in his scent, I felt like I was getting lost.

I think I already am.

"Thank you for listening," I whispered into his shoulder.

"I told you I'd always listen."

Walsh's hand made a gentle, smooth gesture against my back, lulling, hypnotic. I could've stayed in that moment all night, under the glimmer set of stars and in the warm arms of Walsh Hunter. It was our first hug, first embrace. I could feel his heart beating through the fabric of his shirt—or was that my heartbeat, so rushed that it made me feel slightly dizzy? Because he was so close, and he smelled so good, and he was so *warm*. I don't remember Scott ever being this warm.

I wanted closer, and I didn't know what that meant.

Walsh's voice sounded like it was inside my head, a whispery breath. "Sophie, I..." He trailed off, pulling back slightly.

In this moment, this quiet moment where the air became

more charged than before, I found myself leaning closer, straining to hear what he might say next. "What?"

I watched his lips, waiting for them to part, to watch the way they moved when he spoke. And I knew—I just knew—I'd remember the way they curved forever. Because his words were soft, almost drowned out by the ringing in my ears.

"I really, really want to kiss you."

Every part of my body froze solid, all of the air vanishing from my lungs. My stomach literally dropped to my toes, a sharp, rushing warmth flying through my veins. His hand holding mine was the only thing keeping me from falling away along with it.

They weren't words I'd ever thought I'd hear him say, least of all to me. Not when there were no people around. This was the opposite of fake dating, and yet...

I wanted it *so badly*, but something in me hesitated. I knew that my feelings for him—unwise, unbidden, reckless and insane—were real. I couldn't deny the way he made me feel. With just a simple look, he made me feel more myself than I ever had with Scott. Where I hid myself away for Scott, Walsh made me feel like I could spread my wings and fly.

But I couldn't do it. Not without telling him about the article. I couldn't let him kiss me, couldn't open my heart to him and let him have the key, and still dig around behind his back.

If I kissed him, allowed myself to feel what I'd been trying to lock away, and he rejected me?

The effects would be devastating.

"You can't kiss me." I pulled away from his embrace,

tearing myself from his gentle fingertips and seductive mouth in a desperate movement. "We...we made a rule."

It was a rush of words, but they held their effect. This beautiful night started to crack to pieces, and I could practically see the shards falling to the grass.

Walsh scrubbed a hand across his mouth, quickly, roughly, as if he could wipe away his words, my words, all of it. "Right, yeah, the rule," he said, voice sounding quite normal. "I'm sorry, I just—I forgot about our rule."

I felt like I was choking. *Oh, shoot me. Universe, just shoot me.* "It's fine, really. I just...I just don't think...I mean..."

"The stars got me a little carried away." When he smiled, I found my heart skipping a beat. He smiled like there was nothing wrong, like I *hadn't* just rejected his kiss. Like this moment *wasn't* that big of a deal, even though it was to me. The only sign that something was out of the ordinary was that he wouldn't look me in the eye. "We should, uh, put this stuff away. I'll grab the machine and the bat if you want to get the tee and the baseballs?"

Walsh didn't wait for me to answer, turning to gather the equipment. I wanted to join him, but his words were still echoing in my head. I wasn't sure I'd ever forget the feeling before I spoke. The feeling of falling, hoping arms would catch me before I hit the ground, but totally unsure of who would catch me. Or if anyone would.

However, the silence also brought other thoughts. He'd said that the stars carried him away. Did he only want to kiss me because of the mood? Did he only *want* to? Or was he like me, *needing* to?

I guess I'd never know.

nineteen

I was expecting a grand welcoming when I got home, expecting my parents to be camped out, ready to shoot me down with loud words. My parents weren't ones to let things fizzle out, and after our fight and leaving them like that, I was expecting confrontation of epic proportions.

Except my parents weren't camped out. When Walsh dropped me off at the curb with an awkward, quiet goodbye, no parental figure was in sight.

I let myself in, locking the door behind me. The house was deadly silent. My parents hardly ever went to bed this early on a Saturday night, but their door was shut, and all the lights in the house were off.

For a long moment, I just stood in the hallway, breathing in the quiet.

"Sophia?"

I jumped at the sound of Dad's voice, seeing him move into the hall. His hair was tousled, his t-shirt rumpled. He blinked, bleary-eyed.

For a moment, I entertained the idea that he'd been waiting up for me, wanting to make sure I got home safely. But surely that wasn't the case. "Hey, Dad."

We faced off, staring each other down. "How was Walsh's?"

"Good," I said cautiously. I wasn't sure what sort of ground we stood on with each other, not since I ran out earlier. "I met his parents."

"How are they?"

"Interesting." I glanced around the quiet house. "Where's Mom?"

"She's sleeping. She wasn't feeling well." Dad moved across the hall from me and leaned into the railing of the stairs. He looked tired, bone-weary, exhaustion lines creasing his features and making him look ghostlike. "I like him, you know. Walsh. He seems like a great young man. You should bring him around more."

It felt wrong, wrong, wrong to be lying to Dad, which didn't make much sense. We'd just finished an outing of lying to Walsh's parents, we'd been faking in front of his friends for weeks. Why lying to my dad was different, I had no clue. "He's really busy with baseball, Dad."

"We should go to one of his games sometime."

I frowned. "You never went to any of Scott's games."

Dad's response was simple, easy. "I didn't like Scott."

Of course. I couldn't keep from rolling my eyes, heading for the staircase. "I'm going to bed."

"We *are* trying, Sophia," Dad murmured, forcing me to pause. "I want to do what's right by you and your mother."

A wave of tiredness rolled through me, and I bent down

to untie my shoes, needing to look at something other than him. "This is what you two do," I said sharply, bitterly, all the compound hurt and anger hitting me at once. "You argue and you tear down your relationship instead of building it up. Doing your best isn't giving up—it's putting your all in."

Dad raised his hand to knock my words right out of the air. "You're too young. It's hard to understand."

"I'm seventeen, Dad. You may have missed a few birthdays, but I'm not a kid anymore."

Dad's eyes widened at my words, and I couldn't help but wonder if he was shocked at me being seventeen or my other comment. I was in this room, this narrow hallway, with this man who looked at me so intensely, but I never felt more alone, more unheard.

We exchanged a long look with each other before I turned and headed up the stairs, leaving him in the hallway and taking my lonely thoughts with me.

I wasn't sure when I'd started to become a teenage girl who thought idiotically about boys. Especially the teenage girl who thought idiotically about Walsh Hunter. I didn't want to be "that girl," but Walsh's words played constantly, like a never-ending tune that I didn't want to get out of my head.

I really, really want to kiss you.

My skin still remembered the faint trace of his fingertips, his breath tickling my hair as his lean body pressed close.

My response had touched the tip of my tongue, frantic and relieved. *I really, really want you to kiss me.*

Why, oh *why* had I pushed him away? To torture myself,

surely. I should've just kissed him and suffered the consequences. They couldn't have been worse than now, lying in
my bed, replaying the near-moment over and over.

And it was *real*. He couldn't fake that look he gave me.
No one was around to witness it. There was nothing to prove
and no one to prove anything to. He couldn't have been
faking it.

Right?

I threw all my confusion into my writing, trying to
distract myself from the reality that was boggling my brain.
My pen scrambled to keep up with the words as they shot
through my head.

"*'Each spring, the locals are riled up with the smell of
freshly popped popcorn, the smell of fresh grass in the air, and
the clack of a ball hitting the metal bat. Bayview High is no
different,*'" I read aloud as I wrote, trying to get my pen to
move faster. "*'Every school has a sport that brings people
together. Some schools prefer football, but at Bayview High,
they like to play ball. And they're good at it. Four straight years
of county championship trophies in a glass case seem to prove
so, but what if the players praised like gods are more sinful
than angelic?*'"

I heard a car door slam shut outside, immediately
throwing my not-so-fantastic-writing to a halt. My alarm
clock only read just after eleven, and no one should've
been home that early on a Monday. After waiting a few
seconds, I heard the front door open and promptly slam
shut.

Abandoning my pencil and notebook, I tip-toed toward
my bedroom door and peeked down the steps. Nothing. I

didn't even hear anyone, not Mom's footsteps or Dad's breathing.

I sidestepped Shiba on the staircase, gripping the railing and peering into the living room. It was also empty, as was the kitchen. The lights were off, the TV was off, no sign of life existed.

The door to the bathroom hung slightly ajar, the lights glowing from the crack between the wood and the jamb. A shuffling noise came from within, and I slid off the last step, walking into the doorway.

My mom leaned against the toilet, her light hair falling out of her bun, her workout shirt darkened with moisture. The stinging scent of vomit clung to the air, and I pressed a hand to my nose. "Mom, are you okay?"

A lame question, because she clearly wasn't, but she lifted a hand from the porcelain. "I'm fine, I'm fine." She fought to keep her voice even and made a noise in the back of her throat.

I took a slight step back, afraid she'd throw up again. I didn't think I could handle *hearing* her get sick.

"Do you want me to call Dad?" I asked, wavering in the doorway, strangely embarrassed for witnessing my own mother curled against the bathroom floor.

But she evidently wasn't as concerned as me, and she stretched up to pull the handle of the toilet. "No, no need, I'm feeling much better." Mom glanced up at me. Her mascara was smudged like a black eye under her lashes, her cheeks red and eyes swollen. "I've just been queasy for the past few days."

I thought about the day she came home from work sick and napped the rest of the day. "Have you seen a doctor?"

"It's just stress," she assured me, holding a hand out. "Help me up."

I got her to her feet, surprised by how weak her grip was. "Are you going back to the studio?"

Mom gave me a soft smile, like she enjoyed how concerned I was. She patted at her ratty bun, trying to smooth it down. "No, I canceled my afternoon sessions. I'm going to brush my teeth," she told me, moving to close the door between us. "Do you want to make some lunch? Maybe sandwiches?"

Even though a moment like this would've normally bothered me, her asking for something when I hardly asked for anything, I hurried to agree.

I padded my way to the kitchen, the buzzing of Mom's electric toothbrush buzzing growing fainter and fainter. I forced myself to think of other things. Not my article and definitely not Walsh.

So I thought of my parents. Like two pieces of fabric, Mom a wild floral pattern and Dad a thick piece of flannel. At one point, they fit together like puzzle pieces, perfect, sewed to perfection, but the more times they ripped apart, the less perfect it was each time, the stitches failing to hold.

For the first time in a long time, I wondered what it was like when Mom and Dad were young. Whether or not their love story was a spark of a connection or a slow burn. Did they quickly embrace the other's strange quirks? Was it work that drove them apart? Dad's late nights, Mom's early mornings?

I'd grown up wondering if my love story was going to be like theirs. An echo of their music, a cover of their song. Doomed to relive their mistakes. I always wondered if it was inescapable, especially when I was with Scott. Resigned to only be around people who barely needed me.

And even now, I still wondered. But for the first time ever, when I thought about my love story, I didn't feel discouraged. I actually felt...hopeful.

After sandwiches, I left Mom on the couch and retreated back to my room, falling on my bed. Lying there, I was barely breathing as I waited for a message from Walsh. But there was nothing. Not a single text, and not even a missed call.

Why wouldn't he call? After two days, wouldn't he have sent *something*? Wasn't he thinking the same thing I was, constantly replaying Saturday night in his head?

Oh gosh, what if he wasn't? What if that whole ordeal really meant nothing to him?

I let my phone fall to my chest, staring at the ceiling. A crack ran through the plaster near the light fixture, in the shape of a wiggly lightning bolt. I needed to grab a book and read, get my mind off everything, and just lose myself in the words. I was good at that. That was something I *knew*, not boys and ex-boyfriends and fake boyfriends and prospective boyfriends. That was all uncharted territory to me.

But the idea of Walsh not thinking twice about Saturday night left a tight pressure in my throat, like something was being pulled taut inside of me.

Was this all a game to him? Walsh? And Saturday night, just another game?

Ugh, I needed to just call him. Edith would tell me to call him. She'd tell me to stop being a chicken and just call him. Edith—

My phone vibrated, and it about flew out of my hand because I jerked it up so fast that my skin zapped alive. I answered it without even looking at the ID. "Hello?

"Hearing your voice sounds so weird!" Edith's chipper voice rang out from the other line, much too high pitch for my low mood. "It's been too long. How hath the dark ages been, young one?"

I groaned, disappointed.

"Sheesh, that bad? Oh, wait. You thought I was lover boy, didn't you?" Edith clicked her tongue, a loud noise even through the cell phone. "Figures. Can I come in?"

"Come in where?"

"Into your house, silly. Your front door isn't locked, but your mom's car is home early for a Monday morning, and I wanted to make sure the warden wouldn't get mad or anything."

I could almost see her cupping one hand over her eyes, peering into one of the windows, chatting away. "Yeah, I'm in my room. Just be quiet. Mom's sleeping downstairs."

The front door creaked open over the phone, and I heard the quiet *click* as she shut it. "I feel like this is a boss level in one of my brother's video games. *Do not wake the mother unit.*" I could hear her on the stairs. "Don't roll your eyes at me."

"I didn't."

"Please. I could practically *hear* those things rolling through the phone."

And then she poked her head into my bedroom, smiling, her cell still pressed to her ear. I disconnected the call first, setting it back on my nightstand. "Hey."

She stepped fully into the room, eyeing my attire. "Nice shorts."

They were pink with little green cactuses on them, and little green pom-poms dangling from the hem. They *were* nice. "What's up?"

Edith quietly shut the door behind her, making a face. "Why does your house smell like my little brother's upchuck?"

Ugh. "Mom came home from work sick."

Edith sat down at my desk chair, spinning in it. Her two pigtail braids swung out as she picked up speed. "She's not pregnant, is she?"

"Don't even joke."

She tipped her head back and chuckled a little. "So, guess who called me yesterday."

"Miss America?"

"Ha. No. A certain Mr. Perfect."

Hang on a second. I blinked at her, unsure I heard right. "*Walsh* called *you*?"

She couldn't hide her smile. "He got my number from Zach, I guess. Asked if I heard from you. When I said no, he got all quiet and broody."

Okay, hold up. Why did Walsh call my *best friend* instead of me? Here I am stressing about him not calling me, not thinking about me, and he's out hitting up *Edith*? "And?"

"And then he said he had to go. Then he hung up." She shook her head. "Not the best phone skills, that one. But you'd have been proud. I didn't even squeal once at the fact that Walsh Hunter called *me*. I can feel my popularity status building."

Sometimes I forgot that Edith used to think that Walsh was cute—used to rant and rave about him from time to time. Those days seemed like forever ago.

"Did you go on your date with Zach?"

"It wasn't a date," she told me quickly. Edith pulled her legs into the chair, crisscrossing them and leaning back with a hand to her chest. "Just friends. It was fun."

"But—"

"*Just friends,*" she cut me off, gaze serious. "For now, anyway. It's easier that way. That way I can focus on volleyball, and he can focus on baseball."

I couldn't help but smile a little at how flustered she was getting. "Ed, that's a load of crap, you know that? Just because you're saying it again doesn't make it true."

"I didn't ask him about paying off other teammates. It just felt weird. You get that, right?"

I nodded, not blaming her. If the situation had been reversed, I'm not sure I'd have asked either.

"How's your article going?"

The wind in my sails died down a little bit because her expression wasn't a positive one. She wasn't asking because she cared—she was asking because she wanted to try and convince me to stop writing it. "Can we not go into this again?"

"Sooner or later, you'll change your mind. Sophia, I just

don't want you to throw away a good thing. You and Walsh are perfect for each other."

Hearing that made something inside me dance. "Edith, it's—"

"Fake? I know." Finally, thankfully, Edith rose from the desk chair and moved to sit next to me. She nudged me with her shoulder. "You two are still cute. I wouldn't have guessed it in a billion years, because you two are just so different."

I stared at her hands, her nail polish an oddly comforting sight, and I rested my head on her shoulder. My cheeks warmed, and that was because talking about him made me like this. Warm. Happy. "I think..." I chuckled a little bit, the noise just whispering out of me. "I think I like him."

"You *like* him? Like, *like* him, like him?"

With my eyes squeezed shut and my arms wrapped around her to prevent her from escaping, I told her everything. I told her about the Fourth of July, about how he set up the inflatable flamingo so we could sit and watch the fireworks. I told her about how he wanted me to meet his parents, and then going to the baseball field afterward. *I really, really want to kiss you.*

In all those times, I could still imagine the blue hue of his eyes, the intensity of his gaze, the curve of his mouth.

Throughout all of it, Edith stayed silent, letting me cling to her like a child holding onto her mother. Saying everything out loud, hearing the words and hearing the history through Walsh and me in these past weeks, everything became real. Those quiet touches, looks, jokes. It was like speaking the words made our story real, even if the story was only fake. Even if I was the only one who actually felt anything real.

"It's not real," I told her, "but I want it to be. Is that bad?"

She threaded her small fingers through my hair, gently twisting the red strands around. "What does Walsh want?"

"I haven't talked to him. Not about my...feelings." Gosh, I couldn't even imagine. Couldn't imagine being so brave to even mention it to him.

"Have you told him about your article?"

I picked at my pom-poms. My silence was answer enough for her.

"Sophia," Edith said slowly, sounding the word out. "If you like Walsh—truly, deeply like him—you can't use him for information for your article. You have to stop."

I knew that she was right. The dread and guilt that lived in my stomach every single time Walsh and I grew closer was really my subconscious telling me the truth, too. But it was too late now. There was no time to write something else. Today marked exactly one week until the article was due to Mrs. Gao, and on my calendar, the date was labeled "*Do or Die.*"

Dramatic, I know. But I had no other ideas. Nothing.

I shifted next to her, staring up at my ceiling. We were quiet for a moment, the hum of the central air the only sound. "What if he doesn't like me back?"

She snorted. "Now you're sounding like a high school girl. Not trying to dig up secrets, not so focused on academics. A typical girl pining over a guy. I love it."

I swatted at her, unable to keep away a small smile. "Maybe I just need to pick a day and tell him. After their championship game."

"Procrastinator."

"No, think about it. I don't want him stressing about it and *losing*, right?" *Yeah, that's a good excuse. Great job, Sophia.*

Edith looked skeptical but chuckled after a moment. "You're a chicken. But fine, you wait. In the meantime, you need to stop the article."

She was right. I totally was a chicken. Too much of a chicken to tell her that the article was already finished, written on my notebook and waiting to be transferred onto my computer. Too chicken to tell her that I didn't have any other choice.

Too chicken to tell her, too chicken to tell Walsh.

And that rock in my stomach was never going to go away.

twenty

ednesday morning, I decided to go for a walk. None of my dogs needed the extra exercise, but I figured I could just take the time to just think. However, the humidity clung to me like a second skin. The mid-July breeze made my skin feel sticky, pulling at the hair from my ponytail and making it stick to the back of my neck. It was *hot*. Like, *get-me-a-popsicle-so-I-can-stick-it-down-my-shirt* hot. I was about to collapse from heatstroke.

Monday night, after Dad came home to find Mom on the couch, things were...strange. Beyond strange. He'd made us dinner even though it was Mom's night to cook. When I came down to get my plate, I found them cuddled up on the couch together, Dad smoothing his hand down Mom's back, brushing his fingers along her hairline. Seeing them like that together startled me, but it was even weirder when I couldn't remember the last time I'd seen them cuddle.

The general store came into view, and I made a beeline for it. The grocery store was a beautiful beacon of hope—hope of water bottles. As the electric doors slid open, a burst of beautiful, blessed air-conditioned air hit me, instantly chilling the sweat dampening my skin. The water bottles were a beacon of relief in the back, and I immediately made my way to them. I took the candy aisle on the way to the register and ended up plucking a caramel crunch bar from the shelf.

I set both items onto the counter, fishing for the money in my pocket.

"Hey, Sophia."

My eyes lifted at the sound of my name, surprised. Scott came around the side of the counter and into view, greased back hair, stained polo and all. He was wearing a bad smile that somewhat resembled Walsh's but wasn't nearly as pretty. Seeing him startled me for a quick second, mostly because I'd forgotten that he worked here.

"Can't get enough?"

"Of water, no. Of you—" I cut myself off, refusing to say anything that he could assume as flirting. "I'm out for a walk."

"I can see that," Scott said, ringing up my candy bar. He eyed the collar of my shirt. "Unless you were doused with water, that was my guess."

I picked at my shirt, holding it away from my sticky skin. "Why aren't you at practice?" I asked, fishing for something to say. The baseball team had early practices every morning up until Thursday, the team's final game of the baseball season, to get everyone prepared. "Shouldn't you be at the ballfield?"

Scott gestured to his polo. "Couldn't get off work. Coach isn't happy with me."

"Careful," I warned, watching as he scanned the water bottle. "Or you'll be benched for the big game."

He punched a button, and the cash register beeped. "Four twenty-two, and yeah, bet Walsh would love that."

I handed over a five-dollar bill, inwardly groaning at the road this conversation went down. What did Walsh really want, anyway? *I really, really want to kiss you.* Kissing me couldn't have been what he wanted all the time. Perhaps in that one moment, under the lights and stars and while we were high on our laughter, our bodies close together. But now, if he were to walk through the automatic doors, would he still feel the same?

"I want to say that I'm sorry." Scott lifted his head, still holding my change. "For the Fourth. And the party at Ryan's. I acted...well, I acted like a jerk."

"Yeah, you did." He'd acted like more than a jerk, but I wasn't going to push it.

Scott leaned his forearms on the countertop, running a hand over his greasy hair. "I'd like to try and get together again, to talk. About us."

I wanted to tell him that those days were over, long gone, but I knew "no, thanks" wouldn't have gone over well. Instead, I simply said, "Maybe." *But probably* not. Snatching up my candy bar and bottled water, I stepped away. I needed to get out before I said something stupid or he said something stupid, both entirely plausible. "Well, I'd better get going. I've got to get my heart rate back up."

"Looking at me doesn't do it for you anymore?"

I ignored that, trying hard not to roll my eyes. My legs felt shaky as they led me to the door, but I turned around just before it automatically slid open, something catching in my brain. Before I stopped to think about it, I drew in a breath. "Can I ask you a question?"

Scott leaned his elbow onto the countertop. "Sure."

"I heard a rumor that I'm not sure is true," I said, walking back to the counter, turning the water bottle over in my hands. It was starting to sweat, water beading along the plastic. "About the baseball team."

"What kind of rumor?"

Now or never. "That you guys are paying off the other teams."

It was risky, so stupidly risky, to say that to him. To confront him like that. But if I asked Walsh this question, I didn't know how he'd react. And quite honestly, I didn't *want* to ask him, didn't want to use our relationship to my advantage like this. Asking Scott felt like fair game, but that could totally backfire.

Scott's dark eyes remained steady as he watched me, his poker face impeccable. "Where'd you hear that?"

"A source."

"You sounded like a real hard-hitting journalist there, Sophia," Scott chuckled, leaning both elbows onto the counter now, propping up his head. "Why do you care what the baseball team does?"

I lifted a shoulder, trying to feign a nonchalance genuine enough to convince him. "Just curious, is all. Walsh mentioned that Coach pushed you guys to win, so I didn't know if you went to those kind of measures or not."

"So why don't you ask Walsh?"

I gave him a gooey smile. "You've always been honest with me."

Scott's lips turned up into a smile, but it wasn't a pleasant one. It was one that made my insides feel *sick*, like my intestines came down with a bout of the flu. It was an unpredictable one, one I couldn't quite decipher.

"We don't pay off the other team," Scott said finally, pulling away from the countertop. "We choose certain players who would take the cash, and they throw the game."

The way he spoke, so casual, so careless, made my eyes widen. *We choose certain players.* "Throw the game, like—"

"Make a bad hit, miss an easy catch, run too slow, that kind of thing. Works every time to keep us on top."

For a long moment, I felt the need to pinch myself, because no way was he being so forthcoming. The water bottle was slick in my grasp, the coldness of it the only thing grounding me. "Why are you telling me all this?" I was too shocked to keep myself from asking. "This seems like the kind of thing you'd keep to yourself."

"Like you said—I'm always honest with you." Scott winked at me, and my insides flinched in response. "And I know you can keep a secret."

The door slid open, and a young child with two ponytails bounced in, followed by a girl about my age. I stepped back from the counter, almost embarrassed to be seen so close to Scott. "Thanks," I said quickly, retreating to the doors. "I'll—uh—bye."

"See you later, Sophia," he called after me, that strange humor still clinging to his voice.

Walking back into the awful summer heat after being in

there was torture, and if it weren't Scott working, I might've tried to hide in one of the refrigerators or something.

But holy cow. So check getting proof for *that* off the list. I seriously hadn't expected him to be so nonchalant about it all. I didn't expect him to trust me so much with that kind of information. It almost made me feel sick thinking about putting it into the article now. But then again, *why* did he trust me with that information? He wouldn't have told me any of that before when we were still together. Why now?

I took a long drink from my water, the coldness coursing down my throat and settling in my stomach. It did little to chase away the dirty emotion, but it did help cool me down. The candy bar, though, I'd save for later.

On impulse, I pulled my cell out of my pocket, scrolling through the contacts until I found the name I was looking for. I drafted a new text.

Miss you.

There. That was normal enough. Not confronting, not overwhelming. Normal. No smiley-faces, no exclamation points. After reading it a thousand times, I pressed send.

Stupidity became my friend the second it went through. When baseball practice got out, that text would be waiting for him. What would he think when he saw it? Would he smile or would he cringe? Ugh, what if he thought it was *stupid*?

We still hadn't talked really since our kiss since he'd been so busy. And truth be told, I *did* miss him. But I wasn't sure where Saturday night left us.

My phone beeped in my hand, and it was Walsh calling,

and I nearly jumped a mile. "Hi!" I said overenthusiastically, cringing. *Try again.* "H-Hey, Walsh, what's up?"

"I miss you, too." Walsh's voice came immediately and cheerful, almost cut-out by the people talking in the background. People of the male variety. "I'm sorry that I've been a little AWOL lately—things have been kind of crazy at the house."

Oh, so you haven't been dodging me after our almost-kiss? "That's okay," I said faintly, reaching up and brushing a hand over my damp brow. I forced myself to walk in the other direction, toward my house and away from the baseball field. "How's practice?"

"Hot. Like we're playing baseball in hell."

I imagined Walsh in his baseball uniform, sweaty, laughing. Putting his back into swinging at the ball, his muscles tightening. My insides twisted, and my steps faltered. "What are you doing? After practice, I mean."

"Dad's made today a dedicated housework day," he sighed. "But tomorrow though, after practice, we could get slushies. If you want to. I know you can never turn down a good slushy."

I tried to hide the enthusiasm in my voice with a blasé tone. "That sounds amazing."

Yep, nailed it.

Walsh could totally hear my desperation, but instead of calling me out for it, he just laughed. "I'll see you tomorrow, then."

"See you then," I confirmed, and then forced myself to hang up before I said something really stupid, like *I miss your beautiful face,* or *I love you.* Jeez, *definitely* not *I love you.* I'd rather die of heatstroke.

Knowing that my fake-boyfriend was busy, and that my best friend was busy, and I was sitting at home with nothing to do —it sucked. I'd been staring at my journal for what felt like hours now, reading the words I'd written with a detached sort of feeling. I should've been *excited* about the paragraphs I'd formed, thrilled at how close I was.

Less than a week and I'd be turning this article into Mrs. Gao so she could present it to the school board. Less than a week to learn my fate—whether I'd be in the running for that internship or if I'd be sitting at home every night after school, staring at the ceiling.

Walsh wouldn't know of the article right away—surely it would take time for word to get around—but it would be following soon enough.

I stared at the last line of my article for a long moment. *It's no secret that Bayview is a play-ball kind of school, but with all these secrets coming to light, I'm left to wonder—and surely you are wondering, too, dear reader—if the Bayview High School baseball team just swung their third and final strike.*

I ripped my glasses from my nose, pressing my fingers to my weary eyes.

There was a knock on my bedroom door around seven-thirty, and my dad let himself in. "Hey, kiddo. Dinner's ready."

I set down my pen gratefully, pushing my glasses up.

"What are we having?"

"Your mother was craving tacos tonight."

My nose scrunched up.

"Don't worry. I made the vegetable casserole that you like too." My expression—which morphed into utter shock from the fact he remembered one of my favorite meals—must have been comical, because he laughed. "We're sitting at the table tonight."

I stared at his retreating figure, pushing to my feet. "Were you abducted by aliens?"

"Yep," Dad called. "And they're coming for you next. It's better to have a full stomach."

When we got downstairs, Mom was already sitting at the table, smiling down at her cuticles. Her eyes lifted when I hopped off the last step, smiling with teeth. It shocked me more than just a little. "Hi, honey. Come sit down."

I approached slowly to my seat, trying to trick my mind into thinking that this was a normal, everyday occurrence. It didn't believe me. Probably because Mom called me *honey*. "Why are we eating at the table tonight?"

Dad carried a plate full of hard taco shells over from the countertop, rattling with every step of his. In his other hand was the veggie casserole, steaming. "A change of pace," Dad said, setting the plates down and sliding behind Mom to sit. As he passed, I noticed that his fingertips traced her shoulders faintly, and she leaned into the touch.

I immediately braced myself, picking up my knife and fork like they were my weapons in battle.

"Actually..." Mom slapped her palms together, making a loud *pop*. "We have some good news."

"Good news?" I echoed, skeptical. I wasn't sure what really classified as good news to them anymore, and I was worried to find out. But Mom's face held enough of a glow that my heart couldn't help but beat a little faster.

Dad caught my eye as he doled out a portion of my veggie casserole. "So, did you know that your mother's friend, Mariana, is a licensed therapist?"

I looked between them. "Uh, no, I didn't know that."

"I spoke with her over the Fourth," Mom said, smiling wider, "about everything. Things with you, things with your father, and she talked us into it."

"Talked you into *what*, exactly?"

Dad reached over and placed his hand on Mom's, squeezing her fingers. "We're no longer getting a divorce. We've decided to start therapy."

It took several moments for his words to actually register in my brain. *Therapy.* The word didn't make sense at first. They actually signed up for therapy? Like, couple's therapy? Despite their struggles over the years—they'd never done that before.

I was blinking fast, as if fast blinking would somehow make all this *normal.* "You're going to Mariana for therapy?"

"Oh, no," Mom said. "That would be a conflict of interest. But she gave us a great referral. We've been going for the past week."

"She did help us realize, though, that we've been too absent. And I know grounding you was a bit *too* much, but we'll find our balance soon." He dipped his chin a little, staring me straight into my eye. "We're sorry."

Mom reached for my hand across the table, across the

food, and slid my hand into hers. Her eyes filled, rapidly, a dam about to burst. "We love you—love this family—enough to fight for us."

A big part of me just wanted to laugh. Laugh at the absurdity of this moment, how cheesy it could've seemed. But there was something so *genuine* about this. It didn't feel like some theatrical performance, didn't feel fake or forced. It felt...real.

And jeez, maybe that's because I wanted to believe it so bad—wanted to accept their words so easily.

The strange feeling that started to well in my chest, I realized in that moment, was pure and utter *relief.* The old pain of being a silent player in this family was finally going to be resolved. Finally, *finally* going how they were supposed to. We'd go back to the way things were, or something close. I'd finally have my parents back.

Things were going to go back to the way they were. They were going to *try.* Finally, we were really going to be a family again.

"I love you guys, too." They were words I couldn't remember the last time I'd told them. They were words that were a new morning, night turning into day, and I finally woke from my bad dream.

And then we were all crying over tacos and veggie casserole, holding hands like we were going to start praying, and I couldn't remember a time I'd been so happy. I couldn't remember a time where we all held hands, all wore smiles lighting our faces.

I couldn't remember a time when I felt so *light.*

. . .

My mom and I curled up together after dinner, Shiba resting along the arm of the couch. Dad already retired into his room after watching a whole chick-flick with us. He'd claimed the romance made him sleepy, and Mom laughed. On that couch, I was a kid again, soothed by her mother's voice and lulled by her touch. I couldn't remember the last time we'd binge-watched movies like this together, curled up and happy.

When the clock chimed eleven o'clock and another romance movie was about to come on, Mom stretched, absently touching her stomach. "Oh, sweetie, I don't know if I can make it through another."

"Me neither," I said, even though I was still energized from our conversation. "Thank you, Mom. For this." I gestured at the TV screen.

She turned to me, her eyes shining. Her smile was wobbly. "Oh, Sophia, we should have done this a while ago. We haven't done much right. I never realized how much you were hurting in all this. We wanted to give you space to grow up, but it was too much."

No kidding. I pulled the hem of the afghan over our legs. "Can I ask you a question?"

"Sure."

"Was it hard to stop thinking about yourself? Changing your mindset and not being so..." I trailed off, knowing that self-centered would've sounded bad.

Mom pushed a lock of hair behind her ear, clearing her throat. "When the incentive is better than being selfish, I found that it wasn't so hard. One of the first things Dr. Lively taught us was how to stop the situation before it grew destructive. So if there is a point where I put my needs and wants above anyone else's, I need to stop and see how the situation is unfolding."

It felt strange to hear Mom speak like that, self-aware and determined. It made me want to talk to her about everything. About Scott, about Walsh, about the article, about the internship. I wanted to let it all fall out there, hear what she had to say on any of it. But if I told her about my article, what would she say? Would she think it was a good idea or be like Edith and try to talk me out of it?

So instead, I asked, "What made you two think about therapy, anyway?"

"Oh." Mom's voice was soft, and the tears that were in her eyes a moment ago vanished with her own look of excitement. It ignited her whole face, making her look so young in the dim light as whatever thought in her head built. "We didn't tell you."

Another spasm of apprehension went through me, but less cautious this time. "Tell me what?"

"Oh, dinner got so emotional, and it completely left my mind—"

"What did?" I asked again.

"—which is silly if you think about it, the idea that I could actually *forget*."

I frowned a little. "*Mom*. What did you forget?"

If I could've frozen this moment in time, I totally would've. Slammed my finger on the pause button, never allowing this scene to develop further. Mom's fingertips curved protectively over her stomach, the wedding band on her finger winking mischievously at me. "I'm pregnant."

The words did.

Not.

Compute.

Several beats passed, and it still didn't register.

I blinked. "What?"

"I'm pregnant." Her excited expression hadn't dimmed yet, hadn't lost an inch of its glimmer.

"No, you're not."

Her eyebrows slammed down, effectively cracking her excitement. "Uh, yes, I am."

"No," I reiterated slowly, like trying to get the words through to a child. "You're not."

She shifted her position, tucking her ankles underneath her and leaning closer. "Sophia, I am. I have all the symptoms. Morning sickness, weight gain, cravings—"

"That doesn't mean you're pregnant."

"I went to the doctor, Sophia. They confirmed it."

They confirmed it. So she made an appointment, and they did an ultrasound, and there was...a baby. In my mother. *Right at this very moment.*

The urge to laugh hit me, but no sound came out. A *baby* literally a *baby*—was growing in my mother's stomach. Had been there for some time now, if I really stopped to think about all the times she'd been sick these past few weeks.

Dear God, I hoped no one thought to secretly videotape my reaction, because the longer Mom stared at me, the more I felt like the world had been ripped out from underneath my feet, and I was falling.

And I knew now that no matter what people said, I was about to hit the ground. Hard.

I saw this moment like a picture in a book, reading the

little description underneath. *A mother speaks the joys of new human life whilst the daughter, sitting beside her, is about to start screaming.*

It all became so horrifyingly clear. My parents weren't making up for *me*. Well, not entirely. No, it was for *him*. Or her. The baby that was butting its way into our messed up lives.

That was what was happening: they were back to their cycle of playing house.

It was never about being better parents for me.

It was about being better parents for the *baby*.

Shiba meowed as I got to my feet, my head spinning around and around like a top, nearing the edge of a table. And I was about to fall off the edge.

"Sophia—" Mom tried to reach out for me, her hand only finding air. "Honey, please listen."

But I was already dashing for the staircase, my socked feet slipping on the wooden floor, throat so, so tight. I stumbled as I took the steps three at a time, propelling myself with the handrail. My skin itched and stung, like I'd been bitten by a thousand mosquitoes.

I shut myself in my bedroom, leaning against the door and squeezing my eyes shut. It was a stupid soap opera. I was trapped in a stupid TV show where it all revolved around death or new life, breakups or hookups. There was no being normal, having normal parents. No normal relationship with normal boys.

I wanted to scream and scream and scream at the top of my lungs and never stop.

twenty-One

*I*t was official.

I was a complete stalker.

But standing in the middle of Walsh Hunter's yard a little after midnight sounded weirder than it actually was. Probably. At least, that's what I kept telling myself.

I should've just called him. I should've swallowed my stupid pride and asked him what he was doing. Saved myself the embarrassment of staring up at his dark house like a freaking serial killer. And it totally didn't help that the sky was seriously about to crack open, the thunderstorm looming threatening any second. It just made my presence in the dark creepier.

This was a bad idea. On so many levels, just a bad idea.

Granted, I hadn't set out to do this. Pedaling away from my house in a frantic fervor, Walsh Hunter's house wasn't my destination. I didn't really have one. Desperation fueled me—desperation to just *get away*. And I found myself here.

But now that I *was* here, clutching the handlebars of my

bike for dear life, was it wrong that I still wanted to see him? Just to be with him. To feel his arms wrap around me in a way we'd only been once before, hear his voice in my ear telling me everything would be okay. And I would believe it because it was *him*.

The collection of windows on his house only held shadows, a vast difference from that night of the party, when someone had turned on every single light on the premises.

"Sophia?"

In a rush of sensation, I felt my stomach drop swiftly to my toes, the air *whooshing* from my lungs.

Walsh wore long blue pajama pants, a black, loose-fitting t-shirt, and sported his normal mussed hair. His eyes, though, were alert, as if he'd been awake for hours. As if he'd never gone to sleep.

And when those eyes met mine, those beautiful, beautiful eyes, his eyebrows came together, like he couldn't comprehend as to why I'd be here at this time of night.

Breathe, Sophia. Breathe.

"You tripped the motion sensor in the driveway," he said, stepping out onto the porch. "The thing lets out a sound in the house like a doorbell."

Ah, awesome. So he knew I was out here. Or, well, not *me*, but someone. He knew *someone* was being creepy.

Standing in the middle of his lawn, still propping up my bike, I felt insanely shy. Like, *hide-me-under-a-rock* shy. Like, *is-there-a-way-to-disappear-into-the-ground* shy. I wanted to ask him what he was still doing up, but my brain was caught on *him* and how he said my *name*. "Hey."

Walsh started down the steps in his bare feet. "Are you okay? It's, like, one in the morning."

Did I say *shy*? No, I believe the correct term would be *embarrassed*. Insanely embarrassed.

"I'm *great*," I said with way too much enthusiasm, sounding like I was attending cheerleading tryouts. "Seriously. Just out for a little...bike ride."

He didn't quite look like he believed me, and I couldn't quite blame him. "I refer to my previous statement."

I tried for humor. "I wanted to be the first one there when the library opened."

"Sounds like you." He smiled a little bit, but it did nothing to overshadow the concern that was so clear on his face, in his gaze. "What's really going on, Sophia?"

His soft-spoken question chased away any further chance of humor, carrying across the yard. My throat burned, and I swallowed hard. I hadn't been able to let out any tears at home, and not even on the long bike ride over here, but in that moment, I wanted to cry. Maybe it was because my emotional threshold reached its limit or because Walsh was looking at me with his eyes so full of concern that it cracked my heart apart.

The wind, thankfully, was on my side. Icy air coming off the ocean kept my watery eyes from overflowing. "Can I come inside?"

Walsh and I stood about four feet apart in a faceoff, him just off the edge of his front porch and me still clutching the handlebars. His hesitation had me bolstering myself for a rejection. It was one in the morning—why *would* he invite me in?

And yet here I was, asking him to do just that.

And yet there he was, about to say— "We have to be quiet. Janet's sleeping on the couch. She fell asleep and I didn't want to wake her."

Everything inside me lurched again, in a way that wasn't necessarily uncomfortable. *He's actually inviting me in.*

As gingerly as I could, trying to hide my shaking hands, I set my bike down and made my way over to Walsh. Five fingers were outstretched to me, and I took them, his hand warm, calloused in all the places I remembered.

Once we crossed the threshold, Walsh didn't give me a chance to take my sandals off, so they *clack-clacked* on the staircase, despite me trying to tip-toe. As we climbed higher, I could see a little bundle on the sofa, graying hair against a dark pillow.

Potent adrenaline shot through my veins, sending my pulse into high gear. He was taking me to his bedroom. For some reason, the idea of it made me want to simultaneously dig my heels in and go with him. Going to his bedroom felt personal, intimate, a real line that this fake relationship shouldn't cross.

But at the same time, I almost felt eager to jump over it.

Walsh pushed open a door, and my eyes immediately went to a queen-sized bed pushed in the corner, with silky navy sheets that were rumpled, as if he'd just rolled from bed. Looking at it made my cheeks flush.

It was a relatively clean room; no clothes littered the floor except for a pair of wadded up jeans. A desk sat along the far wall with a picture frame sitting on its surface.

For a moment, neither one of us moved. Walsh still stood

with his hand on the doorknob, and I was standing just over the doorway into his room, looking around. I could feel his watchful gaze on me, wary, like he wasn't sure what I was about to do.

Honestly, I didn't know either.

"So, are you getting excited for the final game?" I asked him, feeling horribly awkward with the uncomfortable silence in the air. His unmade bed called my name—pillows fluffed and blankets ruffled. I couldn't help but picture him tossing and turning in it, trying to get comfortable. "You haven't really talked about it much."

"I can't wait," Walsh replied, but there wasn't any enthusiasm in his voice to back up his words.

"Don't do that," I said.

"Do what?"

"Lie." I fell down on the top of his bed, falling back until the back of my head touched the mattress. It was how he was on my bed, lying back to stare at the ceiling. "You can tell me anything, you know. If you're not excited about the game, you can be honest with me."

I heard Walsh draw in a breath like he was about to say something, but the words didn't come. Even without looking at him, I knew he'd be wearing his mask. The one he shrugged on when he wanted to conceal emotion. More than anything, I wanted him to take it off.

Two breaths passed before he tried again. "Why are you here, Sophie?"

Ah, of course. Dodging the subject. For now, I'd let him.

"I wanted to see you." There. The words were out there, spoken to the ceiling, spoken to the universe. "I know we said we'd see each other tomorrow, but I...I wanted to see you now."

"Why? Did something happen?"

It was such a loaded question, and I could've unleashed everything onto him. Staring up at his ceiling, I could've told him everything. I wanted to. Jeez, I wanted to tell him everything—everything with my parents, with the article.

But I was a total chicken. "You have a nice bed, Walsh," I told him instead, stretching out my limbs. His bed *was* comfortable. His sheets were soft on my exposed skin, and I ran my fingertips over the wrinkles. "Feels super expensive. I bet it's nice to sleep on."

"Sophia."

I finally sat up, unable to avoid it any longer. "My mom's pregnant."

The words sounded harsh in the air. Ugly. Awful. Walsh's silence felt so loud. Louder than the buzzing in my head.

And then Walsh took a step closer to me, running a hand along the back of his neck. "I—I don't even know what to say, Sophia. I thought your parents were getting a divorce."

I shrugged again. The bed jostled as he sat down beside me, my attention drawing from the boring ceiling to his features. His hair was sticking up ever so slightly, golden locks silky and soft-looking. I wanted to push my fingers through it. "They were. Not anymore."

"Because now they're having a baby?" Walsh frowned when I nodded, reaching down and tracing his finger one of my hands that rested on his sheets. "How do you feel about that?"

"It sucks. It doesn't matter." I pulled a move from the Walsh playbook, and I wanted to pat myself on the back. Dodging conversations, avoiding it as much as possible, was his thing, and I was totally changing that subject. "How are *your* parents? You said you did housework today."

"We were supposed to, but...plans changed." With his free hand, Walsh tucked a stray piece of hair from my bun behind my ear, his eyes and body exceedingly gentle and warm. I could snuggle up and sleep in that warmth. I could live in that warmth, could stay here forever. "They ended up going somewhere. That's why Janet's here."

I knew I needed to ask him what changed, where they went, but I couldn't think beyond his touch grazing my skin. *Brain, he's just touching my cheek, and barely at that... You need to focus.*

His thumb brushed further along my cheekbone, feather-light and warm. The touch had me holding my breath, afraid to move and startle it away. It unlocked something inside of me, some place in my heart, and the words started to flow untended.

"I don't want to be like my parents, Walsh." The words came out strangled, like they had to be dredged up from deep inside me. It cracked me apart to say it, to admit that fear. Tears made my throat burn and tighten. "Always fighting, always playing games. Trapped in a ceaseless loop of pain and drama."

An endless soap opera with shouting and yelling and crying and kissing. That wasn't love. That was insanity.

I didn't want to be like them, but maybe I already was. I mean, I was playing a game. I was fake-dating Walsh Hunter in efforts to build up my article. I was focusing on my own selfish dreams even though it was ruining someone else's. A wash of horror coasted over me, following in realization's footsteps, leaving me shivering.

Walsh lifted his leg up on the bed to face me fully, body leaning towards mine. "Sophia Vanessa Wallace, you aren't like your parents."

He didn't know. He didn't know how I was, not truly.

But I wanted him to. I wanted Walsh to know how I was, how I could be, just in the way I wanted to know him. Every thought, every desire, every dream. I wanted to know it all, and even though it was a terrifying thought, I wanted him to know all of me too.

In that breath of a moment, I realized how close we were, how close his mouth was to mine, and all those other dark thoughts escaped into the corner of my mind.

I touched my fingertip to the scar on his cheek, bumping over the slight pale divot in his skin. I wondered if he could hear my quick beating heart, could see how I barely breathed.

The Fourth of July did me in, and I fell for him, lost in the universe that was—*is*—Walsh Hunter. Stupid inflatable flamingos and blue-raspberry slushies ruined everything. It ruined the prospects of walking away from this fake dating thing with a written article and my heart intact, with a journalism program and a clean conscience. All of that went down the drain and for the first time ever, I allowed the treacherous thought into my brain.

What if I scrapped the article? What if I made this real?

And then Saturday night, with his mouth so close to mine, his words echoing in my head ever since.

"What's going through that head of yours?" Walsh's eyes were dark, darker than they usually were, pupils seeming to swallow the blue. My fingertip traced down from his scar to his jawline, causing him to draw in a shallow breath. "Sophie?"

With my eyes on his jaw, I didn't even think—not a single thought. "I really want to kiss you."

I refused to look up and meet Walsh's gaze—*refused*. But I watched as his mouth parted ever so slightly at my confession, felt when his hand reached over and touched the side of my knee. A tempting touch, coming as close as he could. "I thought you made a rule."

I was losing heartbeats, misplacing them in the fog in my mind. Half of my brain was telling me to stop, the other half begging me not to. A mild pain gnawed at my chest—the longer I held back, the worse the pain became. "I know," I whispered back, all of the butterflies in my stomach taking flight at once.

And when I leaned in to kiss him, his mouth met mine halfway.

Walsh's lips—oh, his lips were as soft as I'd always imagined, a different kind of thrill running through my veins. Warmth spread through me, starting from where Walsh's mouth touched mine and moving down to where his hand brushed my knee.

He's kissing me back. He's kissing me back. Walsh Hunter is kissing me back.

And then that hand moved. One, two, ten fingers touched my waist with gentle pressure, pulling me flush against him. Not even a centimeter existed between us; the air was absent between our bodies. It made my thoughts even foggier, my own fingers delving into the soft hair at the back of his head.

And it was this ginormous breath of fresh air into my lungs, clean and pure and right. The fog of despair in my head was starting to clear the more his scent and taste infiltrated my senses, filling my brain with a different sort of haze.

Kissing Scott had never been like this, like I was on fire, in the middle of a firework, about to explode. If this was what kissing was like—true kissing, with pure abandon and no hesitation—I knew I'd missed out on this entirely. Those absolutely rare times when Scott kissed me, they were hesitant or domineering, him trying to brand me as his with his mouth. But with Walsh, it was a mutual sort of fire that existed between us, and I loved every moment of it.

My teeth grazed Walsh's bottom lip, and the low noise he made in his throat had every single thought in my head scattering. His lean body moved over top of me, positioned so he maneuvered his weight off of me. The soft fabric of his pajama pants brushed against my bare legs, the silky sheets embracing my arms. I couldn't keep up with each emotion that flew through me: desire, happiness, relief. *More, more, more.*

Walsh's mouth brushed my lips, my jawline, where my pulse beat in my neck and then back to my lips. It was a path of fire and ice, there and back, and I never wanted him to stop. My hair tugged as Walsh threaded his fingers through it, popping it out of its bun and fanning amber locks onto the pillows. I could feel his chaotic heartbeat under my hands, like his heart wanted to jump from his chest. My fingertips brushed the edge of his shirt, grazing his bare side.

I had no warning. One minute, Walsh's mouth curved around my own, our legs tangling in the knottiness of his sheets, and the next he pulled away from me, the spell broken like a splash of ice water to a sleeping figure. He drew in a sharp breath, edging just out of reach.

A deep, haunted look lived in Walsh's eyes, so dark that it was almost unrecognizable to me. It wiped away the magical moment, the buzz fading fast.

I sat up, air refusing to drag into my lungs. My hair hung in front of me, wild. "What's wrong?" I asked him, almost afraid to ask the question. "Walsh?"

"I..." His voice was rough, scratchy, and his chest was heaving like he'd just ran a marathon. The fire quickly faded from the surface of my skin. "I just—I can't kiss you."

"Did I overstep?" I pressed a hand to my forehead as embarrassment flooded through me. "I'm sorry, I didn't mean —I just thought that you—"

"I knew Scott was cheating on you."

Walsh said it quick, the words almost rushing together. Like he was trying to rip off a bandage. It took my brain several tries to catch up, to fully understand what he said. Because what he said—it didn't make any sense. "Uh —what?"

"I knew Scott was cheating on you with Jewel. I-I knew they were together, the night of the party."

My lips tingled as I tried to figure out what he was talking about. The night of the party. He caught Edith and me at the door, directed us toward the dancefloor.

"Bayview is a big school," he said quickly, almost desperately, where I still felt confused. "When people talked about Scott's girlfriend, I just assumed that was who Jewel was. I'd seen them together a few times before, at parties or at games. It took me a while to realize you were his girlfriend."

Uh, okay, but I didn't see the big deal in it. Why did he sound so nervous?

"How long?" I asked as if he hadn't spoken. I mostly wanted to know how long Scott had been seeing her while seeing me. "How long did you know about Scott and Jewel before realizing?"

For a moment, Walsh didn't speak. It was a blissful moment, full of silence and anticipation as I held my breath, before he finally answered. "Two weeks before you and Scott broke up. You were in the hallway with Edith and Zach...he pointed you out."

The words punched the air from my lungs. *Two weeks.* Scott cheated on me for *two weeks.* Or more. Everything was screwed up between us, but I never really understood how much. And Walsh knew about it. *Zach* knew about it. And if Zach knew, did Edith know? Did everyone know? Everyone but me?

Walsh finally looked into my eyes, his own wide and wary, a crease forming between his brow. "Scott's a jerk, Sophia. Worse than a jerk. He's a cheater. You didn't deserve the way he treated you. He needed to realize how much he messed up."

There wasn't going to be an argument from me there. Scott *was* a jerk. But honestly, why did Walsh look so tense? Why was this something that he'd stopped kissing me for? I mean, cool that he wanted to be honest, but why was that so important at that moment? Because my tingling lips didn't think so.

Until my brain snagged on his final words. "He needed to realize *what*? What's that supposed to mean?"

Walsh, from those few inches away from me, said nothing.

"He needed to realize how much he messed up," I echoed in a voice that resembled a whisper. Slowly, so slowly, the pieces started to click into place. One by one, like puzzle pieces. "You invited me to the party because you knew he'd be there. With Jewel. Did you invite me so I'd see?"

Walsh just watched me figure everything out, jaw clenched so tightly that I could see the muscle pop from here. He looked the same as before, but never in my life had Walsh seemed so unrecognizable. It was like looking at a totally different person.

Everything stopped. My heartbeat stopped, the pounding in my head stopped, my thoughts came to a terrifying halt. "You did. You *planned* this fake relationship. You knew it would rile him up, throw him off his game, if he thought that he lost his girlfriend to *you*. It wasn't because you wanted to help me. It was just to rub his face in it." The more I spoke, the louder my voice got. "You came in and declared your love for me—it was all on purpose. It was all part of your *plan*."

Scott's words came back to me in that moment, words that I'd immediately brushed off. *He's only dating you, Sophia, so he can mess with me.*

"It's not that simple," Walsh told me, drawing in a shallow breath. "I know it seems and sounds like it, Sophie, but it's—"

I shoved up from the bed in a swift, jerky movement. *"It's Sophia."*

The moment rapidly cracked apart like glass, and I inhaled the broken shards in, cutting my lungs. All the times Walsh asked about Scott came running back to the front of my memory, and everything just clicked. All along, he hadn't been trying to help me, to keep Scott from being rude to me. No, all along he'd been trying to make Scott *jealous*. That was why he picked the dog park—he knew Scott played basketball there. That's why he took me to Ryan's party. Why he posted pictures of us together.

I stared at his figure in this perpetual state of disbelief, blood pumping so loudly that I could barely focus. My voice sounded strangely normal when I spoke, as if I were unaffected. "This'll go great in my article."

Confusion was the first emotion I saw cross over his expression, cracking apart the wariness for a split second. "What?"

"Oh, you know, my article." Looking down at him still sitting on the bed, I felt my knees begin to shake, my fingers following suit. I clenched them into fists, clamping down on the wave of emotion. "The one I'm writing for the newsletter? This will go nicely between the Royals paying off opposing teams and stealing extracurricular funding. See how perfect people think you are then."

"Paying off—what? What are you talking about?"

"You never did ask me why I'm writing about baseball." Anger made my heartbeat loud in my ears, my words nearly drowned out by the sound. "Haven't you ever heard of undercover journalism, Walsh?"

He just watched me, confusion clear in his features, but not a single hint of anger showing through. Why wasn't he *furious*? I was threatening to ruin his reputation—and my own in the process—his carefully threaded rep that he *thrived* off of. And he was acting as if I were talking about the weather. As if he didn't care. He gets to upend my life and isn't the slightest bit bothered—what kind of a robot was he?

Walsh said, "I didn't mean to hurt you, Sophia."

Oh, no. He didn't get to say things like that. Things that made my heart begin to thaw, made the furrow in my brow ease slightly. My lips still tingled from the memory of his, and in that moment, I *hated* him. I was right about him before, standing in the hallway on the last day of school. He may have a pretty smile and great hair, but everything inside was just selfish, selfish, selfish.

"Right," I said finally, voice like acid, "because you didn't think of me at all."

I woke from this dream where Walsh Hunter was someone I understood, cared for, when in all honesty I had no idea who he was. I was starting to think that I never did. It was strange to think that, just a few minutes earlier, everything had been fine. Normal. I'd come to his house expecting...well, I didn't know what I'd been expecting, but it wasn't this. Not even remotely close.

"Be on the lookout for the article," I told him, resting my hand on the doorknob. Walsh saw the tears in my own eyes; I could see the exact moment he discovered them. Walsh looked at me with a gaze so full of pain it was like his heart was the one that was breaking, shattering. As if he were the one whose life was being turned upside down. Just another lie. "I heard it's written by your favorite nerdy author."

And I turned and walked out, shutting the door behind me. And even though I'd left him behind in his bedroom, as much as I hated it, I could still taste him on my lips, a numbness that I couldn't rub away.

twenty-two

Rainwater poured off my clothes and pooled in my sandals as I stepped underneath Edith's porch, my sandals making a squelching noise whenever I took a step. My bike wheel spun from where I'd thrown it down in the grass, rushing to find cover.

I knocked, hard, wondering if Edith would even come and answer the door. I had no idea what time it was, but since it was one-ish when I was at Walsh's, no doubt it had to be close to two in the morning by now. I didn't bring my cell phone with me—because that's just how my life worked—so I couldn't call her for a ride or a heads up.

Her bedroom light was on, though muted by her curtains. I could've walked over there and knocked, though I wasn't totally convinced that she wouldn't call the police. Or at least sic her dog, Roxi, on me.

So, instead, I knocked. And I knocked. And knocked. "Edith, it's me," I called as loudly as I dared. "Edith!"

And then I heard it—the glorious sound of the deadbolt

flipping over. But when the door pulled wide, it wasn't Edith on the threshold, not her father or even her little brother.

It was Zach.

And his eyes were so, so wide. "Uh—hi," he said, blinking rapidly. "W-What's up, Sophia?"

"Sophia?" Edith's head appeared on the other side of Zach, peeking around him. Edith blinked, and it gave me time to take in her appearance. Like I said, it was probably two in the morning—surely my bike ride in the rain lasted as long as it felt—but she still wore her day clothes, a pair of denim shorts and a tank top. Eyeshadow still glistened on her lids. "What are you doing here? Why are you wet?"

I didn't wait to answer them before I shoved my way inside, causing Zach to back up a step. That was when I noticed his feet were bare—no shoes, no socks. "Why is he here?" I demanded, my residual anger from Walsh transferring. And the way Zach was staring at me, like a deer in headlights, just made me feel angry. "It's late."

"Shh, little brother's sleeping," Edith whispered quickly, glancing at the back of Zach's head. "Um, maybe you should get your stuff, Zach."

He didn't need further encouragement. Without another word, Zach turned, almost ran into Edith, and started down the dark hallway. He probably wasn't even out of earshot before I went into it. "Why is he over at two in the morning? Why are his socks off?"

"He was keeping me company until Dad gets back," Edith said, tucking a curled strand of hair behind her ear. She even still had her studded earrings in. "He went out to a concert on a date—a concert, can you believe it? I think he's having some sort of midlife crisis."

Thinking about Mr. Bradley going on dates was strange, but not the most important thing on my mind right now. "You have a boy in your room without your dad being home? He doesn't allow boys even if he is home."

Zach came back into the foyer, this time with his shoes on and his jacket slung over his arm. He glanced at Edith. "Thanks for, uh, the advice."

"Don't worry about it." Her lips pulled into a warm, gushing smile as she looked at him. I noticed that she looked into his eyes, scanning for each emotion there. "If you need a shoulder to lean on, you know where I live."

And while Edith was looking into Zach's eyes, he was grinning back at her with a few crinkles by his eyes. The two of them looked like love-struck fools.

Of course, it only made me feel angrier.

"See you later, Sophia," Zach said to me, edging around my figure with a nervous expression. I moved a little bit to let him pass but didn't answer.

Neither one of us spoke until the door softly clicked shut behind him.

"Why are you mad?" Edith demanded, crossing her arms over her chest. "And don't tell me you're not, because it's clear on your face."

"I broke up with Walsh."

Edith blinked quickly, surprised. "What? You ended your fake relationship? I thought you liked him."

That made me laugh, dull and hollow. "This entire time, he's been using me, Edith." I explained every terrible truth to her, feeling my voice shake. Heck, *everything* was shaking. My hands, my knees, my breath. "All those dates, those pictures. He wanted to rub it in Scott's face that he was dating his ex. How messed up is that?"

Edith's gaze remained steady on me after I fell silent, a small crease taking root between her dark eyebrows. Her quietness seemed to ring through the house, knocking against the walls and my brain. I waited for her mouth to open, for her to come back with an equally enraged response.

I waited, but it never came. "Well?" I demanded, a little more than impatient. "Aren't you going to say anything?"

"I'm trying to figure out why you're mad."

I flinched back from her, my turn to frown. "Why I'm mad?"

"You're saying that Walsh used you to make Scott mad, right?" Edith crossed her arms over her chest. "How is that any different than you using him for your article? How is what he did worse, even?"

No way. No way was she taking Walsh's side. She was my best friend. "You've got to be kidding," I snapped at her, for what felt like the first time ever. I couldn't remember ever raising my voice at her before. "You don't get how important this article is. It's my ticket into writing for the *Blade*, to jumpstarting my career."

"I do get it, Sophia. But that's your dream. What about Walsh's?" she demanded. "The rest of the team? You'd be tanking their dreams of playing on the county league once this got out."

"They forfeited that when they started cheating. The school is cutting the newspaper to support them!" I said back, exasperation and hurt making my throat tight and my voice rise. "They're taking my funding and just handing it to them —I have no choice!"

My loud voice rang through the house, and I held my breath, hoping that Edith's little brother didn't come wandering out to see what was going on. Again, I'd mentioned choices. Edith's words from before came back to me, about how we all have choices. She was right. Walsh made his, and I made mine.

Edith's lips pinched tight, whitening near the corners. I'd always been able to practically read her thoughts, gauge her emotions. Being her best friend for nearly ten years gave me the upper hand in that department. But right at this moment, with her brown eyes heated and glaring, I couldn't figure out what she was thinking. "You're so mad at your parents for being self-centered," she murmured, the quietness of her voice a stark contrast of mine, "and you're mad at Walsh for using you to make Scott jealous, but what about you, Sophia?"

Everything in me stilled. "What are you trying to say?"

"When was the last time you asked me about me?" she asked, deadly quiet. "About Zach? I mean, come on, Sophia. You could've asked what he needed advice about. I would be curious if the roles were reversed! When was the last time we talked about anything other than Walsh and your article?"

"That's not fair," I all but gasped. "You don't talk about any of those things."

Edith threw her hands into the air, expression cracking into a look of exasperation. "Gosh, these past few weeks, it's like I'm my own best friend. You've been gone. Off with your fake dating Walsh, and I was happy for you! I was rooting for you! But Sophia—do you seriously think you get to be mad at him when you're using him to your own advantage?" She let out a sharp breath, an annoyed sigh, but she was not done. "You're so mad at your parents and Walsh, but in reality, if you want someone to blame, you should look in the mirror."

I recoiled from her, jerking back, my sandals slipping on the damp floor. A chill worked its way over my skin, raising goosebumps along my arms, tugging the hairs at the back of my neck. My muscles trembled as I stood stock-still, frozen, tensed for another blow of harshness.

But Edith didn't speak again. Though her eyes softened as our stare-down continued, her lips didn't part.

I watched my best friend for a moment longer before turning on my heel, simmering and steaming as I tugged the front door open. At the last second, with a nagging thought passing through my mind, I stopped, turning back. "Did you know?"

Edith hugged her arms around her middle, a crease between her eyebrows. "Know what?"

"About Scott and Jewel? Did you know and not tell me?"

I waited and waited for her to deny it. To open her mouth and tell me that I was silly for even considering such a thing. To tell me that no way would she break girl-code like that. To tell me that she had no idea.

I waited and waited for her to deny it, but Edith, with a pinched expression, never opened her mouth.

Rain still plummeted from the sky, and my bike was soaked from where I'd left it in the grass. Left with no other choice, I walked out of the house, chin low, the rain instantly pelting down on me.

First my parents, then Walsh, and now Edith.

This truly was a night from hell.

I didn't go to sleep that night. From the time I got home dripping wet until the dawn broke the next morning, I spent the time typing my exposé up on the laptop and read it over one last time.

I'd written about how the teachers favor the baseball players while school was in session, giving them early dismissals as well as good grades on assignments. In Bayview High's student handbook, it's said that an athlete must maintain a minimum of a C+ average to play. And even though I *knew* at least one of the players had failed a class before, I'd never known a baseball player to have to sit out on game day ever.

"*At Bayview High School, baseball is more important than grade-point-average. At least honest grade-point-average. Why else would players receive more extensions on assignments and more extra credit opportunities than the average student?*"

In the next paragraph, I'd highlighted the Royals' nefarious methods when it came to cheating.

"*Though cheating is a direct violation in the Code of Conduct, during the baseball season, it's encouraged. Thus, the team takes creative measures to cheat—like paying off opposing team members to throw the game. All to win the beautiful, fifty-dollar trophy.*"

And of course, I couldn't leave out the money involvement. With Walsh's confession about Ryan's parents' donations, it didn't take me long to decipher the bar graph I'd printed off. After digging a little deeper, I found that the "Fund Modification" that skyrocketed the Bayview High's athletic fun had come from four individual checks. This last one took time, but after reviewing the handbook, I found the perfect way to highlight it.

"Baseball funding has significantly gone up in the previous years, three times more money factored into the account than given to the football team, the volleyball team, and even the softball team. And while private donations to one specific sport are prohibited—according to section 34.b in Bayview High School's handbook—four separate deposits were listed on the income sheet in the last school year alone, all with the invoice Baseball Fund."

I stretched my fingers, hesitating to transcribe the ending over onto the computer. I could practically feel the animosity seeping off of the words that were composed, written with such a heavy, exploitive hand that even the letters were slanted.

Though I said I was going to, I couldn't bring myself to put what happened with Walsh onto paper. From a professional standpoint, I didn't want to risk using a personal example in fear that it would degrade the piece. But that wasn't the whole truth. I couldn't bring myself to write it down because thinking about Walsh's words, his expression, made everything inside of me tense.

Edith was wrong. I wasn't the selfish one, using Walsh for my article. In all honesty, he hadn't even helped that much. Sure, going out with him got me a few little tidbits—especially with the players paying off the other teams—but nothing overly important. No, Walsh was the selfish one, all the way. And Scott. And the freaking baseball team, and the school board that supported the baseball team. It wasn't me.

Coldness worked its way over my skin. *Lots of finger-pointing, huh, Sophia?*

No, no finger-pointing. Just being honest.

I set my pen down, reaching up to rub my eyes behind my glasses. For a moment, I just sat there, listening to my breathing, the anger that I'd held slowly morphing into a thick cloud of guilt.

"I'm doing the right thing," I said aloud, turning to glance at where Shiba sat on the windowsill, her personal spot. "Right?"

She didn't look at me as I spoke, but watched outside, as if that were more interesting than my mental struggle.

Unable to help myself, I swiped up my cell phone, opening up a social media app. My fingers pressed the buttons almost blindly, opening up a certain profile. *Walsh Hunter.* All the photos he took of us were still uploaded to his timeline, and the tightness in my chest almost reached an unbearable degree of pain as I scrolled through them. A photo from our time walking dogs, a photo of me sitting in the passenger's seat of his car, a book open in my hands. A picture of me at the beach volleyball tournament, slushy in hand.

I couldn't bring myself to look at the captions on the photos, but I moved to the one from the Fourth of July, the only photo Walsh took of the both of us. I gave a wide smile as I looked up into the camera, lips stained from the slushy, but Walsh didn't look at the lens. No, that watery blue gaze cut to my direction, his own lips tipped up as he looked at me. The caption read, "*Who needs fireworks?*"

"Sophia?" Mom's voice came muffled from the other side of my closed door, quiet. I glanced towards my alarm clock, wincing at the time. Just after seven in the morning. "Sophia, are you in there?"

"Yeah," I called to her, my voice rough from disuse. My shaking fingers caused my cell to slip as I set it against my desk, and it clattered loudly. "You can come in."

When the door pushed open, I saw that Mom still wore the clothes from last night, her loose-fitted blouse and a pair of leggings. She hadn't changed out of them into her pajamas. Her hair, still up in its bun, hung a little lopsided. She let out a breath as she saw me, and I half expected her to start yelling.

Instead, though, she wrapped her arms around me, cutting any more words off. "I've been wanting to do that all night," Mom said against my shoulder, voice muffled. "I wanted to give you space, but I'm sorry."

I patted her arm a little awkwardly, not knowing what to say. My anger had been spent; I just felt so drained now. "It's okay, Mom."

"It's not. It's really not." Mom pulled back slightly so she could see into my eyes. Her own were glassy, a sheen of tears over the brown. I had her eyes, but on her, they looked full of life and warmth. I, on the other hand, felt the exact opposite. "I know what you must be thinking, Sophia, but we didn't plan the baby. And the baby didn't make us rethink our decision about a separation."

A wave of pain rushed through me as everything hit me, one by one, like tiny little pinpricks. "Mom—"

"It was *you* who made us think about it. Your words, as harsh as they might've been—and we have to work on your tact—got through. *You* saved our little family, Sophia."

Our little family. It sounded strange. A family implied something that felt foreign to me, something foreign to us all. Me, my parents, and a little sibling. The idea made my throat feel tight. Her arms weren't as constricting as they were before, but I felt even more strangled.

But not by her. *If you want someone to blame, you should look in the mirror.*

"Sophia?" Mom squeezed my shoulders. "Say something, okay?"

The prospect of talking to her was terrifying, mostly because last night was terrifying. One deviation from my path of *push-it-down* caused my lungs to seize on whatever oxygen they pulled in. "Why did you and Dad never pay attention to me?" I asked, looking straight up into her dark eyes. For how constricted my throat felt, my voice sounded fairly even.

"Oh." She passed her fingers over my temple, touch gentle. Her eyes began to water. "Oh, Sophia. We paid attention. We never wanted to be helicopter parents—we just wanted to give you some space. To grow up, to make your own decisions."

I drew in a shallow breath. "I never asked for space."

"I know, sweetheart. And I'm so sorry." She pulled me closer once again, my desk chair squeaking with the movement. "It wasn't right, and I'm sorry."

I let her hug me, let her scent embrace my senses. I basked in the rarity of the touch, in the warmth it spread. My mind reeled as details from last night hit me, punched me, almost knocked me to my back. My lips tasting the softness of Walsh's, his hands slipping gently on my skin.

Those memories instantly warmed me, but the ones after that made me feel cold as a piece of snow falling from the sky. And it *hurt*. Edith's harsh words that came after also bit at me, causing me to burrow closer to Mom.

"I remember when I painted those butterflies," Mom whispered, and I noticed her gaze was turned up to the top of my wall, where there were two butterflies. "Do you know what kind of butterflies those are?"

I sniffed, glancing up at the red and black painted butterfly. "A monarch?"

"A *Vanessa atalanta*." Mom pressed her lips to the crown of my head. "A red admiral. My favorite kind of butterfly. I guess you can guess why your middle name is Vanessa, hmm?"

Mom never told me that before. The breath I tried to drag into my lungs clogged in my throat, tears tipping down my cheeks, and there was no holding them back. No holding back the tears, no holding back the emotion that was suffocating me, and no holding back on my words.

"Scott cheated on me," I told her with a stuffed voice, clinging tighter so she couldn't pull away. I didn't want her to see my face, all splotchy swollen from tears, no doubt. "Edith knew. *Walsh* knew. No one told me until it blew up in my face."

Her hand moved in circles on my back. "And I bet you're mad at them."

"Of course I am!" I pulled back then, forcing her hand to fall. She was blurry as I looked at her. "At Edith especially. It's girl code. I don't get how she'd keep that from me. I'd never do that to her."

A little line formed between Mom's eyebrows. "Do you think maybe she just didn't know *how* to tell you?"

"Even if it was like that, she could've found a way." Heck, *anything* would've been better than pretending it wasn't happening.

"What would you have done if the roles were reversed?"

It was a fair question, but hearing Mom say it made me want to shrug away from it. To ignore the question. I tried to think about how Edith acted before our breakup. She kept encouraging me to break up with him. Before I thought it was just because she thought I could do better, now I realized. She knew he was a gross cheater and wanted me to get as far away as I could.

My gaze fell to my desk, to the scattered papers. Edith tried to get me to break up with him. She encouraged me to dump him because she knew. And even though she couldn't tell me for whatever reason, she'd still been looking out for me. That was her way of telling me without telling me.

I leaned back in my chair, hearing it squeak underneath me. "I'm...selfish," I all but whispered, my blood icy under my skin.

Mom passed her hand across my hair, voice worried. "What makes you say that?"

Oh, how could I explain the whole situation? I'd been

hiding so many things from her that I wasn't even sure where to start.

"Walsh and I broke up." It was the closest thing to what happened, even though it wasn't necessarily the truth. And Edith—were we even friends anymore? The whole "look in the mirror" thing. Was that her way of severing ties? I'd been such a horrible best friend—a horrible person in general. "I'm too self-focused, Mom."

I deserved this pain, this pinching in my legs and chest and arms and throat, all over my body.

Mom pulled my body to her again, and this time, her arms were cobra-constricting tight, trying to squeeze the pain out of me. I tried to imagine that I was an orange, the juice spilling from my insides from being squeezed.

"You know, it's always been hard for me to let your father be your father. To not try to control every aspect of our relationship. Down to even him eating my leftover spaghetti. Your grandparents were like that," she said quietly. "Dr. Lively and I had a session about learned behaviors. She said that my desire to control the situation came from my younger years." Her hand smoothed up and down my back, a lulling sensation. "It's hard to let others in when it's been only you for so long."

Though the words were promising, tears filled my eyes. "What do you mean?"

"You've only ever had to focus on you. It's like you said—you never asked for space. But when you're only focused on you for so long, it's hard to switch over when more people come into your life." Mom framed my cheeks with her warm palms, wiping away any tears that fell. "I always thought that giving you all that space would make you strong. Independent. Not needing to rely on anyone to make you happy. That's not how you raise your child, though. I know that now."

I clung to my mother for the first time in years. I'd been praying for a day like this to come for a long time, where she'd take me into her arms again, kiss the top of my head, and tell me that everything would be all right. Give me motherly advice. Never had I ever needed it more than I did right now, and she was happy to oblige.

She had good intentions over the years, her and Dad both. They wanted me to have space, to make my own decisions—they never meant to push me away. In their eyes, they were giving me freedom to be who I needed to be, even though I needed them.

Knowing all that now made the heavy weight in my chest somewhat more bearable, a pressure I never realized until it rolled away and the oxygen poured into my lungs. "I screwed everything up," I told her, my words barely distinct as they mashed together. Tears pricked the corners of my eyes. "I've been so selfish all summer. I let the one guy who actually understood me slip through my fingers."

Walsh was the one person who made me feel like me. When I was with him, I forgot how quiet or nerdy or shy I am. I just felt like *me*. He was someone who saw me for what I was—a nerd who loved quality time, who rolled her eyes at silly things, who was goal-oriented to a fault. He helped me find strengths in those qualities, ones that for so long I thought made me *weird* or *boring*. And I'd gone and thrown that away.

The second I started falling for Walsh, I should've thrown out the article. But I hadn't. I continued because, for some reason, I thought my needs were bigger than Walsh's. And they weren't. Bashing the baseball team was low, and not at all the type of writing that my heart longed for. And what was the point in doing what I loved when it ripped away someone else's dreams?

Especially when they involved the boy I cared about.

I could see now how hypocritical I truly was. I couldn't be mad at him for doing the exact same thing I'd been doing. His actions were no more despicable than my own. I *knew* I was doing the wrong thing, and I did it anyway.

Edith had been right about everything, and I'd been too selfish to realize it until it was too late.

"We all make mistakes," Mom replied softly, reading my mind and tucking my hair behind my ear lightly. "But they only stay mistakes if you don't try to make them right."

"I doubt he'll ever forgive me," I told her.

"Walsh seemed like the understanding sort when he was over here, Sophia. You should talk to him. A simple apology could go a long way."

An apology. The idea seemed so small, useless. I'd threatened to end his baseball career—if he'd done that to me and my writing, I don't know what I would've done.

No, he deserved a grand gesture. A gesture that would've touched his heart.

Something like an electrical shock coursed through me, and I pulled back, eyes wide. "Mom. Can you drive me to the store?"

twenty-three

The morning of the final baseball game, it rained. Giant, fat raindrops that somehow felt like they were the clouds' way of mocking my predicament.

Except there was no wallowing in the Wallace household. No, there was only *doing*.

"Here." Dad came up to me with a white trash bag in his hand, flapping it wide to open it up. "Put it in here and it'll protect it from the rain."

I curved the edge of the wide poster board so that it easily slid into the plastic, fingers shaking. "Thanks, Dad."

"That was very thoughtful, Richard," Mom said from where she leaned against the stairwell, hand absently on her belly. Shiba sat on the stair that was level with Mom's knee, joining the conversation as well. "Are you sure you don't want us to drive you?"

"Thanks, but my ride should be here any minute."

I checked my phone to note the time, my stomach somersaulting. It'd been two days since showing up on Walsh's doorstep, and there'd only been radio silence since. No texts, no phone calls, no nothing.

Dad glanced in Mom's direction and then back to me. "And you don't want us to come?"

I couldn't hide my smile at the supportive words. "I know you wanted to go to one of his games, but I think I've got to do this myself."

No, I *needed* to do this myself. As much as the idea completely terrified me, I had to do this myself.

"Well, your mom and I will be here if you need us," Dad said, walking over to Mom and picking up her hand. "Probably making dinner. Loaded potato soup?"

"No, I was thinking—" Mom stopped, looking up into Dad's eyes. She took in a little breath, but not like the reset breaths she used to take, the long and exaggerated inhale. It was slower and more contented. She gave a small smile. "Actually, loaded potato soup sounds good."

The past conversation with Mom came back to me, where she said in therapy they were taught to make sacrifices. Over the past two days of being at home, I noticed them putting small practices into place. Volunteering to take out the trash, Dad coming home from work a little earlier, Mom sticking around in the mornings to have breakfast before going to the studio. They weren't perfect. There was still a long way to go for all of us. But these were all steps in the right direction.

And it would be much different sooner or later. This time next year, a baby's cries and laughs would fill these walls. Which was crazy, crazy, crazy to think about.

A car horn honked from the driveway, reawakening my nerves. "Wish me luck."

"You don't need luck," Mom said, reaching out to squeeze my shoulder. "Just be yourself."

Be myself. Sophia Vanessa Wallace, journalist. Sophia Vanessa Wallace, writer. Sophia Vanessa Wallace. *Just be yourself.* And more importantly, I needed to be *honest.*

With the plastic bag tucked underneath my arm, I pulled up the hood on my sweatshirt, covering my hair and keeping my head tucked low. The rain didn't fall as heavily as it had the other night, diluting to a faint trickle now. Dad pulled open the door for me, and I hurried out into the driveway, finding the familiar navy sedan parked.

I slipped inside, shutting the passenger door behind me and pulling off my hood. "Thanks for coming."

Edith leaned back against the driver's seat, watching me closely. She'd pulled her dark hair into a high ponytail, a purple ribbon weaved through it to match the Royals' team color. She also wore a purple and gold oversized t-shirt, tied into a knot at the front. "Please. I'll always come when you call."

"Even when you're mad at me?"

"You were mad at me too," she pointed out, hesitating before putting the car into gear. "I should've told you about Scott the second I found out."

"I get it," I told her, and I did. "I don't know what I would've done if our situations were reversed. Probably encourage you to dump his butt, too."

Her nose scrunched up a little bit when she smiled, like it always does. "You still love me?"

"Only if you still love me. I should've listened to you all along about the article."

Edith leaned across the armrest that sat between us and wrapped her arms around me, her bracelets jingling loudly. "Yeah, you should've, but I forgive you."

I pinched her in the side, causing her to jerk away, laughing. She settled into her seat and backed out of my driveway, her windshield wipers making a suctioning noise as they swiped across the glass.

"So," she said, glancing my way as she started down the road. "What's this super-important mission you're embarking on again?"

Ah, yes. The super-important mission. "If I talk about it, I might chicken out."

"Sophia Wallace, the chicken?"

"We both know that's not a surprise."

Edith's lips curved, just a little bit.

"So let's not talk about me. Let's talk about you. What's new with Zach? How's volleyball training going? Did your dad ever say how his date went?"

She laughed, holding a hand up. "Slow down, hotshot. I can only take one question at a time. Volleyball's going good. Tryouts are next week. I've been practicing down at the beach with a few girls a couple times a week, and it's been really helpful."

"That's good. I'd offer my help, but I'm not good at volleyball. If you need a target, though, I volunteer."

"It's the thought that counts," Edith said, grinning sideways at me. "Dad's date went well, I think. He came in a little after you left. He doesn't talk about that kind of stuff with me much—he says it's *inappropriate*—but I think he's just nervous I'll disapprove."

"Do you? Disapprove of him dating?"

Edith flipped on her blinker as she slowed down at a stop sign, her tires squealing as she cut across the pavement. "No, I don't. I think it's good for him. It's been almost a decade since Mom died—he needs someone to keep him company."

"And...Zach? Did you ever find out if he's with Celia?"

I watched as Edith tensed, but she tried to shake it off by shifting in her seat. "They're not together, but they do hang out sometimes, which is probably not a good sign. But Zach and I...we talk here and there. We talk until it's late sometimes, but the other night was the first time he's come over. It's...I don't..." Edith took a long breath and let it out. Color flooded into her cheeks, and I watched her try to turn her face away to hide it. "We're just friends."

My lips curved up a little bit, and I nudged her. "*Just* friends?"

"Just friends," she repeated, swatting at my hand. "For now. And that's okay."

"For now," I echoed, crossing my fingers.

This time when she glanced at me, there was a gleam to her eyes. "I mean, who knows what the future holds?"

Edith took the last corner that led to the baseball park up town, slowing down for a flow of pedestrians crossing the street. A lot of them carried fold-up chairs and soda bottles, either wearing Bayview's colors of purple and gold or the opposing team's blue and white.

But they weren't walking *towards* the baseball field—they were walking towards their cars.

"What's going on?" Edith asked, glancing toward her dashboard. "The game is supposed to start in five minutes. Why is everyone leaving?"

"It couldn't have been rained out, right?" No way it'd rained that much today. It was just a sprinkle, really.

"I wouldn't have thought so." Edith eased her car over to the side of the road, pressing the unlock button. "Go see if you can find out what's going on. I'm going to go park."

I held my breath as I pulled my hood back over my head, grabbing my plastic bag and pushing out of Edith's car. There was a line at the ticket booth, but as I got closer, I realized that the people in line weren't paying for their tickets. The person behind the counter handed back five-dollar bills to those who stepped up.

Too busy watching the line, I didn't notice someone cross my path until I ran into them, putting my arms out to catch myself. "I'm so sorry," I said as I looked up, jerking when I met their eyes. "Mrs. Gao?"

Mrs. Gao smiled as she took a step back, and I realized she held a toddler's hand. The girl was small, probably two or three, with dark hair and eyes. "Sophia, it's good to see you," Mrs. Gao greeted with a small chuckle, reaching up with her other hand to smooth back her hair. "What do you have there?"

My poster board made a sound when I slapped it close to my stomach, the plastic bag crinkling. "Something for a friend. What are you doing here? Aren't you boycotting baseball?"

She lifted the hand of the toddler slightly, swinging it in

the air. "Oh, not at all. I love baseball, and so does this little nugget here."

The little girl giggled at that, snuggling closer to Mrs. Gao's leg.

"But...what about baseball getting our program's money?"

Mrs. Gao's features softened a little. "That was the school board's decision, not the team's. They had no say in the matter. It's not fair to blame them, is it?"

I swallowed hard when she finished speaking. Her attitude towards everything did make sense. Yeah, baseball got a lot of unfair perks, but Mrs. Gao was right. They had no vote in cutting the newspaper. That was all the school board.

All at once, my resentment toward the baseball team felt really, really ridiculous.

"How is your take on the Back to School article coming along?" she asked.

A small pinch took home behind my ribs at her words, but it wasn't necessarily painful. More resigned. I could've told her about the baseball article, about how I had it finished on my desk just yesterday. That it was perfect in format, great in detail. I could've even told her how I spent my entire summer working on it, finding out new ways to perfect it. I could've told her how I teamed up with Walsh Hunter to finish it, and what came from that partnership.

But none of that was the truth. Though if I said the truth, that would be it. It would close the door to the Bayview High Report. No more newspaper, no more journalism. No more title for my résumé, no more internship.

I'd rather lose all that than lose Walsh's respect forever.

We may not end up together, but I couldn't bear the idea of him never looking me in the eye again.

"I scrapped it."

There was no missing the shock on her face. "You...you *what?*"

"I scrapped it yesterday morning. I'm sorry I couldn't tell you sooner, in case you were waiting on it."

Scrapping the article meant a lot of things. Officially a forfeit, I surrendered to the war I'd been fighting all summer. No more newspaper, no more internship, no more outlet to catch my breath.

But I *wasn't* alone. Before, my love of writing had been a way to feel less lonely. It always felt so good to have those words to keep me busy, keep me company. Now I had both my mom and my dad, both dedicated to making this work. And though there were no guarantees, though they might slip up sometimes, never had they ever opened their eyes to me like this. Though I'd have no journalism class, no internship, I had a family for the first time in a long time.

And besides, having my internship would've meant nothing if I knew that I cost Walsh his dream.

"What's going on, anyway?" I asked, glancing around at the people leaving. "The game—isn't it supposed to just be starting?"

Mrs. Gao glanced over her shoulder at the empty baseball field, not a single player in sight. "It's been canceled, actually. Greenville ended up winning by forfeit. Someone accused our baseball team of cheating, so the umpire investigated, and he ended up disqualifying us."

"Cheating?" I echoed, and though I knew I took in a breath, I couldn't feel it. "Someone said the Royals cheated?"

"They must've found proof, too, or else they wouldn't have canceled the game." Mrs. Gao looked down at the toddler. "I should get her home. It was nice talking to you, Sophia. I'll see you when school starts."

I shook my head a little bit, trying to clear it, but the action didn't help. My grip tightened on my trash bag.

Since there was no admission, I slipped past the gates with ease, standing on my tip-toes to see over the heads. I didn't see any players anywhere, green for Greenville or purple for Bayview. They hadn't left already, had they? There was no way. If parents were only just leaving, wouldn't the players still be here? A raindrop fell on my glasses lens, spattering against the glass, and I hastily pulled them from my face to scrub it off.

"Bad news, Sophia," Scott said, his voice immediately recognizable before I even got my glasses back on. "Your boyfriend's a loser."

I slipped on my glasses, looking up to meet Scott in the eye. Jewel stood just behind him, hair frizzing from the dampness in the air. For the first time ever, she had a pinched expression to her face, one that was less than happy. "What are you talking about?"

"He found out about the cheating and quit," Scott shrugged, folding his arms. His baseball uniform looked pristine, not a speck of dirt or dust anywhere on his jersey or his pants. He'd managed to grow the scruff out longer than before, leaving a patchy and uneven dotting of brown. "And completely screwed his team over in the process."

Screwed them over? Wait. "*He* told the umpire you guys cheated?" *Why would he do that?*

Scott gave me a look. One eyebrow raised, lips pursed, looking at me like I was stupid. "No, Walsh *walked*. Just before the game started, he just *left*. Quit. See, I would've been a better captain than him. I never would've walked out on my team."

"Why did he walk?" I was alarmed now. Walsh wouldn't have quit the baseball team, ever. That was the key to being on the county league. I looked around the sea of people, hoping his face or golden hair would stand out.

Scott let out a soft chuckle. "You know, when I told you to keep a secret, I expected you'd hold it in at least a *few days* before spilling the beans."

The longer I listened to Scott talk, the more I couldn't think straight. He threw curveball after curveball my way that kept smacking me upside the head, making my thoughts scatter. "Wait...Walsh didn't know about the team cheating?"

"Of course not." He gestured toward me. "Well, not until you told him."

And just like that, it all clicked. With the way he was staring at me, an expression torn between smug and unkind, I understood. "You told me about the cheating so I'd tell him. You *wanted* me to tell him."

Scott spread his hands wide. "I was hoping you'd wait until after the final game so we could win, but in the end, I got what I wanted. Winning the game is good, but beating Walsh Hunter is better. Way better. Walsh quit the team, and Coach Glassmore doesn't offer second chances."

Oh my gosh. Another raindrop fell on my glasses lens,

but this time I didn't try to rub it away. I could barely move; I was surprised I even still held the trash bag. Waves of guilt and shame washed over me. How could I have been so stupid to play right into Scott's hands? No wonder he gave me that information so willingly—he *wanted* me to blab.

"Where's Walsh now?" I had to find him.

Scott raised a shoulder, not a care in the world. "No clue. But I'm definitely having a celebration tonight. A 'Beating Walsh Hunter' party. I like the sound of that."

"Ugh," Jewel sighed loudly, stepping out from behind Scott's shoulder.

Her eyebrows were pulled together in the meanest look I'd ever seen from her. Honestly, I didn't think her face could contort into a frown. But there it was, in full force, and totally directed at Scott. She came to stand by my side. A united front, a wall of the girls Scott had dated.

"You're so childish," Jewel said. "Going on and on about how Walsh doesn't deserve to be captain, but he does. Because he's worked for what he's gotten. He's *earned* it. You don't work for anything—you just *complain* about everything!"

My gaze darted between the two of them, torn between shocked and amused at the way things were unfolding. It honestly felt like I was dreaming.

"You can be mad at Walsh all you want," she went on, not losing steam. "But he's a better guy than you could ever be. And if it's not obvious, this is me dumping you."

No, not that I was dreaming. It felt like I'd been thrown into another soap opera, watching this dramatic, heated scene unfold. *Just Desserts.*

I bit down on my lower lip before it split into a grin. *Yeah, definitely amused.*

I watched as Scott's raised eyebrow fell. "You're—"

"Breaking up with you." Jewel enunciated each word carefully.

"She's tried to fix it," I told him, unable to help myself from mimicking his own words, and it felt so *good*. "But she just can't do it anymore."

Scott's glare wavered from me to Jewel before he rolled his eyes. "Fine by me," he scoffed. "I got what I wanted. Have fun with your issues, crazies."

Then he stomped away, dragging his shoes through the grass as he headed for the gate. I took a moment to watch him go, to watch his tense posture. It's funny how a fake relationship could feel so much more genuine than my actual relationship with Scott. And how fitting—Scott broke up with me to find someone "better," and she ended up dumping him anyway. *Universe, I owe you one.*

I turned to Jewel, raising my free hand. "I think you deserve a high-five for that."

She smacked my palm lightly, giving me the smallest smile I've ever seen from her. "Thanks. So you're crazy too, huh?"

"Apparently. But I've heard that being crazy is more fun." I nudged her arm. "Besides, if we're going to talk about crazy, it's most definitely the guy who is so cutthroat about being team captain."

She laughed. "Definitely agree with you on that."

I smiled, happy that this situation with Scott brought about one good thing. Even though Jewel was supposed to be the "other woman," she never felt that way. If anything, she'd be a great friend.

"Sophia!" Edith called as she hurried in through the gates, her makeup smudged slightly from the rain. "Walsh—he's out by the fence talking to some guy. He's by the corner, away from all the people."

He's still here. I clutched my plastic-covered poster board tighter, nerves chittering to life. "Jewel, help Edith find Zach. You can tell her about what just happened and how you rocked it. I've got to go."

"Wait, what *did* happen?" I heard Edith ask Jewel as I hurried away.

twenty-four

$\mathcal{M}$ost of the crowd had already filtered from the baseball field, heading home. The line at the ticket booth dwindled down to only a few people, and I passed them, eyes peeled.

All the air *whooshed* from my lungs as I spotted a figure down near the far end of the fence, Royals uniform, hat backward with blond hair peeking from underneath.

Walsh.

My body refused to move forward, but my brain started to immediately soak up the details.

Walsh didn't have his bat bag with him, but he did have his mitt tucked underneath one arm. He fiddled with his fingers as he spoke to the tall man in front of him, one who, I noticed, held a clipboard. Walsh nodded to whatever the man said, his attention totally captured.

Until his gaze slipped past the man to mine.

I was thrown back to a moment so long ago when the same thing happened, back in the hallway on the last day of school. Walsh, completely in his element, looking directly at me as if I'd spoken to him. Back then, I'd glared at him with all the anger I could muster.

Now, looking at him evoked a kaleidoscope of butterflies to stir in my stomach.

The next few moments happened in rapid succession—Walsh's lips moved quickly, my brain too slow to try and read what they were saying, and the man passed over a small business card before walking away.

And then Walsh strode straight to me.

Part of me almost wondered if this was a dream; the boy coming toward me could've been a mirage or someone else entirely, but my heart knew. My heart would know him anywhere.

Walsh's lips twitched a little, and he stopped a few feet away. His expression was filled with a nervousness that made my blood hum, holding his baseball mitt between his hands. "Sophia."

I held my bag tightly to my chest. "Hi." Despite my brain willing me not to, I found myself taking a step closer, the blood rushing to my head. The last time I was this close to him, his skin had been slipping against mine, his lips touching my lips, intoxicating. It brought a stinging feeling to my throat. "Who was that guy over there?"

"His name's Tom Fletcher. He's the coach for the Fenton County baseball team." Walsh's voice sounded a little stunned. "He was asking me a few questions."

"Did he ask you why you quit just before the final game started?" I asked, my malfunctioning brain forgetting what tact was.

One corner of his mouth quirked up. "He did."

"And?"

Walsh shrugged. "I told him what happened. About how I didn't want to play for a cheating team. I'd rather never play baseball again than be grouped in with a team of people who cheat their way to the top. I told him..." His lips twitched again. "I said that I love the sport."

I almost smiled at his words. "But you hate the game." I wanted to kick myself so badly in that moment for ever thinking that Walsh knew about the team's methods of winning. "And what'd he say?"

Walsh lifted up the small card Tom gave him, and I watched as he turned it over. "Told me to call him on Monday."

A wave of relief flooded through me, one that nearly made my knees weak. "The fact that he wants to talk to you more is a great sign."

"Yeah," he chuckled almost incredulously, looking into my eyes. "I guess it is."

We stood regarding each other for a moment, neither one of us talking. "Was it scary telling the umpire about the cheating?"

Walsh raised his eyebrows a little bit. "I didn't tell him. Zach did, actually."

Zach confessed about the cheating? I wouldn't have seen that coming. But it made me look at him in a different light, in a different way. He stood up for something that was right, and I admired him for that.

I wanted to go on, to say what I'd been rehearsing for the past day and a half, but my mouth refused to open, my tongue refused to cooperate. It seemed that the erratic heart-beat in my throat swallowed my ability to speak.

Walsh cleared his throat first, shifting on his feet. "I'm sorry. About what happened."

I began shaking my head. "You don't have to apologize, Walsh. *Seriously*. I do. I never should have written that stupid article—especially not after we spent so much time together. That was messed up of me."

Walsh blinked like I'd been speaking a mile a minute. Maybe I had been. He took a small step forward, slipping the business card into his pocket. "I haven't stopped thinking about Wednesday night, Sophia. I haven't stopped."

Wednesday night. Heat flooded through my cheeks.

"The house was deadly silent that night, and I was thinking and thinking and thinking. About a lot of things. Dad took my mom to rehab that night, did I tell you that?" He shook his head, dragging his cleats along the grass. "No, I don't think so. That's why Janet was over—that night, Mom asked if Dad would take her. She...she asked for help."

I reached out with my free hand and slipped my fingers into his, squeezing it. "Walsh, that's great news."

"It is, but I couldn't stop thinking. About my mom, about the final game, about you. I kept wishing you'd call me or text me because I just needed to hear your voice. And then you just showed up at my house."

I had been the one needing to hear *his* voice. After Mom's truth bomb, all I wanted to do was hear his voice. And he felt the same way. "I'm sorry for everything," I told him, my voice unsteady. "For writing that stupid article. And for getting upset with you. That wasn't fair."

"It was completely fair. I should've told you the minute I realized what was going on. Once I knew about you and Jewel, I should've said something, brought it up."

In all honesty, if Walsh approached me before Scott broke up with me I wasn't sure I would've listened to him. I probably would've told him where he could shove it.

"I didn't plan the fake relationship," Walsh said, this time dropping his voice. "The way Scott spoke to you that night was so...I couldn't help myself. I wasn't even thinking—I just stepped in." He shook his head. "After I saw how shocked he was, my motives became a little less selfless. But I started out with good intentions, I swear."

Seeing Walsh here, opening his heart out to me, felt like a dream that I was just about to wake up from. I watched him for a long moment, trying to burn this memory into my mind. It recorded over the last memory I had of him, of our argument, of me being so angry.

I looked down at the plastic bag, watching as a lone raindrop slid along the side. "I threw away my article."

"*What?* Why?"

"It was selfish," I said, and even though the words felt ugly in my mouth, I knew I had to be honest. "Though the school is seriously messed up when it comes to idolizing baseball, what right did I have to take away your dream to fund my own? And it wasn't the kind of writer I wanted to be, you know? That's not who I am. I write about how plastic straws are damaging the environment, not exposés that can hurt someone's feelings. That's not me."

"Too bad," Walsh said, causing my gaze to jerk to his. "I could've given you some juicy content."

"I wanted to tell you so badly, but I was afraid you'd never talk to me again."

Walsh reached over and grabbed one of my hands with his own. He had to feel the clamminess, but clung tightly, almost like he was afraid I'd pull away. "Sophie, I don't think I could stay away from you if I tried. I...I love being around you. Yeah, we started hanging out to sell our fake relationship, but along the way, I just wanted to be with you. Without others around, without having to show off. Because being with you, I could just be me. I wasn't *Mr. Perfect* or team captain or anything like that. No one was looking at me other than you, and I could be *me*."

Everything inside me screeched to a halt. My heartbeat, the air in my lungs, the blood pumping in my veins—everything stopped because that was exactly the way I felt. He'd repeated my own thoughts back to me without even knowing it.

I pulled my hand from his, reaching for the ties on my bag. "I made this," I said as I pulled the board out. "You were supposed to see it from your pitcher's mound and swoon, but you had to go and mess up the game."

Walsh laughed at my attempt of humor. "I'm pretty good at messing things up."

The board shook from how bad my fingers trembled, but I dropped the bag to the ground, turning the board so he could read it. "I'm not the best at making signs," I told him quickly. "So don't laugh."

I watched as his blue eyes roamed across the white poster board, as the expression on his face fell into a stunned sort of shock. In that moment, I totally could've thrown up. In the second between him reading and realization crossing his features, I could've thrown up all over his fancy little uniform.

"That circle thing is supposed to be a baseball," I pointed out, words coming rapid-fire, feeling ten thousand kinds of silly. "It was dumb. I just—"

"*He stole second base and my heart*,'" Walsh read. And then the corners of his lips pulled high, showing me his beautiful smile. It lit a blue-flamed fire in his eyes, and it had that scar by his eye crinkling up. The butterflies were back in my stomach, making me feel like I couldn't breathe. "Sophie."

"*Welsh*."

Walsh's lips twitched, remembering that nickname from once upon a time, but he kept going. He reached out and put one of his hands on the sign, lowering it until it touched the ground. "Give me a chance. A chance for you to roll your eyes at me a million more times and for me to call you Sophie, a thousand more lame parties and baseball games and dog walking and fireworks. A real first date, where we can read more romance books that you love and eat Janet's cookies. I want to give you everything because you deserve it. You're worth it all, and I'll prove it to you." Then, quietly, almost self-consciously, he added, "Please?"

I couldn't breathe for several moments—the thought of inhaling would've been laughable if I had any air inside my lungs—so it seemed like I was deliberating. I tried to play my silence off like he hadn't just struck me speechless yet again. Like my heart wasn't about to explode inside my chest and my knees weren't about to give out in front of the baseball field. Like everything that I'd been wishing for wasn't coming true.

"Did you recycle the speech you used the night of the party?" I found myself asking, insides quivering.

Walsh's eyes curved as he smiled. "I bulked it up a bit."

I stepped closer to him, stepping over the trash bag on the ground. "I'm not sure I can roll my eyes a million more times," I said, reaching for him. "But I'd love to try."

Walsh leaned forward and pressed his mouth against mine, lips just as velvety and wonderful as I remembered. His one hand found the dip of my waist, holding me to him. And this—oh, this wasn't like our first kiss, all fire and desire. This was so much softer and slower, and technically the first real kiss of our relationship. This was the kind of kiss people wrote about in books—the toe-curling, heart fluttering kiss I'd always dreamt about.

I only heard the dull sound of applause when Walsh pulled away, and I turned to meet the eyes of Edith, Jewel, and Zach, all watching us.

"That was beautiful," Edith said, leaning against Zach's side. I noticed that his hand brushed hers. "Seriously adorable."

"I second that," Jewel added, clasping her hands together.

Zach didn't say anything, but he grinned.

Yeah, I know. *Mortifying.*

Walsh ghosted his fingers along my temple, his skin cool against mine. If someone presented this moment to me months ago, I would've claimed I were high, drunk, or acting, because never would I ever be kissing Walsh Hunter in my right mind. But this was the realest thing I've ever experienced.

Totally threw that no-kissing rule out the window.

"Let's go get ice cream," Edith suggested, and Walsh picked up my sign, holding it close. "All of us."

"We'll meet you over there," Walsh said, grabbing the plastic bag from the ground and pulling on my hand.

I didn't glance over my shoulder as we walked away, but I heard Edith's voice trailing after us. "You riding with Jewel and me, Zach?"

"Only if I get shotgun," he said immediately in response, and I couldn't help but smile.

Walsh tucked my hand close, giving it a squeeze. "I found something yesterday, something that I think you'll love."

Most of the cars were gone as we crossed into the parking lot, and Walsh's rusting SUV stood out as we walked up to it. He fished the car keys from his pocket, and the car clicked as it unlocked.

"Is it better than my sign?" I asked, watching as he tucked it safely into the backseat. "Well, probably a lot could be better than my sign. My baseball kind of looks like a basketball."

"I love it," Walsh said, pulling something from his car and offering it out to me. "So, I went walking around my yard yesterday, just needing to think. I went out to the railing and saw it, plain as day. When you threw it, it must've landed on a rock. It didn't get washed away with the tide."

It took me a long, long moment to recognize the rectangular object in his hand for what it was—with the stickers emblazoned on the front and the scratch along the bottom corner.

It was my writer's notebook.

The edges of the pages were wrinkled a bit from the heavy rain we got, but since it was hardbound, it was relatively okay. I flipped open to a random page, the ink still intact.

I didn't realize the significance of seeing it until something turned over in my chest, like a lock undoing itself, allowing a tidal wave of pressure and relief to burst through my bloodstream. My journal. My writer's notebook. It was *here*. It hadn't been eaten by the sea. Walsh found it, saved it, and was offering it out to me.

He couldn't have known how important this was to me, how desperately I'd been missing this bundle of paper. A part of my soul. I was itching, desperate to get my hands on it, to feel it solid underneath my fingertips. Maybe even more importantly, I wanted to kiss Walsh.

So I did both.

I grabbed onto the journal while pushing onto my tiptoes, finding his lips with my own. His other arm came around me, holding me close against the fabric of his jersey and the firmness of his body. It was the most comfortable place in the world, being in his grasp. And I fit so perfectly, like I'd always meant to be in his arms.

My eyes closed as every inch of me hummed with happiness. I realized I'd experienced it with my mom the other morning, being in her arms, hearing her comforting words. "Thank you," I said, reaching up and tracing the angle of his jaw with a fingertip. "You have no idea how much this means to me."

"I might have an idea," he murmured in response, kissing that finger, sending a flicker of flames down my spine. "Every writer needs their notebook."

I wrapped my arms around Walsh's waist and held on tight, basking in his embrace, even as the rain still sprinkled from the sky.

I'd been so close to losing this, to missing out on this. On never feeling his arms around me again, never feeling his lips brush the top of my head, never feeling his fluttering heartbeat through his shirt. I'd been too consumed in my own life, my own world, that I almost lost this entirely.

But Mom and Edith were right. I wasn't by myself in life; others were around me. It wasn't just about me and my dreams, and I thanked the universe and all the stars in the sky that my eyes opened before it was too late.

twenty-five

$\mathcal{I}$ didn't have an article to submit to Mrs. Gao by the deadline, but I didn't feel sad about it. It really felt bittersweet. Before, I'd been dead-set on reinstating the newspaper at school, that that was the only key to my future in journalism. But it wasn't, not by a long shot. Just because Bayview High didn't have a newspaper didn't mean I had to stop writing. Just because I wasn't going to get the senior internship at the *Blade* didn't mean my career was over.

This summer gave me something I didn't have before: perspective. Everything happened for a reason—I knew that now, from how everything worked out with my parents and with Walsh—and I believed that my writing would work out, too.

Positive Thinking and I were now BFFs.

The day after the school's board meeting, Mom, Walsh, Dad, and I all sat in the living room watching a movie. Walsh and I cuddled up on the chaise lounge while Mom and Dad sat on the couch together.

My cell chimed with an email going through, and I saw

that Mrs. Gao sent me an email that read "*Stay by your phone today.*" I brushed it off, thinking she'd sent it to the wrong person.

Well, I'd thought that until my cell phone started to ring.

"Hello?" I said, taking a glance at Walsh. He'd been running his fingertips along the side of my leg, which was pressed against his, but now stilled, eyes on me. Dad paused the movie, filling the air with silence.

"Is this Sophia Wallace?" The voice was light and feminine.

I pushed my glasses up my nose, wary. "This is she."

Walsh's lips twitched as he went back to tracing my leg.

"My name is Leanne Ferris," she said. "I'm the editorial director at the *Bayview Blade*."

The phone nearly tumbled from my grip as my fingers spasmed, and then I froze, still as a statue.

"Last night I was at Bayview High's board meeting to report for the paper and I ran into a Mrs. Gao. She talked a lot about your writing skill and showed me your article about paper straws you wrote a few years back." She paused. "It was very insightful and informative. I was hoping you'd allow us to run it in next week's issue."

My hand slapped over Walsh's hand on my leg and I squeezed, nearly grinding his bones together. "R-Run my article in the *Bayview Blade*?"

"*What?*" Mom gasped, eyes wide.

"I understand that your journalism program at school was cut this school year," she went on as if she couldn't hear the building freak-out in my voice. "To apply for our senior internship, the school must have an active journalism department."

Words, Sophia, spit them out. "Um, right."

"I'd like to extend a direct internship at the *Bayview Blade* for you personally. That is, if you were thinking of applying." I could hear her chuckle slightly over the phone. "With an article like that, Ms. Wallace, I'd be surprised if you didn't."

"You're offering me an internship?" I repeated, unable to keep the mad grin from my face. She'd said *Ms. Wallace.* So professional and real. *Am I dreaming?* "At the *Blade?*"

She sounded amused. "Yes, I am."

I blinked at the frozen image on the TV screen, my brain short-circuiting. Dad nodded his head eagerly at me, mouthing at me to answer her.

It wasn't until Walsh squeezed my hand that I snapped back to reality, the words coming out in a rush. "I-I accept. Yes, I accept wholeheartedly." *I'm mere seconds from screaming.* "Thank you so, so much, Ms. Ferris."

"Come by the office when you can and I'll give you a tour," she told me, and then added, "The *Blade* will be lucky to have you, Sophia."

When she hung up, I held the phone to my ear still, savoring the moment. Savoring the feeling. The fire that was still in my veins, the elation that was consuming me. My body was hot, hot, hot, and everyone in the room was staring at me with wide, impatient eyes, sharing these emotions with me.

Walsh still gripped my hand, waiting for my reaction. "Let it out, Sophie," he said with the biggest grin on his face. "Let it out."

After trying so hard to hold it in, to hold all the excitement and energy back, I started to squeal. When the rest of them joined in on my cheering, it was a while before we stopped.

And I'd never felt so at home in my house, with Walsh's arms around me, his lips against my temple, and my parents grinning from ear to ear. I'd never felt so loved.

epilogue

The November breeze was comforting and cool, lingering on any skin I'd left exposed. I shivered a little, thinking about how Mom would say I should go inside before I caught a chill. But I didn't want to. Not yet.

Mom hit her five-month mark yesterday in her pregnancy, her baby bump as round as a basketball. The argument nowadays was that a perfect bump meant it was a boy, but Dad was sticking with his hopes of another girl.

And they were getting excited—baby things littered the whole house, bassinets and toys and unisex clothes, since they were determined not to know until the baby was born. "It'll be exciting," Mom would say, trying to convince us. "It'll make the day that much more special."

If it were two against one, Dad and I totally would've won. But, of course, Walsh sided with Mom.

"It's her decision," Walsh said for the millionth time now, his breath warming the top of my head. His arms around me pulled me closer still, my back flush with his chest. "But, c'mon, Sophie, you have to admit that knowing takes some of the fun away."

We were sitting out on the porch swing in front of my house, one Dad installed for Mom toward the end of summer. It was nice when the weather was still warm, but since it was now late November, it seemed insane that Walsh and I were out here. But as the wind tipped us slowly forward and back, I found I couldn't care less.

We both wore jackets, a heavy blanket over our legs, and Walsh's body heat enveloped me. I was more than content. "She just likes to do things the hard way."

"Like someone else I know," Walsh teased, pressing his mouth against the crown of my head. His warm breath caused a shiver to break out over my skin, slipping down my spine. "Your article in the *Blade* last week was one of your best ones yet, Sophia."

The internship at the *Bayview Blade* originally started out as a *learn and write on your own* sort of deal, but once the editors read more of my work, they gave me a little column in the back twice a month. This past week I'd written an open letter to my selfish self at the beginning of summer. "It felt strange writing it after everything that's happened."

"I loved reading it."

I made a face. "You say that about every article."

"That's because I love everything you write," he murmured. "You're my favorite author."

I snorted, cupping my hands over his. "That's an easy pedestal to stand on when you don't read."

Walsh lightly tickled my side and I yelped, grabbing his fingers to get him to stop. They were icy to the touch, and I exhaled onto them, much like he had once upon a time. "When are we leaving to meet Edith and Zach?"

We were going to see a movie down at Buckley's Theatre for a double date, something we tried to do once a week. Edith and Zach had come a long way from where they'd been at the end of the summer. Their whole "just friends" spiel lasted until the beginning of October, until they both realized how stupid they were being. Thankfully. They were so adorable together.

I grabbed at Walsh's wrist, pushed his jacket sleeve up, and exposed his forearm to look at his watch's face. "Probably leave in ten minutes."

"Probably?"

"I like sitting here with you." I snuggled deeper, glancing up. "I may never move."

His cheeks were red from the cold, making his skin look ten times paler, but he grinned down at me like I was the sun sitting beside him. "I *love* sitting out here with you." And he grinned, tracing the frame of my lens with a light touch. "And I love your glasses."

I rolled my eyes at him. "You always have to one-up me."

He kissed the tip of my nose. "Is your family still coming over for Thanksgiving dinner next week? Mom has been researching recipes for the past month."

"Hopefully 'turkey' is on her list."

"Sounds familiar," he chuckled. "It's been keeping her busy, which is good. When she came home from the rehabilitation center, they told her to take up a hobby. I guess cooking was her choice."

"Janet will just have to be housekeeper/nanny/therapist

now. Take the title of 'chef' off."

"As long as she still bakes her cookies."

I turned back to face the street, settling against the steady heartbeat that thumped along my spine. "We're still coming— we wouldn't miss it. And *I* wouldn't miss Janet's peach pie."

"Right." Walsh dragged the word out. "Her peach pie. That's all you're coming for."

The swing creaked slightly as a small gust of wind knocked it backward, and I shivered against Walsh. "I'm surprised you didn't freeze your butt off today. Practicing in this weather must suck."

When Walsh called the coach of the Fenton County league the Monday after the final baseball game, Tom had immediately asked him if he'd like to play for their team for the following season. Of course, Walsh said yes, but on one condition. He needed a promise that they played for the love of baseball, *not* for the love of winning. They'd said that they admired his honesty and sportsmanship, and loved that he did the right thing rather than just join in.

"It's not too bad. We're moving to a gym once snow falls."

"Probably a good thing." I smiled. With those words, I pushed up from the swing, tearing the blanket from my legs and standing. The cold air hit me, and I fought back a shiver as I turned to stretch my hands out to him. "We should go."

Walsh's golden eyebrows were pulled together as he looked up at me. "It definitely hasn't been ten minutes."

"I know, but Edith will get mad if we're late again. You know how she gets if she misses a preview."

Walsh swiped my hands up in his, but instead of stand- ing, he pulled me down into his lap. The porch swing groaned as it swung backward, rocking us closer. Walsh gave me a wicked grin, his blue-green sea eyes heating deeper, pupils threatening to swallow the color. "We still have a few more minutes," he insisted, voice pitching lower. "Besides, it's payback for all the times they've been late."

I was going to tell him that most of the time it wasn't her fault—her volleyball practices had kept her later while they were still in season—but I pressed my mouth against his instead. I loved that a spark still electrocuted my skin when we touched, when we kissed, the air between us zapping to life as if struck by lightning. I wanted to stay like this for hours, just him and me.

Walsh tugged his lips only a centimeter from mine, chest rising and falling in an uneven breath. When he smiled, it was wide and terribly cute, filled with a happiness that I'm sure mirrored the budding I felt inside. His words brushed my lips. "I love you, Sophie."

Four words filled with so much emotion it made my head spin and my skin flush. Walsh Hunter gave me the grin that was designed just for me: a smile that lit the sun, put a glow to the moon, and ignited all the stars.

I moved to press my lips to his, speaking softly against them. "And I love you."

If you enjoyed this book, I would so appreciate if you could take the time to leave a review.

Check out the next book in the Love in Fenton County Series now!

Before You Go!

Reviews are so important for authors, especially for indie authors. If you enjoyed this book, please head over to Amazon and leave a review!

Sarah Sutton

ALSO BY SARAH SUTTON

LOVE IN FENTON COUNTY:

WHAT ARE FRIENDS FOR
OUT OF MY LEAGUE
IF THE BROOM FITS
CAN'T CATCH MY BREATH
TWO KINDS OF US

WHAT ARE FRIENDS FOR?

What Are Friends For?

Who said falling for your best friend was a good thing?

If the Broom Fits

The handsome prince always chooses the princess, never the witch.

CAN'T CATCH MY BREATH

Can't Catch My Breath

Can love break free from the past?

Made in the USA
Middletown, DE
19 March 2022

62929745R00196